Married to the Bad Boy

Vanessa Waltz

CONTENTS

ACKNOWLEDGMENTS

Thanks to Faith Van Horne for editing and Kevin McGrath for the cover design.

TONY

"C'moooooon, Tony."

Blondie sighs into my ear, her vermouth and gin breath gusting over my nose as she tries to shimmy over my legs, a feat that sends a lot of raised eyebrows my way considering this chick's dress is practically hiked up to her panties.

It makes my cock stand to attention when her little ass rubs my lap. She's wearing the same panties as yesterday. Dirty. Sexy.

But if I thought for a second that I had a good chance of running into yesterday's one-night stand, I would've never come to this bar. I fucked her last night, and the needy bitch wants seconds.

Of course she does.

She grips my waist with surprising strength and lands a sloppy kiss on my cheek. I sweep a hand over her bare shoulders and a row of goosebumps sprouts over her skin.

"Sweetheart, *listen to me.*" I smile, painfully.

"No."

She pouts her small lips for a moment, and then erupts into giggles.

"No? What the fuck do you mean, no?"

"I don't wanna listen. *I wanna fuck.*"

My cock wants to fuck her, too. It swells in my slacks despite how much I want it to calm down. I don't fuck girls twice. Ever. Whatsherface is making it extremely hard for me to turn her away.

Blondie slides her manicured hand over my thigh and grabs the bulge between my legs. It twitches in response and I groan out loud, embarrassed for my cock. Blood roars through my veins, pounding through my head:

Shut up and fuck the girl.

It's hard to ignore that fucking voice when it's hissing in your ear, over and over.

Goddamn her. I grab a fistful of her hair and bend my mouth to her ear. "Fucking listen to me or I'll spank you in front of this whole bar."

That captures her attention. Finally.

She shuts up and her doe-like eyes find mine, but they drop away almost immediately, focusing on my chest and arms. She places her hands on my chest and feels me up. I don't want her, but it's hard for my cock not to get excited when I've a half-naked chick bouncing on my lap.

It's hard to keep her eyes locked on mine. She has the attention span of a goldfish and is just about as bright. I tap her cheek lightly and she turns her head toward mine again.

"We had fun last night, *but it's over.* I don't go out with girls more than once."

I'm distracted by her nipple, which slips out of that thing she calls a dress, and my cock jumps in my slacks.

"It feels like you want me again."

Then her hand tightens around my stiffening cock and I am less and less aware of the fact that there are people gawking at us.

Jesus.

Blonde hair tickles my neck as she leans in, smiling drunkenly. "I'll leave you alone if you fuck me one more time."

One more time?

I blow air out from my cheeks and consider it. She's a lusty broad, and willing—and I could easily bring her to the back and fuck her in one of the VIP booths. Or the storeroom. I can just imagine her slick, pink pussy wrapping around my cock like a glove, just like it did last night. I could fuck her cunt nice and fast, and as long as she didn't spread out word that Tony Vidal could be persuaded into a second fuck, I'd be all right.

"You're the best I ever had, baby."

You're not the best I ever had.

Still, she was a good, hot fuck and she came real nice for me. Sometimes, they come in the bar looking for me because they know who I'm connected with, and they think that if they flash their tits at me I'll loan them money or beat the shit out of their boyfriends—no. Other times, they're danger whores looking for a hot piece of action. They know I'm a bad boy, and they'll fuck me if I pretend to tell them some secrets about the mob. It gets me off to see them hot for my cock. I stick my fingers in their cunts and make them scream for me. They twist and writhe, and I make them come before I get my dick wet. I've got a real reputation for scoring pussy. Tony—the great fuck. Hey, it's not a bad one.

Her fingers splay over my chest and her fingers coil around my cock. It thickens in her hand and she gives me this coy little smile, because she knows exactly what she's doing to me.

"You just want me balls deep inside your cunt, don't you?"

She doesn't bat an eye. "Yes."

All right. Fuck it.

"I'll bang the shit out of you—*again*. But that's it. No more. You know the rules."

She nods drunkenly. "Yeah, I know the—the rules."

We slide off the stool and her tits practically pop out as

she stumbles next to me. The guys in the bar wheel their heads around like sharks smelling blood, but she's my meal for tonight. Actually, only a snack, really, because I'm interested in the piece of ass I briefly spotted. If I see anyone else talking to her when I get back, I'll tell him to fuck off right before smashing his fucking face into the wall.

I drag her bony ass behind the bar, looking for Tommy before I open the door to his storeroom. It's a small, dusty room with boxes of liquor. There's nothing really important, but he'd bust a nut if he knew I was fucking in here.

"Tony."

I turn around after closing the door, and the crazy bitch stands there, already naked. Her pink dress pools at her feet. My eyes follow her bare, slim legs to her trim waist—not an ounce of fat, and then her small, firm tits. Seeing them now reminds me how I nailed her tight little cunt, how her tits almost seemed to fit in my mouth and how she squealed when I sucked on her perfect skin. She opens her mouth, but all I want from her lips is to have them wrapped around my cock. Her shaved pussy gleams as I approach her, slapping her inner thigh. She spreads her legs apart and I run my fingers over her swollen clit.

My cock throbs as she tilts her head back, her blonde hair hanging as her chest pulses.

"Fuck me, Tony."

The request makes my mouth water, but not as much as her glistening pussy. I want her swollen lips in my mouth. I want to taste her while she cums on my tongue.

"Do I look like the kind of guy who takes demands from women?"

Still smiling stupidly, she shakes her head. "No."

"Then why are you trying to treat me like a bitch?"

The question is too complex for her to answer in her state. Still, I enjoy watching the puzzlement on her face as she struggles to figure out an appropriate response. She lifts her small shoulders in a shrug.

I sit down on a box and beckon to her with a single finger.

"I want to taste that beautiful cunt of yours."

Blondie smiles coyly as she approaches me, her small feet curling against the cold floor.

"I want you to grind your pussy against my face. *Move.*"

I reach around and give her a vicious slap over her ass. Her muscles twitch as a bright red burn flushes her skin. She giggles and moves forward. I smell her musk—it's all over her thighs. She spreads her thighs and I grab her ass cheeks, loving how firm they are, and then my tongue darts out, tasting her. Her musk swirls around my tongue as I press my face to her greedy cunt, reaching back and eating her pussy for all I'm worth. She lets out a long moan and digs her fingers in my hair, which I hate, but I allow because her antics turn me the fuck on. I catch a glimpse of myself eating out this chick in the mirror across the room, and I laugh into her heated pussy. It doesn't get much fucking better than this—scoring hot chicks every fucking night.

A sharp intake of breath from her tells me that I'm on the right track. She yanks hard when I plunge my tongue inside her slippery walls, using my finger to rub her clit.

"Fuck—*Yeah*, right there."

"You like that, baby? You want to come?"

"Y—yes!" She gasps out, her chest dotted with red.

I laugh into her pussy and use my hands to bring her closer to the edge. They dive into her wet cunt, curling forward until I hit that sweet spot. She gasps, clinging to my hair. My tongue swirls around her swollen nub, sucking the juices that spill from her. Then I insert a third finger and her thighs twitch on either side of her. She lets out a long groan as she comes over my fingers, her pussy clenching me hard. My dick strains against my slacks as I feel her come undone. I slide my fingers out of her and wipe her juices on the inside of her thighs.

"Holy *fuck*," she says, sounding as though I fucked the drunkenness out of her.

"All right. Now get the fuck out of here."

I give her another slap across her ass and push her back as she gasps for breath.

"But—you said you'd fuck me!"

I grin at the confusion clouding her face. "And I did."

"That's not what I wanted!"

"I wanted you to leave me the fuck alone, but I guess we don't always get the things we want in life."

"Fuck you!"

A smirk tightens my face. "Already have."

Then I leave her standing there, naked and stunned. It's a bit of a dick move, but I told the girl about my rules. I was very clear. One night. No repeats.

I duck into the bathroom to wash the pussy juice from my hands and face, laughing as I catch a glimpse of my disheveled appearance in the mirror. My dick is still half-hard, but I decide to leave it alone. I walk out, passing the storeroom as I reenter the bar and take my seat.

Pussy and the mob are pretty much my life.

My nights are pretty much the same.

It starts with a look.

One glance across the bar. A giggle, a smile, a shadow

of a wink.

I'm into you.

Really what they're saying is: *Let's fuck.*

It's a language I've got down to a science over the years.

Then I look at the girl. She's sitting at the far end of the bar. Is she my type? Too thin? I'll take a woman with curves any day over some stick-thin model with a bony ass. Red lipstick. Cherry-red. I've got a theory on lipstick color. The redder it is, the more wild she'll be in bed.

Long, slender neck. Like a swan. She has dark brown eyes—I can see their color all the way from here. Nice thick lips. A black dress with thin straps clings to her shoulders. Jesus, the shit girls wear when it's -10 outside.

My eyes slip right down to her plunging neckline.

Nice tits, honey.

Yeah, I'm checking them out. So what? She notices and a pretty blush blooms over her porcelain cheeks.

The chair squeaks as I shift myself uncomfortably, my cock stirring as I think about what she'd look like naked. What will her tits feel like in my hands? I imagine striding to her right now and pulling down that tight cocktail dress to free them.

Oh, *Maddon.* I can feel my cock throbbing as I imagine

11

the filthy things I'd like to do to her body. Tie her up, loop the rope around her tits, and make her bend her knees to suck my cock, then I'd return the favor and stick my tongue between her legs until she comes. Vivid images flash through my head, slowly getting my dick hard, but I stay here and sip my drink, giving her a friendly smile.

Right away, I can tell that this girl is not used to being ignored. She keeps trying to catch my gaze, but she won't budge. Fuck, she's one of *those* girls. I'm tempted to wait her out, to let her come to me, but I can't risk some other asshole hitting on her.

Draining my glass, I set it down and slide off the stool, making a beeline for her. She pretends not to notice as I slide in right next to her. A pleasant citrus smell wafts from her neck and I bathe in it for a moment.

"How's it going, hon?"

Her delicate face turns toward me and my heart flips inside my chest. Wow, she's gorgeous. She doesn't wear too much makeup. Great skin. She's average height, with long, thick dark brown hair, a few curls teased around her face. Nice pouty lips and big eyes. They're animated—full of emotion. Large, golden hoops for earrings. Beautiful face and body. She looks like a hyper-sexualized version of the Italian girls I grew up with. I can almost see her nipples through the fabric, and a vision of me bending her over the bar table consumes my mind.

"Not that well, actually."

A loud New York accent shakes from her mouth. She plays with the almost empty drink in her hand and gives me a fleeting look. Then she does a double take, a slow blush spreading over her cheeks as she checks me out.

Take a good look, hon.

"Can I get you a drink?"

My lips pull into a grin as her blush deepens. She wraps her fingers around her drink and gives a little shake of her head.

I want her hair wrapped around my fist as she kneels on all fours, her tits swinging as I nail her from behind. The heat of that vision almost makes me groan, because she is, without a doubt, one of the most beautiful girls I've ever seen.

I ignore her dismissal and lean in closer. "Damn, I didn't think a girl like you would get so hot and bothered over a small request."

She worries her lip and catches me staring. "I am *not* hot and bothered."

A deep chuckle rumbles through my chest. "Sure you aren't, sweetheart."

Fuck, I can't stop thinking about how those full lips

would feel wrapped around my cock. She parts her lips and gives me a long look, a strand of hair hiding her face. I'm tempted to reach out and brush it behind her ear, just for an excuse to glide my fingers over her perfect skin.

Her eyes are slightly glazed over as her gaze meets mine. "You don't know me."

"I don't need to know you to buy you a drink."

I flag down the bartender, ordering us a couple drinks. Then I turn back to this smoking-hot broad, wondering what's the best angle I should use to take her home with me. Though, it doesn't look like I'll have to try very hard. Desire rolls off her shoulder in waves, like a heat lamp. The way her eyes can't seem to stop glancing at me—yeah, this chick wants my cock.

"What's your name, beautiful?"

She narrows her eyes. "Elena."

"I'm Tony."

Elena accepts her drink from the bartender and takes a long sip. "Listen, I'm not in the mood."

Yeah, right. That's the most feeble brush off I've ever heard.

I raise my eyebrow, toying with her. "In the mood for what?"

Long, brown hair swings in front of her tits as she leans toward me with a half-drunken smile. "For you to list reasons why I should go home with you."

"There's only one reason, actually."

"Yeah?"

My voice lowers down to a slow growl. "I think that you've had a very long day, and you're desperate for a nice thick cock to pound your pussy. You want a reason? I'll give you one. I'll fuck you so hard and good that your clit's going to feel my cock thrusting underneath long after I'm gone."

She coughs into her drink, her cheeks blazing like a fire engine. "*Wow*. Does that line ever work for you?"

It clearly did. Despite her unimpressed tone, she keeps her face buried in her drink. I can see the way she presses her thighs together and the color of her cheeks says it all, really.

"Sometimes. So far, I think it's working pretty well on you."

She snorts into her drink and shifts in her seat, her leg bumping into mine. "Well, you got my attention."

The slight touch of her leg against my slacks makes me think of having her naked, our bodies intertwined together. Blood pounds in my head and I can't think of anything else but the desire roaring through my veins.

Keep it together.

"Are you actually good in bed, or is it all bullshit?"

The way she shivers under my gaze gets my cock so goddamn hard. "Ask around, sweetheart. I'm a great fuck, any girl will tell you that."

"Hm—that's not very enticing."

"Why, because I've fucked around?" Disappointment seethes my insides. I can't stand prudes, but she doesn't seem like one. A small smile lingers on her lips. Teasing. She's teasing me. "I'll make you come on my tongue and lick every drop from your sweet pussy."

Her face heats up like a lamp and she hurriedly swallows the rest of her glass, sputtering slightly. A drop lands on her tits, and I'm tempted to lean over and lick it right off.

"What makes you think you can talk to me like that?"

"I'm sorry, hon. You told me you weren't in the mood so I thought I'd get right to it. I'll make you forget every asshole who didn't treat you like the goddess you are. Is that what you want to hear?"

A small smile flits across her pretty face. "You should have started out with that one."

Her eyelids flutter as I reach out and touch her shoulder. That thin little strap just begs to be ripped off. Elena looks at my hand and her lips part slightly. Fuck, it's hot.

"I like to cut to the chase. Life's too short to spend it talking about bullshit."

"Me too. And the answer is no."

"I'm pretty sure you're coming home with me tonight."

She cocks her head and crosses her legs. "I'm not interested."

"Your body tells me something different."

Then she raises a middle finger with a shadow of a grin ghosting her face. "How about now? What is my body telling you right now?"

My chest shakes with laughter at this little spitfire. "It tells me that you like the chase."

"Uh-huh."

She rolls her eyes again at me, brushing an errant strand from her head, and I catch her wrist in mine. Elena sucks in her breath slightly and blood rushes to my chest when I feel her heartbeat through her skinny wrist.

"You like the filthy shit I keep whispering in your ear. Admit it."

"Maybe I do, but I'm still not interested."

She says one thing, but doesn't make a move to pull from my grasp. Like a flower starved of sunlight, she opens up to me. Wants more. There's a vein jumping in her neck: I. Want. Him.

17

A flash of irritation sears my chest. "You have a boyfriend, right?"

Elena sips her drink quietly.

"*Fuck him*. Come home with me instead."

"He's more like an asshole ex." Her eyes darken at the mention of him.

Ah, even better.

"Didn't I tell you? I'll make you forget about him."

Her eyes shine like dark gems as she stares at me, her bottom lip trembling as if she dares to believe.

Fuck, I want to get closer to this girl, but I want her without all the guys gawking at her, so I stand up.

"Take your drink. C'mon."

"Where are we—?"

I take her hand and pull her from the bar stools, bringing her to the back rooms with VIP booths. The noise drops away slightly as we enter the mostly deserted VIP room. I sit down, still holding her hand. She looks hesitant, but my smile wins her over. It always wins them over.

She slides over the booth, and I don't throw an arm over her like I want to. The leather couch squeaks as she moves closer to me, her thigh gently touching mine as she turns her body toward me. Her big, expressive eyes tremble in the low light. This girl is fucking scared.

Nervous?

I push it aside as I take her in. My eyes can't get enough of the smoothness of her skin, the way the dress folds over her tits and ass, and her lips, slightly puffy as though from a bee-sting.

"So is this where you're going to make me come with your tongue?" The last bit shakes from her voice in a nervous laugh.

"If that's what you want, sure."

She inhales deeply and exhales it in a shuddering breath. "I don't know what the hell I'm doing."

"I do."

My finger runs along her jaw, turning her face toward mine so that those stung lips are right under mine. I hold her there the same way I'd hold her over the edge of a cliff. She trembles, waiting for me to make the first move. Her breath mists over my face, and then she shakes her head.

"No, I can't."

No. Yes. No. Yes. Make up your fucking mind.

"I'm sorry. I can't while he's still in my life."

Like I give a fuck about stepping on some other douchebag's toes.

Her brown eyes widen. "Seriously, if he saw me with

someone else he'd—"

"*Elena.*"

My thumb moves across her cheek, under those beautiful, blowjob lips that I'd love to give a test run.

"What?"

"Shut up."

Then I kiss her.

It's like an instant high the moment my lips touch hers. The heat I've been watching flush her skin burns into my mouth. My hands drops down her silky neck, and I take a fistful of her hair and sweep it aside. My fingers run down her skin as she gasps into my mouth. My tongue sweeps over her bottom lip and I grasp the base of her neck, my cock pounding with blood.

She pulls away from me with a painful yelp, her hands flying to her neck, where I notice shadows of purple. What the *fuck*? Are those bruises?

My chest slowly fills with heat as I connect the dots. Elena lets her hands fall from her neck and shakes her hair back into place, flattening it nervously.

"I—this is a bad idea."

My cock screams for me to keep going, to pin her down and lick her from head to toe.

"If it's a bad idea, why did you follow me in here?"

Elena's fingers tentatively touch my chest. A flare of

warmth spreads where she touches me and she lifts her head.

"I was selfish."

A weak feeling seizes my chest when she says that. I don't know why. "You're not selfish for wanting me. Ditch the loser and come home with me."

A sad smile twitches across her face. "You make it sound so simple."

"It is."

I bend my head again, taking her lips in mine before she can utter a protest. Ah—fuck, the way she feels, her body rubbing against mine, her soft lips. Her palm rides my chest, the heel digging into my muscles. I just can't wait another moment without knowing what her tits feel like, so I brush my palm against warm curve of her breast. My thumb kneads her hard nipple as I deepen the kiss. She makes a moan against my lips that makes my dick throb. I squeeze her, and then my hand moves to her waist and I take a handful of her flesh.

"Ow!"

Elena breaks off the kiss with a painful cry, and I snatch my hand away as if it was burned. Jesus, is she covered in bruises?

Small tears bead in her dark eyes and a surge of rage

21

flashes across my eyes.

"I didn't mean to hurt you."

She shakes her head, dismissive. "It's fine."

Like hell it is.

"Who is your ex?"

"Why?"

"So I can beat the shit out of him."

I bursts out of me before I can really think about what I'm saying, but it occurs to me that I really want to do this. I want to find the prick and bash his fucking head in. What kind of man hits a woman? It boils my blood to see this kind of shit. I'm no white knight, but I want this girl to not flinch when I touch her.

"Yeah, that's not a good idea."

Surprise rattles through my head. "Are you one of those chicks that keeps running back to the guy who beats you up?"

The icy glare she shoots me says it all. *"Fuck you."*

"Then why's it not a good idea?"

"Look, you seem like a tough guy and all, but my ex is—ah, *connected.*"

Connected. He's in the mob? Huh. Interesting.

"You can say the word, you know. It's not a bad one. *Mafia.*"

Her tongue darts out, wetting her lips. "He's a

wiseguy."

"So am I, hon."

The energy shifts between us. All of a sudden, it's tense. I reach down to my ankle and show her the piece I have strapped there. She sits up straighter and I have to laugh at her startled expression. An apprehensive look overcomes her face.

"Are you—are you with Johnny's crew?"

Her wispy voice trembles from her uncertain lips, and I incline my head.

She knows Johnny—knows who I'm connected to. This is getting more and more interesting.

Elena drops her voice, adopting a frightened timbre. "Could I ask you—I mean, are you the right person?"

"I work for John. You can ask me anything."

Elena bites her thumb anxiously, shooting me looks before she finally sighs. "I need to put a hit on someone, and I've a lot of cash."

A hit.

My head turns so violently that I pull a muscle in my neck. I study her. It's not often that I get asked for a hit from a woman. Her eyes burn with a quiet intensity that instantly raises my suspicious. Is she with the cops? Nah, I fucking doubt it.

"Let me guess, your boyfriend?"

She nods.

Plenty of women have hired my services to 'take care' of violent boyfriends. My fists. Their face. That's all it takes for them to walk away forever.

Not this guy.

A violent surge of energy pounds through my veins, making the ones on my hands swell.

"I think I have a pretty good idea, but why?"

She slowly licks her lips and just the small motion is enough to my dick throb.

"I left him and he's coming for me. He won't stop until I'm dead. It's him or me."

I breathe in her tantalizing scent, my eyes all over her generous cleavage and my balls seize when her thighs bump against mine. I reach up, brushing back her dark brown hair and I touch one of the bruises on her neck. She flinches, but doesn't pull away.

"Sure you want to do this? I've handled guys like this before."

Her voice hardens and her big eyes narrow at me. "I want him dead. I have ten thousand American dollars in cash."

Well, this isn't quite how I imagined my night ending up. Fuck. I can't quite believe what I'm seeing. This angelic, little Italian girl who looks like she would shrink from the sight of blood is asking me to kill a man. Her boyfriend.

"What's his name?"

The intensity from her eyes finally drops as she glances away and murmurs the name. It's so soft that I can barely hear it. "R—Rafael Costa."

My insides blaze when I hear the name. I only know one Rafael Costa, and he's in New York. He's one of us— *La Cosa Nostra*. The new boss, Vincent, would chop my head off if I made a move against one of his made guys.

Disappointment settles in my guts like lead as I lift myself from the couch and grab a couple glasses along with a huge bottle of vodka.

I can't help her. Fuck.

"Will you do it?"

I sit back down next to her, my eyes on her beautiful body. I imagine it sprawled on a floor somewhere, a hairline crack in her skull, a red pool of blood behind her head.

My jaw aches. Turning back to the table, I pour a couple glasses and press one into her questioning hands.

"Drink, sweetheart. You look like you could use it."

Elena lets out a sigh and brings the drink to her lips.

"You're not wrong."

Heat burns down my chest as I swallow the alcohol, the warmth glowing in my cock as her body jostles next to me. She drains the glass and reaches the bottle before I can pour her another. The crazy broad just takes it as if she owns it.

I like her already.

"Will you do it?"

I hate saying the next few words.

"He's a made guy. I can't."

Elena's face falls horribly for a moment right as she brings the second drink to her mouth. For a moment I'm horrified that she might cry, but the look disappears. She shrugs, assuming a look of complete indifference.

"Whatever."

Whatever. Yeah fucking right.

Fuck. I don't want to know anything about this woman. I don't want to feel sorry for her, and I shouldn't want anything to do with her. She's another guy's girl, but he doesn't respect her, so why should I respect his claim?

I catch a strand of her dark hair dangling in front of her face and twirl it in my finger before gently tucking it behind her ear. Her nostrils flare as I stroke the side of her cheek.

"I'm going to go."

I catch her hand as she stands up. "No, come on. Stay."

Elena tugs it out of my grasp, shaking her head. "I can't."

I don't have the heart to lay more filthy lines on her, not when pity tightens my chest. I watch her leave the VIP lounge, her head still held high. It's as though she's not a victim.

Then I'm left uncomfortably alone with my thoughts. Instead of picking up another chick, I go home. I wander to my bedroom and lay flat on my bed, staring at the ceiling.

It's the most empty moment of my day. I feel my heart beating, but nothing much else.

* * *

My boots slide through grey slush on the streets as my breath puffs out in white clouds. I reach for the door handle of *Le Zinc*, Johnny's restaurant and headquarters. It's a swanky, upscale French bistro with an antique zinc bar. I step inside the warmth gratefully, the sudden heat prickling my frozen fingers and toes. Pierre, a young guy who watches the door, nods at me as I enter.

It's noon and the place is packed. A mixture of Johnny's crew and oblivious civilians fill the restaurant.

Pierre takes the wool coat from my shoulders and I smooth the suit over my chest. Johnny sits at his usual table in the back. He stands up, smiling, his arms outstretched.

"Tony, how are you?"

Tommy, the new soldier, sits nearby, along with one of Johnny's captains—Fred. At first sight, Johnny doesn't look like much. He's slender and slight of build, and usually wears a small smile, but he's the thirty-five year old boss of the Cravotta family. At the age of twenty, he bought out all the payment companies and had all the construction companies in his pocket. At twenty-five, he bought out a dairy company up north and began extorting all restaurants and grocery stores that didn't use Salerno cheese. Now every grocery store only stocks his cheese, and restaurants that fail to make protection payments go up in flames. When he was thirty, he backed *Les Diables,* a biker gang in the city, during the biker wars. They work for him now. He gets a taste from every construction company, restaurant, casino, and racetrack in Montreal. He's invincible.

It's for those reasons that I always seem to forget to breathe in his presence. I'm not the kind of guy who gets nervous, but Johnny's a fucking legend.

He smiles at me as though I'm his best friend and pulls

me into a fierce hug, and I kiss him on both cheeks. It means nothing. I've seen him smile like that to a man he pulled into an embrace, right before he dug his pistol into his chest and killed him.

"Hey, John."

"Have a seat. Do you want something to eat?" Always courteous, Johnny waves over someone even after I shake my head.

He gives me a menu, but I know the thing by heart at this point. The waiter bustles to our table, his pen poised over a small notepad.

"No, really, John. I'm good."

"At least have a drink with me."

The waiter grabs the bottle of wine, a vintage from Tuscany, and pours a glass for me. "All right."

He swirls his glass over the white tablecloth and lifts it to his lips. "*Tabarnak, c'est bon.*" Fuck, it's good.

My hand curls over the stem of the wineglass, and I take a small mouthful. It's pretty fucking good—dry and full of flavor. I set the glass down, avoiding his painful stare.

"I've bad news about Turner Construction," I say finally, lifting my head to meet his eyes. "They won't do business with us."

Johnny doesn't say anything for a moment, but a sudden, caustic, burning heat flares from his eyeballs. "What the fuck are you talking about?"

I swallow hard. "They're an American company—they don't do business like us. They can't accept bribes."

"Then you make them understand how it's done."

I grit my teeth from the rumble in his voice. "I tried leaning on the boss a little, but I think they're just going to leave Montreal. They just don't want to deal with us. I'm sorry, John."

There's nothing but the sound of people talking, the clatter of silverware, and John's frozen stare boring into my skull. He opens his mouth.

"I'm really disappointed with you, Tony. I thought you were a better negotiator."

I clench my hands over the table, feeling a surge of anger.

Don't get angry at the boss.

"There was nothing else I could do. Americans don't do business with the mob. It's just that simple."

"Do you think I got to where I am now because I gave up that easily?"

Quiet resentment builds inside my chest as he stares at me.

I never wanted this life for myself.

"There's something else I need you to do."

He reaches in his jacket and I tense for a moment, because he could easily be reaching for a gun. Johnny smiles at me as he takes a photograph from his inner jacket and shows it to me.

It's a family photo of Jack Vittorio, the former New York boss, and his wife and—the girl I met yesterday. Holy shit, she's Jack Vittorio's daughter?

"This girl showed up in my restaurant yesterday, trying to contract a hit on a made guy."

"Yeah, I met her in Tommy's bar. She asked me for the same thing."

Johnny smirks at me. "You're fucking kidding me?"

"Nope. I told her no, of course."

"Anyway, I need you to watch her. I don't want anyone fucking up my relationship with New York or *Les Diables*. She might try going to them next. Do not let her."

An unpleasant feeling leaves me feeling gutted as I stare into the photograph. She's beautiful, really—the type of girl my Ma would love. Dark hair and innocent, big eyes. Italian.

"And Tony?"

"Yeah?"

"Try to keep your dick in your pants."

31

"I can't promise that," I respond, grinning at the photo.

He sighs loudly. "Go. Get the fuck out of here and start your collections."

The cold, dismissive tone freezes my jaw shut. I somehow manage to grunt out a good-bye, and then I stand from the table. He's already looking somewhere else. It's as if I'm already gone.

Fucking hell, I need to get a new job.

But that's just it, isn't it? I can't just quit—not after becoming a made member. It's not just a job, it's a way of life.

I gather my wool coat and shrug it over my shoulders, eager to get out of there. At first, it was great. All the pussy I could want and more money than I'd ever had, but after a while you start to notice that all the girls kind of look the same. They act the same, and they want the same things from you. Namely, your money. But I still want some to fill the gaping hole that girl nailed into my chest the other night.

* * *

The warmth slowly unfreezes my fingers as I flex them, pain prickling all over my skin as they thaw. I clench my jaw, thinking of the sickening sound of cracking bone. It replays over and over in my head. The image of the lead pipe in my hand repeats in my head as I smash it against

32

his knees, producing a thick, meaty sound. His face contorts with pain as his knees explode into fragments. The gag I shoved down his mouth only partially muffled his screams.

Fuck, the sounds.

I take my seat at the bar, and Genevieve, the curly-haired bartender, slides me my drink almost immediately, knowing that I'm in one of my moods. She doesn't even meet my gaze. I slam back the drink, that awful burn reminding me of gasoline, but I swallow it down. It's like adding mulch over fire. Drinking drowns it out for a little while, but it's still burning underneath. The flames lick through, and my head starts to pound and I keep drinking. I don't remember if I'm drinking to numbness, or whether I'm drinking to feel something or whether I'm drinking just to drink.

It doesn't matter, anyway. It always ends up the same.

I take a look around, trying to take my mind off of it— trying to find something sweet to alleviate the bitterness in my mouth, and then I see her.

It's her again.

I freeze as she whisks by me, a citrus breeze wafting across my nose. I turn around to watch a slim waist, her shirt riding over her hips, giving me a nice view of her perfectly round ass, which bounces in her black leggings. She slides right over the stool next to me without realizing that I'm looking at her, a slight frown creasing her forehead.

Try to keep your dick in your pants.

If Johnny really cared about that, he would have been more clear.

She's involved with a made guy. You could get killed if you touch her.

Dying for fucking a girl seems like a good way to go. Actually, I'd prefer to die *while* fucking a girl, but beggars can't be choosers.

Johnny could kill you.

I don't give a fuck.

She's the daughter of a boss. You don't fuck daughters of bosses. You don't look at them. You don't talk to them except to say, "Hello, how are you?" and "Goodbye." She's the forbidden fruit. A conquest.

I have to bang this broad.

My first instinct is to touch her shoulder, her waist, to overwhelm her with my presence. I'm a master at getting girls to come home with me. Before long, I'll have her begging to suck my cock.

I lean in slightly, and I let my hand grasp the head of her chair. "Hey, beautiful. What's got you down?"

She doesn't even look at me. "Fuck off."

So the Mafia princess has a mouth, doesn't she? Intriguing. Genevieve hears the exchange and grins at me behind that bar counter.

The energy burning from her body is completely different from last time. Last time, she was scared. Defeated. Today, she's pissed. Did Johnny turn her down again?

I give Genevieve a nod, and she pours a drink for the girl.

"What's this?"

"I'm buying you a drink."

She pushes it away. "I don't want your fucking drink."

Then why did you sit right next to me?

"What's with the tone?"

"You're just trying to get into my pants."

"Is it a crime that I think you're gorgeous?"

She turns her head, her long, black hair snagging on her creamy shoulders. Brown eyes look at me under her long lashes, and they widen as she takes in my appearance. Gently parted lips beckon to me, and I smile at her. My cock makes an impatient twitch as her lips lift slightly.

Her slim body slides off the stool and she walks close to me. Close enough so that blood pounds in my ears and

I'm face to face with an amazing view of her cleavage. Her lips, slightly wet with pink lipstick, tremble. The citrus scent floats over my like a cloud, not overpowering, but pleasant.

"I'll do whatever you want if you get rid of my ex for me."

Goddamn. The desperation in her voice makes my stomach sink, but I'm tempted to say yes. Fuck him— Fuck the mob, I'll kill him for you because I want to suck on your lips and feel the warmth of your tits in my palms.

Instead, I shake my head, hating the disappointment in her eyes. Her hand slides away from mine.

Don't let her go!

"I'm sorry, hon. You're not going to get anyone to agree to do that for you."

She shakes her head, her eyes watering, and she gives a hopeless, sharp intake of breath that makes my insides clench.

I take her shoulder, half-expecting her to throw my hand off, but she lets me touch her skin. My fingers just graze over her and her eyelids flutter.

"Come home with me and you'll forget all about that asshole. I'll make you feel really good, Elena. I promise."

Her body shivers and she steps back from me. Temptation brews in her eyes like a storm gathering. I see it shifting and receding. She wants to, but she doesn't want to.

Then she opens her mouth, her eyes hardening into marbles.

"I want nothing to do with you."

Frustration gathers in my chest when she shoots me down. I want this woman—she's a goddamn prize, and I would gladly shoot her ex-boyfriend in the face if it wouldn't get me killed.

Elena turns to leave, grabbing her coat, but I grab her tiny wrist. I pull her into my chest and she utters a gasp. My arm wraps around her waist and she swallows hard.

"At least have a drink with me."

"No."

"*Come on.* One drink."

She wets her lips, and for a moment I imagine them wrapped around my cock. My fingers tease around the hem of her shirt, and then her eyes glint with pain and she reaches behind herself, grabbing my hands to rip them away from her body.

"You don't know how to take no for an answer, do you?"

I grin at her, loving how ferocious she is, and the way her brown eyes seem to sparkle with electricity. Girl's got fire.

"You kissed me back the other night and left me with a raging hard-on. I can't leave you alone."

Her mouth parts almost as though she's about to give in, but then her eyes harden. "I don't want you. End of story."

Yet she doesn't pull away when I grasp her chin and lean down close enough to feel her breath over my cheeks, and to see her neck pulsing with her racing heartbeat. My fingers run along her jaw, moving to the back of her head, into her silky hair. My lips fall against hers, and her mouth opens in a gasp. It's intoxicating. This girl makes my body hot, and my other arm snakes around her tiny waist. I pull her smoking hot body into mine, and her tits crush against my chest. I smile against her mouth as she sighs into mine. Her palm flattens against my chest.

And she shoves me.

I have a brief view of her red, furious face before a sharp sting hits my face, her hand a beige blur. The slap echoes in the bar, despite the noise and the people everywhere. They turn to look at us, but they hardly give me a second glance. I've been slapped before. So what? They always go home with me.

I didn't even fucking see it coming.

My chest shakes with laughter as she stands frozen with

a semi-paralyzed look on her face, and then she turns around and bolts from the bar.

This isn't over, honey.

ELENA

TWO WEEKS AGO

The world undulates in my head, continuously roaring as I stumble past New York City traffic. I feel like I'm walking inside a bubble that distorts everything I see. Everything's too loud, too fast. My head pounds, still echoing with the blows. Everything sounds hollow.

I trip on something hard and fall on my knee. My jeans tear open and I feel a sharp sting. There are bits of gravel digging into the red gash. I brush them away carelessly and turn toward my sister's apartment. How the hell did I ever make it here?

My balled up fist hammers on the frozen door, my fist shaking in the cold. It's freezing outside, but for once I'm grateful for that. It soothes the aches on my face and my swollen eye. For a moment, I think about pressing my face against the wood, but then the heavy door flies open.

My sister stands in the doorway of her brownstone, baby in arm, looking leggy and fabulous. Her gasp of horror suddenly chokes into laughter.

A cold feeling stabs my gut.

"Jesus, what happened to your face?"

Now that I'm so close to the entrance, the last bit of

adrenaline fades and I clutch the iron rail to steady myself.

What the fuck do you think happened?

"Rafael hit me," I say, swallowing hard when a triumphant smile stretches over her face. "I really need a place to stay."

"I told you a thousand times, didn't I? I warned you about him, but no, you had to have the bad boy."

Yeah, she warned me about dating Dad's associates. I didn't care. He was intoxicating and full of life—Dad gave him his blessing. If Dad liked him, so would I.

I was so naive back then. He's a monster—they're all monsters, and the only thing that kept him from eating me alive was my father. Everything changed so quickly.

"I know you warned me, but I really need your help now. I need a place to stay."

Hating the tremble in my voice, I stand up straighter to make me feel less weak.

Maria adjusts the baby on her hip and narrows her eyebrows, the high arches fixed in an expression of contempt. "You got yourself into this mess, and you can get yourself out of it. Too bad Daddy isn't here anymore to fix it for you."

A gust of icy wind blows across my face, almost as if summoned by magic by her cruel words. Her perfect indifference stuns me. It hurts so much that my legs tremble and freezing wetness gathers at the corners of my eyes. For God's sake, she needs to push aside her sibling rivalry or whatever fucking grudge she has against me. This is serious.

"I need your help. *I'm desperate.*"

"Go to Mom's house."

I shiver violently in the cold, wishing that my goddamn sister would let me in the damn house to continue the conversation.

"The feds seized it. They're giving her a couple weeks to move out. They're taking everything. We don't have any money. They froze the bank accounts."

"I know. I've been giving Ma cash for a while, but you're on your own." Her face twists in malevolence. "You always were a spoiled little brat."

Fine, I could live without money, but I can't keep living with Rafael.

"At least give me a place to stay! I *really* need to get away from him."

A sad smile flickers on her sour face.

"You know as well as I do that he'll just drag you back."

My eyes burn as the truth of that statement sinks in. The air swallows my choked sobs, and Maria reaches outside for a moment to pat my shoulder.

"He'll get bored of you eventually and move on to someone else. They always do," she adds bitterly. "Now, go. If he finds out you've been here, you'll be in worse trouble."

She closes the door and the Christmas wreath bangs loudly in my face.

Where the hell am I supposed to go?

* * *

They called me the Mafia Princess.

I was the boss' daughter.

When I was old enough to realize Daddy wasn't exactly living a normal man's life, I started reading the papers. All the violence splashed over the pages and my dad's name interwoven with the stories horrified me, at first. Why did so many people hate him? Why were the cops always harassing him? Then I remember watching him shake hands with the mayor, and I was in awe. He was a tough guy. He was a villain, yes, but he was my villain. Nobody could touch him, or me by extension. His men were always respectful toward me, afraid of saying anything that could get their heads chopped off.

I'm not an idiot. I know who my dad was, even though he sheltered me from the life—from the violence. The boys I grew up with, who later became his associates, were like family to me. They were always around the house, picking up dad to drive him places, even to have dinner with the family.

And then he was murdered and they completely disappeared.

Shame weighs on my heart as I trudge up the icy subway steps.

There was only really one rule in our family, growing up.

Don't ever talk.

Don't talk to the press, don't talk to outsiders, and definitely, never, ever talk to the police. It was like a mantra in our house. Every time there was an indictment, Mom would drill the rules in our skulls.

But he talked.

He talked to the feds. I found out from the agents who visited our home just before they raided it and began taking everything that wasn't bolted to the floor. They told us that my dad's body was found in an abandoned farm in east Jersey, riddled with bullet holes.

None of his friends came to the funeral.

I know he was a rat, but he was still my dad. He adored me, and yes, spoiled me a little more than my brother and sister. Now he's gone, along with his protection. I'm not the boss' daughter anymore. I'm just the daughter of a traitor.

My hand trembles over the handle of the pork deli store where my father used to hang out. We used to get our meat here all the time. Vinny, the new boss, should be there. A wave of self-disgust rises like caustic acid in my throat.

Worse of all is that I know who's responsible for my father's murder, and I'm about to go to him for help. The idea sickens me, but I am literally out of options. Last resort.

This could be a huge fucking mistake.

I try to glance inside, to check the moving shadows and see if one of them resembles Vinny. A large, warped form suddenly appears at the frosted glass and the door swings open, revealing a young man who I vaguely recognize.

"Hello—holy shit!" His eyes widen as he takes in my appearance.

I grit my teeth to stop the chatter against the cold. "Can I please see Vinny—Vincent?"

He steps aside and I sigh as warmth washes over my frozen limbs. Hours of walking in New York City's streets made them numb with cold. The young man gazes at me in concern and takes my arm, as if he's afraid I'll keel over.

We move past the few customers dallying in the cafe, who shoot me alarming looks, and head toward the back of the store. It's a place I've never really been.

Please, let Rafael not be there. Please, God, he'll kill me.

Fear boils in my stomach, making my stomach turn as the coffee I had for breakfast burns holes inside me. I stop at another set of doors and try to see whether Rafael is in there. The young man opens the door before I can decide whether to go in or not and pulls me in a large room with a pool table, chairs, desk, and a dining room table. I spot Vinny hanging near his pool table, stick in his hand, as he laughs at something Nicky said beside him. Vinny is a tall, good-looking man about ten years older than I am. His laughter used to fill me with a warm glow, but now it grates against my ears. He has no fucking right to laugh when my father is dead. Everyone knows that he killed him. I know it was him—or at least one of these bastards.

Dad talked to the cops, so they killed him.

"Vince."

The young man's voice rings out, and I do a quick scan of the room. Sitting there on the edge of the pool table is the man I'm trying to avoid. He wears a black leather jacket over a red button-up shirt that I ironed for him this morning. Despite his little coke habit and alcohol problem, he always looks clean-shaven—just like you expect the devil to look. Handsome, attractive, and deadly. He stands up immediately, hands wrapping around his pool cue as if it's my throat.

Oh no. *Oh no.*

Rafael takes a furious step forward, his handsome face twisted in a cruel grin. It says: *I'm going to kill you later.*

A loud, obnoxious voice rings across the room.

"Jesus Christ!"

Vinny finally notices me, the laughter evaporating from his face as he scans my face.

The boy next to me faces him. "She said she wanted to see you."

I would give everything in the world to make him take back those words. All the heart leaves me in an instant. Oh God, it was stupid to come here. I must have been delirious. Rafael stands right there, *right there,* and he knows exactly why I came.

"That's not what I said! I just wanted deli meats—and to say hi. My mother and I, you know, we really don't, we haven't seen you in a while, and—"

Vinny raises a hand, cutting off my babbling nonsense as he walks closer to me. A mixture of fear and revulsion makes me want to vomit. Concern knits his face and he lifts a hand to my jaw. I flinch as his fingers touch the swollen area.

"I'm not gonna hurt you, hon. Who did this to you?"

Tears slowly well in my eyes because the first person to show concern for me is the man who probably killed my father. I glance at Rafael, whose features are taut with rage.

"N—nobody. It was an accident. I fell on some icy steps of the subway."

Oh what a lame lie. You can't think of something better?

It doesn't fool Vinny. His hand drops from my face and he turns around to look at Rafael's smooth, unconcerned one.

"You did this?"

"He didn't!" Oh God.

"Of course not."

But his tone is way off. I'm his girlfriend. If he didn't do it, he should be apoplectic with rage. He should be throwing chairs across the room and screaming that how dare someone touch his girl? Instead, he just stands there. It's as though he doesn't care if Vince puts two and two together.

Vinny turns around, his fists clenched. "You've got some fucking nerve, lying to a boss."

Rafael crosses his arms and makes a brave attempt of a smile. "It's my fault she's a klutz?"

The boss takes several strides toward him and Rafael's

48

fist tightens around the pool cue, and then suddenly Vinny's fist smashes against the side of Rafael's skull. My screams echo in the room as he topples to the ground with a cry of outrage.

No, no, no! He's going to make it worse for me.

"I didn't do shit to her!"

Enraged, Vinny brings back his foot and kicks out hard. Rafael's face contorts with pain as his mouth makes a horrible, gasping sound.

"You want to fucking lie to me again? Huh?"

Rafael turns to his side and snarls at the boss. "What the fuck do you care about Jack's daughter? I'm a fucking made guy, you have no right!"

The other men grab Vinny's arms before he can do more damage, even though the boss looks like he would like nothing better than to beat him to death.

"Degenerate fuck. Do it again, and you'll be fucking sorry."

He makes other furious moves toward Rafael, but the others shove him back.

"Vince, calm down."

They let him go and Vinny stands there for a moment, chest heaving. Then he runs a hand through his dark hair and walks away from Rafael, who picks himself off the floor and gives me a murderous look. I turn away from him, shaking, and almost jump when I feel Vinny's hand on my shoulder.

"Come, I'll get you some meat for your ma."

Some sort of numb shock propels my feet forward, through the doors and into the cafe. "Vince, I—he was telling the truth. He didn't hit me."

Energetic, black eyes cut right through me. "You don't have to lie to me. People don't get bruises like that from falling down. You don't have to stay with him, either."

Something in his voice compels me to drop the bullshit and just tell him the truth. Maybe it's the faint anger I feel rustling in my chest. I don't know if I want to accept help from the man who, well, murdered my father.

You killed my dad.

"If I leave, he'll kill me. I don't have anywhere else to go, anyway."

The clerk behind the counter hands me a large package of deli meat wrapped in paper and I take it. "Thanks, Vincent."

"Hey, wait—"

My face already burns with the hopelessness of it all, and I shrug off his hand on my shoulder and head toward the icy storm outside, hoping that it'll swallow me.

* * *

The door opens.

It's the worst sound in the world—a sound that fills me with terror, a sound that makes me want to scurry to the bathroom and lock the door. I dread it every day. Dread the moment his boots walk through that door, and even worse is the noise when he slams it shut because he's always pissed these days.

Just go away. Just leave me alone.

But he won't, especially after today.

I sink into the leather couch, hoping that I'll become invisible. I stare straight ahead into the burning TV screen, hoping that something on it will distract him from his rage. I try to think back to when the sight of his face made me feel warm instead of cold with fear. He was never like this when Dad was alive—never laid a hand on me. He would never have dared—Dad would have killed him. We used to talk about getting engaged.

A painful twitch on my face makes me grimace.

"Are you fuckin' laughing?"

Something in my body turns my face toward his reddened one. His once handsome face seems wasted away by rage. The leather jacket he wears makes him look like a cartoon villain, and I think for a moment how funny the whole thing is. Me, the boss' daughter, stripped down to nothing but some whore for him to use and abuse. Whose own sister resents her for being the favorite, and won't even save her from her abusive boyfriend.

It's not really that funny.

"I'm not."

The shorter my responses are, the better.

Don't even look at him.

"You humiliated me in front of the people I work with. Do you have any fucking idea how bad that is?"

The sound of his footsteps makes me cringe, and then finally he stands in front of me, blocking the TV. I'm still paralyzed with memories from the past, refusing to confront the ugly present. He stoops down and makes me. He seizes my painful jaw, forcing it upward.

"*Look* at me, you fucking cunt."

"I didn't mean to, Raf. I swear to God, I was just there for deli meat."

He sneers at me. "And you needed to see Vincent for that? Fucking liar."

A heavy hand slaps the wound on my face, sending me flying. He laughs as I catch myself on the couch. A surge of poisonous rage runs through my veins that I'm unable to act on.

Oh, what I would give to make the son of a bitch suffer like I have.

Instead, I use the only tool left in my arsenal. Tears. They fall down my face freely, because it's so easy to cry these days. Normally, I'm dead to the world, twisting in agony inside.

"Y—you used to be so sweet with me. I don't understand why you're like this."

His weight sinks into the couch and his hand curls around my shoulder, pulling me upright and into his chest, where I just feel cold. I shrink from his closeness. For a moment, I think it worked. That maybe some tiny human part of me hears my distress and feels guilty.

His lips sear the swollen side of my face as he kisses it, leading a trail to my ear. "I was sweet with you because your daddy would have killed me if I laid a hand on you." His teeth bite down hard on my earlobe, and I grit my teeth.

Don't cry out. Don't let him win.

"You're not the boss' daughter anymore. *You're nothing.*"

It shouldn't hurt me to hear that from his worthless lips, but it does. It really does.

"You're fuckin' lucky I let you stick around."

A small thrill rises in my chest. *Why don't you just leave me?* I want to ask.

"Why do you?"

He plants another hot kiss on my neck, biting down hard enough to leave a bruise. This time, I make a small squeak of pain and he lets me go, laughing. "I like being able to do whatever the fuck I want with you. Besides," his voice drops down to a whisper, "I know about the money."

A sick, swooping sensation curls around my stomach as feeling disappears from my limbs.

How could he know about that? Dad left it for me!

I turn my face toward his, hoping that I can distract him. My arm wraps around his neck and I bury my hand in his short, bristly hair, leaning into his body as our lips touch. "I don't know what you're talking about."

He smiles against my lips.

My body flies over the coffee table, his hand wrapped around my neck. A gasp leaves my throat as my back slams into the hard table, knocking the breath from my lungs. Then his fingers bite into my neck, squeezing hard as my throat closes up.

My lungs wheeze as he leans over my body, slowly crushing me of life. I can't let this fucking asshole kill me like this—fuck him. My fingers rake over his face, nails digging into that furious visage. Maybe it's because I'm losing oxygen, but his face looks deformed in the low light.

His grin spreads a little too wide, his teeth pointed like tiny daggers. His eyes are completely black, and I wonder how I ever thought he was human. It's like the darkness had the effect of throwing a lantern on his face, revealing every ugly scar he kept hidden.

The fingers release my throat and I gasp for air, clutching at my skin and coughing. The vision disappears, and Raf sits up straight with a crooked smile that used to send butterflies flying in my stomach.

"I know Jack hid money in his house, and I know that you know where it is. You're going to take me to it." He leans in, enjoying watching me squirm on the table as I try to get away from him. "Oh, and if you ever go to my boss again like that, I'll kill you."

A flash of heat burns my face. I hate the arrogance on his face. Weeks ago, he wouldn't have fucking dared to say that to me.

Who's the real coward?

"No, maybe I'll fucking kill you!"

I shouldn't have said it.

Raf's nostrils flare as he stands up suddenly, the abrupt shift of weight making the table creak.

I really shouldn't have said it.

"You have balls, Elena, I'll give you that, but it's very

unbecoming for a wiseguy's girlfriend."

I know that tone in his voice, and my teeth clench together as he balls his fists. I'm so fucking tired of being scared all the time.

"Stand up and take your beating like a good little bitch."

Hating him, I stand to my feet, but I don't remain standing for long. He grips my jaw in his massive hand and squeezes. Then he shoves me hard enough for my head to crack the plaster on the wall. He howls in rage when he sees the damage.

"Look at what you fucking did!"

His boot slams into my side and I feel something inside me break—it's not a physical thing, but a mental collapse. Heavy blows rain down my back and sides. The pain radiates throughout my body, but it's as if there's a brick wall. I can't feel it. It must be some sort of miracle, or I'm very close to being dead and I should really, *really* fight back.

My neck slams against the wall and I suddenly feel an electrical shock of pain down my spine as he squeezes my throat, crushing my windpipe. A gust of his breath, stinking of alcohol, blows across my face.

"Say it again, *bitch*. I fucking dare you."

My eyes slide to his and I fight the impulse to smile as

my broken body screams with pain that I can only dimly feel. My ribs are probably fractured and I might have a slight concussion, but I don't feel a fucking thing.

This is the best you can do, you piece of human garbage?

I want to say it again, just to prove to the asshole that he can't wear me down. I'm Jack Vittorio's daughter and, yeah, I might be a little bit of a spoiled bitch, but no one treats me like this.

My limbs tremble against the wall and an ache pounds through my ribs, spreading agony through my torso, but I don't say a word. It's okay to let my ego take a blow for now. He'll get what's coming to him.

"I expect you to lead me to the cash *tomorrow*," he says, his face finally smoothing over.

His fingers unstick from my throat, and I collapse like a stone to the ground, crumpling like a heap at his feet. Rafael's cold laughter brings another surge of fury to my heart, but I force myself to calm down.

Don't let him see.

The fridge opens and I hear the clinking sound of bottles. Dread sinks my stomach as I hear the telltale hiss of a bottle opening. He's going to get drunk and stupid again, if he isn't already. I pick myself off the floor and limp toward the bathroom, hoping that he'll stay in the living room and zone out in front of the television. A vision of myself confronting him with a weapon burns my mind.

I'm going to die. Sooner or later, he's going to kill me—whether by accident or on purpose. I could see him kicking me one too many times and breaking my neck.

The bathroom door closes behind me and I twist the lock, wincing at the sudden beams of light overhead. The mirror reflects the image of a broken woman. Her dark brown hair hangs like a nest around her face, which looks like a disaster. Swollen cheeks and blood in her left eye, whose eyelid is sunken over. Busted lip. I lift up my shirt, revealing a large, angry red mark on my abdomen.

I don't recognize the girl in the mirror. She looks like those women you feel sorry for—the ones who keep going back to their abusive partners, over and over again.

When did it get this bad?

There were little things. Signs. A disrespectful comment here and there. Then, finally, he hit me. He slapped me across the face when I disagreed with him about something. My dad was still alive then. He was overcome with remorse. *Please don't tell your dad!* I remember well how he cried and blubbered like a baby. At the time, it touched me how strong his remorse was, and I decided to forgive him.

Now I know that I was just a moron. He wasn't fucking sorry. He was piss-scared that I was going to tell my dad, who would have gutted him, and he would have been absolutely right to do it.

Any idiot could have seen through him, but I actually thought I loved him. He was the guy brave enough to ask me out, before asking my father for permission. In the beginning, he made me feel special.

The horror in the mirror reflects only a few months of abuse. *What do you think he'll do in a few more?* Coldness slowly freezes my veins like liquid nitrogen.

If I went back to Vincent, maybe he'd be able to help.

And maybe he wouldn't.

He told me he'd kill me if I went back to his boss. Christ, my own sister won't even help me. How pathetic is that? What should I do?

You need to get him before he gets you.

Simply running away won't work. Raf is psycho enough to follow me wherever I go. No, I need help.

You have a hundred grand buried in the back yard at Mom's house. Dad showed you where he buried it because he trusted you above everyone else.

My insides freeze, my mouth suddenly dry. I'm horrified by the cold voice in my head, but it keeps talking.

You could hire someone to take care of him. Someone who might understand your situation.

Hire someone to kill Rafael? I swallow hard, studying the cuts and bruises on my face. Am I willing to walk down that road?

This is life or death. Yours or his. Choose.

Mine, I reply to the voice automatically. A twinge of guilt stirs in my chest at how quick my reply was. Going to the police is not an option. My dad went to the police, and look what they did to him.

I shut my eyes and think hard, trying to think of any friends of Dad's who might be able to help. Sometimes, there would be visitors from out of town at the house. A man—the boss in Montreal—was close with my dad. He spoke with an Italian-French accent, and was always friendly to me.

It's a desperate move.

I don't really have anywhere else to go.

* * *

I don't sleep all night. My body curls on the side of the bed, facing the blank wall. Everything inside me is like a coiled spring, ready to bounce the moment the coast is clear. In my head, I think about where everything is—my passport, the duffel bags, my clothes, shoes, and most importantly, the cash in the backyard.

Rafael's hand lays on my shoulder heavily. "Hey, what's wrong with you?"

I hope that he can't see my face in the dark, because if he did, he'd be offended by the disgust curling my lip. "I'm in pain."

It's not untrue. My whole fucking body aches, especially my head. The two aspirin I took didn't make a fucking dent.

The bed shifts with his weight and the pressure on my shoulder increases so that I lay flat on my back. A moan shakes from my lips as the pounding ache in my abdomen doubles. He hangs over me in a black t-shirt, the alcohol finally purged from his bloodshot eyes. His face bends lower and I flinch from his closeness. He pauses.

"I'm sorry, babe. I shouldn't have laid a hand on you— should never," he stops for a moment to swallow. "I love you."

The words sound so empty. Once, I believed them.

How many times must we go through this? The beatings, the apologies, the gradual buildup, the beatings.

I knew the moment that fuckface hit me that he was no good, but I couldn't leave him. It was the first time he left a bruise. When it happened, I stayed at my mom's house. He marched over there with flowers and sweet talked my mother into agreeing with him that I should 'give him another chance' and then I really had no choice but to follow him back to his apartment.

"I love you, too."

His fingers lightly stroke my cheek. "You just make me so pissed off sometimes."

Fuck you.

"I'm sorry." I hate myself for apologizing to him, but it's necessary.

Kill or be killed.

"I forgive you."

Fuck your forgiveness.

He says it with a slight smile on his face, and I try not to make my smile a grimace. God, I'm so pissed off that I'm praying he doesn't notice anything. I hope he's too blinded by his own arrogance to notice that I *hate his fucking guts.*

"Elena, I love you," he repeats it again as his lips fall on my bruised ones. I turn my head away with a cry of pain, but he continues kissing me in that passionate, possessive way that used to thrill me.

Everything he does hurts me. His weight presses into mine, and he's either oblivious to my injuries or doesn't care. His cock grinds into my thigh, painfully digging into me like yet another weapon he uses against me.

Oh God, no. Not now. I can't handle this.

The thoughts inside my head get more and more hysterical as he gropes his way down my body, and then his cell phone vibrates on the nightstand. He lifts his head, stopping for a moment. It vibrates noisily on the wood.

"Fucking hell."

I swallow my sigh of relief as he rolls off me and snatches the phone from the nightstand, pressing it to his ear. "Yeah? All right, I'll be there."

Profound relief almost makes me throw up, right then and there. Raf tosses the phone back on the nightstand and rips back the covers, swearing.

"Fucking Nicky always has the worst timing." He stands up and pulls a suit from the closet, quickly getting dressed as I pull the covers back over myself, feigning sleep.

When he shrugs on his jacket, he moves to my side of the bed and leans over, kissing my cheek.

"I'll be back for supper."

Good. Gives me plenty time to escape.

"Make something nice for dinner, something with meat. See you later, hon."

I take a good look at him as he turns around, whistling a merry tune. As his shoes flash around the corner, I realize that I'm not sorry to see the back of him.

Hopefully, I'll never see you again.

* * *

Elena, where are you?

I found the empty drawers. Where the FUCK are you? What makes you think you can just leave me?

CALL ME BACK RIGHT FKING NOW YOU STUPID BITCH!

How about I visit you mother? I bet she'll tell me where you are...

Sickened, I click on all the texts and hit the delete button. The vague threat toward my mother has me worried, but I hope that Vincent keeps an eye out for her. She won't hesitate to complain to him if Rafael gives her any shit.

It took me hours to dig up the carefully wrapped hundreds of dollars in the backyard, and then replace all the dirt. I did it right under my mom's nose, which probably bothers me the most. There wasn't enough time to say goodbye.

It's for her own good. If she knew where I'd gone, she would tell him, and then I'd be dead. The flashing, blue light illuminating the depths of my purse sends another wave of sickness through my body. I end the call, but it's no use. He just calls again. Voicemail after voicemail pops onto the screen, until finally I shut the damn thing off and settle into my seat.

"Any coffee, miss?" The train conductor tries to stifle a gasp at the look of my face. "Ma'am, are you all right?"

Not really.

Her face crinkles with sympathy as I just stare at her. "I fell down." I've no energy to summon a less lame excuse. "Ice would be great."

"Of course, yes."

Stares from the other passengers just make me want to throw a hood over my face.

Montreal. I wonder what it'll be like. I know French is the official language there, and I'm a bit worried about getting by. I place my hand against the windowpane, the cold stinging my skin. I'm probably not dressed for the harsh, Canadian weather. I just grabbed whatever I had—a single wool coat, some shirts and jeans, panties, etc. No matter. With the money I have, I'll be able to buy everything I need.

"Elena, honey. I've got something to show you."

That gleam in Dad's eyes sent a thrill of excitement through my chest. He always treated me different than the other guys' daughters. I was a bit rougher around the edges than Maria, a bit more tomboyish. Once, he brought me to the woods to shoot the new assault rifle he got as a gift. He taught me how to use it. Mom hated it.

"She's not a boy," she'd say over and over.

I expected it would be something like that as I followed him outside. It was a crisp, spring day. He placed both hands on my shoulders and squeezed them.

"I'm going to show you something that you need to keep secret. Don't tell anyone, even your mother."

I nodded my head rapidly, eyes wide. Whatever it was, it sounded important. He wrapped his arm around me and led me down the property. We passed the dying pomegranate bushes and stood over the red mulch, hidden by two evergreen trees.

"Underneath this mulch, between these two trees, I've got about a hundred grand buried. I want you to dig it up in case anything happens to me—"

My biggest fear slammed into my chest as if I'd been tackled. Without him, I'm nothing. I knew that.

"Dad, what are you saying? Did something happen?"

He held up a hand, smiling. "No—I'm just telling you in case, you know, I get sent to the can. Or God forbid, I get killed—"

"Don't say that!"

"This money is for you, Elena. You and your mom. Promise me, you'll take it if something happens."

Speechless, I watch his eyes crease as he squeezes my shoulders again.

"Promise!"

"Okay, Daddy."

The whole time, he knew he was going away. He was already in talks with the FBI—they were going to relocate us, and then he was dead. Overnight, I went from Mafia Princess to Daughter of Miserable, Cock-sucking FBI Informant.

Dad filled me with so much hot air growing up that I never believed he could die. He was a boss. New York City fit into the palm of his hand. I went to many charity dinners with him, and even met the mayor and the chief of police. In the end, all of his connections weren't enough to save him.

You're fleeing to Montreal. Then what? Kill him, and you can never return to New York.

I can't think of the future. All I can think of is right now, and the man lusting for my blood.

Eight hours into the ride, I turn the phone back on because I can't take it anymore. There's a stream of violent, expletive-laden texts. Only one makes my breath catch in my throat.

I know where you went, and I'm coming to get you. I'm going to fuck that cunt of yours until you bleed, and then I'll kill you.

* * *

It's a bluff. It has to be a bluff. I told no one where I was going, and used a fake name to book the hotel. Paid everything with cash. There's no way he knows.

I walk the icy, crumbling Montreal streets, horribly underdressed in the freezing weather. It doesn't matter. I block everything out. Cold? Who the fuck cares about cold? I have a psychopath hot for my blood, a spurned ex-lover who wants me dead. God, what if he found me with another man?

He doesn't contact me for a week, and I spend the time hiding out in a hotel, nursing my injuries and working up the courage to meet the Montreal boss.

So much is riding on this meeting with Johnny that I instantly crush the doubts that keep floating to the surface. He has to do this for me. He will.

My life depends on it.

I open the door to *Le Zinc*. It's a wonderful, posh place and I instantly feel uncomfortable and underdressed. The hostess immediately takes my ragged coat, but stops at the sight of my face.

"Miss, you need a hospital?" she asks in a thick, French accent.

"No," I say in a hurried voice, ignoring the looks thrown my way as I search the white tablecloths for Johnny. "I'm looking for Mr. Cravotta."

He's a young guy, and handsome, if I recall correctly. He should be here, my father always talked about meeting him at this place. Then I spot him surrounded by two other men, and I take a determined step forward.

"Miss, you need an appointment with Mr. Cravotta."

"It's urgent," I bark at her.

"You need an—what the fuck?"

I shove her skinny ass aside and barrel toward the table. Two guys I didn't even see suddenly take my arms and shove me back before I'm even five feet from the table.

"Mr. Cravotta, please! I need to speak with you!"

Johnny looks elegant in his pinstripe suit. Every aspect of his appearance is immaculate. His hair is slicked back into rolling waves, without a wayward strand of hair. There's not a single piece of lint on his suit, or a wrinkle, or anything that would mar his image of perfection. He stares at me with dagger-like eyes. It was always hard meeting his gaze, even though he always treated me with respect.

Looking as I do now, I don't find it hard to look at him. He can't say anything that makes me feel worse than I already do.

"Mademoiselle, you need an appointment."

The hostess appears at his side. "*Excusez moi, Monsieur Cravotta. Elle a*—"

"I saw the whole thing. Relax." He gives her a flick of

his hand, and the extremely harassed hostess returns back to the front, giving me a dirty look.

"Please, sir, it can't wait."

The men surrounding him laugh as they look at my face, and amusement flashes over his face before a faint note of recognition finally glimmers in his eyes.

"You're Jack's kid."

"Yes!"

He gives the others a meaningful look. "*Tabarnak de câlisse.*"

I have no idea what it means, but judging from the look on his face, it sounds like a swearword.

"Sit down. Guys, take a walk."

They rise to their feet obediently and the brutes holding my arms finally let go. I nearly crumple to his feet, but I manage to sit across from the table. He eyes me with a burning curiosity.

"What are you doing all the way here?"

I open my mouth, but stop immediately when the waiter fills the glass in front of me with water. He moves away like a ghost.

"Running."

"I can see that."

His eyes linger on the ghastly green bruise on the side of my face, the one I had before I met with Vincent. I'm

70

sure that my eye is still purple, too. Good lord.

"I need your help." My voice squeaks out, and I take a long draw of water to quell my nerves.

Johnny seems to pull away suddenly, his lips curling unpleasantly. "Look, I don't know what you expected from me, but you're mistaken if you think I'm going to help—"

"I have fifty grand in cash, and I need you to put a hit on a man."

Suddenly, his demeanor completely shifts. He leans forward, smiling, clasping his hands together. "If you have business to discuss, that's a different story. His name?"

This is the part I'm worried about.

"Rafael Costa."

Please don't say no.

He takes a small notepad and pen from his jacket, writes down the name, and frowns at it. He recognizes the name.

Please, please don't say no.

My hands grip the edge of the table. "Please, Mr. Cravotta. I'm desperate."

"He's a made man. Part of Nicky's crew in New York." He taps the pen against the notepad restlessly as he looks at me. "He's your boyfriend?"

The frown on his face deepens and I clench my teeth as he shakes his head. "I'm sorry, sweetheart, but the answer is no. You belong to him, and he's a made guy. If you were related to someone in the family, we could arrange something, but…"

But my dad is a traitor.

"Seventy-five grand," I whisper harshly. No, he can't just do this to me. I'll give it all, for fuck's sake. Anything to save my life.

Pity. It's all over his face. "I'm sorry, *ma cherie*, but I'm not going to start a war with New York because of some Yank."

"I—I don't *understand*! Why can't you? I have the money!"

"I just told you that it's not about the money. It's politics." He watches me seethe, his face blank. "Maybe you should call the police."

Is he fucking crazy?

Besides the fact that they wouldn't do anything, Raf would kill me the moment I waved the restraining order in his face. And if he didn't, Vincent might.

"I knew your dad," he says suddenly. "I liked him until he talked to the cops. He gave me a lot of problems."

"I'm *not* my father!"

My voice rings out in the restaurant, momentarily

cutting through the pleasant babble. Johnny's face hardens.

"I still find the idea of helping you repugnant." He nods to the men standing behind me, who grip my shoulders and lift me up.

"Please!" I scream to his rapidly disappearing face. "At least don't tell him where I am!"

Johnny gives me an apologetic smile as they drag me from the table, shoving the small of my back until I'm practically thrown outside.

The cold engulfs me like fog, coming in at all sides, seeping into my skin and making my bones ache.

Is this it, then? I can't go over Johnny's head. He was my only shot. Game over.

No, I refuse to accept this. My dad didn't raise a quitter, and I'll be damned if I let some hopped up jerk take my life because he can't fucking handle that I don't want to be with him anymore. I'll buy a gun—I'll buy an arsenal.

I'll look over my shoulder for the rest of my life.

The unfairness of it all seethes my guts. I whirl back around at the restaurant, half-wanting to sprint back inside and slap Johnny to make him understand how badly I need his help. Oh, he understands, but the asshole just doesn't give a shit about me.

Who else is there? Think.

I chew my thumb viciously as I walk down the street aimlessly, my eyes searching each storefront as though I'll see something or recognize someone, and after a while my legs tire and I'm just so fucking cold. I had no idea how cold it was here. My fingertips are numb and sharp pains shoot through my toes. I can't stand it anymore.

The door to a nearby bar opens and I rush toward it, grabbing the handle and disappearing inside the dark interior. Warmth painfully unthaws my fingers and toes. It feels as though my blood splinters like ice. It's a rustic bar—trendy, with battered wooden tables and clean, metal chairs. I pull one on the edge of the bar and sit down, cradling my head in my hands.

There aren't many people in the bar at this time—it probably just opened. Someone enters the bar from the backroom, and a distinct, New York accent suddenly makes my head snap up and my blood pound.

A hand curls around my shoulder, and I'm a second away from screaming. It's Rafael. He caught up with me already.

"If you came here looking for revenge, I suggest you get in line," he growls in my ear.

It's not him, but I still recognize that voice.

I turn my head and recognize Tommy's playful, hazel

eyes. God, he used to come over all the time. Dad loved him. Talked about him all the time. I haven't seen him in months—I thought he was dead. Then my mind flicks to what he just said. Revenge for my father's death? Heat strikes my chest. He must have had something to do with it, but so what? Everyone did.

"Do I look like I'm here for revenge?"

He releases me as if I've burned him and he steps back, disgust all over his face. "Raf did that to you?"

Tommy, of course, knew all about my relationship with Rafael. Hell, we had Christmas dinner together. We used to play cards. I always liked him, and he seemed to be devoted to my dad.

"Yeah. I just managed to escape."

Pity shines all over Tommy's face, and hope soars inside my chest like a balloon lifting to the sky.

"I know what you want to ask me. Johnny already called ahead. The answer's still no. I'm sorry."

He stands there, looking healthy and happy in his fucking two-piece suit, giving me a sad smile as though he wish he could help me.

Fuck you.

"*You owe me*—"

"I don't owe you a damn thing."

I can't believe how cold his voice is, how devoid of human emotion it is. Why is it that every one of my dad's friends treats me as a parasitic extension of my father? Did I talk to the cops? No.

It hurts more than it should.

"I don't understand why you would do this to me." The pain breaks through my voice and emotion finally cracks through his hard gaze. "Fine, hate my dad, but don't I deserve your help? We practically grew up together, and—you're just going—you're going to let him kill me?"

The anguish of being abandoned by virtually everyone I know twists my heart, and I dig my nails into my flesh. He flinches at the word "kill" and uncrosses his arms, looking at a loss.

Fine.

"Elena, I'm sorry, but there's nothing I can fucking do."

Nothing?

"That sounds like bullshit."

"If I touched a hair on his head, I'd be dead," he says flatly. "Those are the rules."

I search his desperate eyes.

"Give me a job here."

"What?"

I said it without really thinking, but the idea grows in

my head. It's a connected bar. Someone's bound to have a gun at all times here.

"Please. I'll feel safer if I'm surrounded by—guys like you."

"You don't know the language, hon."

"Neither do you!"

He gives me a wry smile. "You're just delaying the inevitable."

"Tommy, *please.*"

The plea in my voice gets through to him and he frowns, sighing. "Fine. I'll get you set up, but I don't want you to come in until you've healed. You look like hell. You'll scare my customers."

"Thank you, Tommy. *Thank you.*"

It's not much, but it's a start.

"Tommy, I need to ask you something else."

He moans and rubs his face hard. "What?"

"I have money that I need you to keep safe for me."

At once, his face brightens. "How much are we talking about?"

I lower my voice. "About a hundred grand."

"I'll be happy to do that for a small fee. Ten percent."

Ten percent? That's ten thousand dollars!

Not like I have a choice.

"Fine."

"I'll send some guys to pick it up. What's your address?" He frowns when I give it to him. "Raf will be able to find that, easily."

I don't know what he expects me to do about it.

* * *

Even after all this shit with my ex, I can't stop thinking about that man in the bar. Here I am, sitting in my new apartment in Montreal, fantasizing about another man.

There are bigger fucking problems in my life, but I can't stop thinking about his rugged face—so different from Rafael's—and his five o'clock shadow, which gave him the perfect balance of disheveled and sexy. He's the kind of guy who haunts your dreams after only one glance. Tall, dark, and handsome, but so gentle with his hands. He said things to me that I should hate for how fucking rude they were, but they gave me such a thrill from his honest voice. There's something really sexy about a man who knows what he wants and doesn't hesitate to go after it.

Tony was a breath of fresh air right when I needed it. He told me I was beautiful, promised me to make me come on his tongue, and I wanted to let him. It was like feeling a ray of sunshine after a really long winter. I wanted to feel desired by a guy like that. Who wouldn't?

But I panicked.

I slapped the most gorgeous man I've ever seen, and I can't stop obsessing over it. It's *ridiculous*. My ex-boyfriend wants me dead and this is what my brain chooses to obsess over.

I fantasize about that sexy bastard while I get ready for work in the apartment Tommy hooked me up with, hoping that Tony will be there.

No, stay the fuck away. Rafael was a nightmare, remember?

A grim sort of satisfaction stretches my face when I look in the mirror. Maria would be so proud. Here I am, making the same mistakes over and over again. The last thing I want to do is start dating, but when I think about how it felt to have Tony's hands squeeze my tits, all reason flies out the window.

Maybe Rafael moved on. All week, he's been silent.

I eye the dark phone sitting on the white sink. A thrill of apprehension runs through me when I pick it up and turn it on. He hasn't left any messages for days, but then I see a new voicemail and it's from my sister.

I play it.

"Elena, where the fuck are you? Your psycho boyfriend has been over here three times—he's completely out of his mind. What the fuck were you thinking, just leaving like this? You can't just—"

I end the voicemail message, breathing hard as I stare

at my whitened face in the mirror. It feels like live snakes are twisting inside my guts. My hands grip the edge of the sink and blood pounds in my ears. I *never* meant anything like this to happen. Why can't he just leave me alone?

My phone rings on the hard counter, and I watch it like a bomb. Even though I deleted his name from my contact list, the numbers don't lie. It's him.

I need to talk to him—to explain to him that it's over. Maybe then he'll leave me alone. A stab of fear clenches my heart painfully, and I pick up the phone gingerly. It's going to explode in my hands. I accept the call, cringing as I press it to my ear.

"I just got out of jail. Your cunt of a sister called the cops on me—Where the fuck have you been?"

So that explains his silence over the last few days. Fuck.

"Raf, it's over. I don't want to be with you anymore."

"So this is how you do it, you dumb fucking bitch? You just get up and leave in the middle of the night like some coward?"

Fuck him.

"Right, I'm the coward. You're the one beating on a defenseless woman. Go fuck yourself!"

"What the fuck did you just say to me, bitch? I'll cut your fucking tongue out!"

"LEAVE ME ALONE!"

The phone trembles in my hand. His voice strikes me

to my very marrow, infection me with fear. It's as though he's standing right outside my bathroom.

"Did you really think you could hide from me in Montreal? Did you really think that would work, that I wouldn't fucking find out? I'm on my way right now, and when I get there you better have my fucking money—"

"I'm not giving you anything—it's my money, so you can go fuck off and find some other bitch to beat up on!"

"FUCK YOU! I'LL FUCKING KILL YOU—!"

I rip the phone away from my ear and end the call, tossing the phone away from me as though it's a live snake. The bathroom echoes with my gulping breaths, which sound unnaturally loud.

Don't fucking cry.

The room spins and I stumble to the toilet, sitting down hard as blood rushes to my face. It's over—it's all fucking over. He's going to go straight to Johnny, who will tell him exactly where I am, and there's no defending against him. I'm fucked. Fucked!

The loud, buzzing sound of my phone vibrates in my ears as if the sound is inside my head. On silent, the phone rattles against the sink and finally falls to the floor. I have the strangest impulse to smash it—to kill it.

I can't spend the night here. That's an easy enough

problem to fix, isn't it? I could find a hotel or something easily.

But if he finds you there, you're just as fucked as you are here.

I slowly deflate, thinking hard. It shames me to admit it, but I need someone to protect me. For tonight, that'll be easy enough, right? Just find someone at the bar— and—my face suddenly burns.

You're that fucking desperate?

The pale shadow of a bruise stretches down my white face.

Yeah, I am.

* * *

It takes me three minutes to take off my boots and put my heels on until I realize I'm trying to put it on the wrong foot. Rafael is coming for me. It's only a matter of time before he finds out exactly where I am. I need to be in another place, but more than that, I need to be protected.

Basically, I need to go home with a guy.

My face burns as I stare at myself in the mirror, imagining my sister's voice.

Typical Elena. Always relying on someone else to fix your problems.

This plan is so fucking pathetic. One night isn't enough.

The horrible, clenching feeling inside me trembles and

almost breaks. A sob rises in my throat and I stamp it down.

No. Do not do this. Do not give up yet.

I want to give up.

You can do this.

But that voice sounds weak.

I'm wearing a lovely blouse I picked up with a diving neckline and leggings tight enough so that they won't miss a curve. High heels. Hair teased into a dark, messy mane.

It's a funny thing. When your life is in danger, you really stop giving a shit about everything else. Pride. Ego. Decency. Whatever. All you care about is making it through the next day.

The panic pulses inside me, fighting to claw its way out of the clenched muscles around my stomach. I shouldn't be here. I should be miles away, running for my life.

Fuck's sake—just go to work.

With a shaky sigh, I turn the knob and leave the bathroom, passing by the office on the way to the bar. Tommy does a double take from his desk and gives me a friendly smile. It warms me for a moment, and then I feel a swooping, guilty sensation.

"You'll get nice tips tonight."

"Tommy," I say in a heavy voice. "We might have

83

trouble."

He frowns and sits up straighter. Before he can say anything else, I head out into the bar, limbs shaking.

The bar isn't packed, but it's getting there. Men in business suits hang out near the bar, talking in rapid French. Young guys dressed in casual clothes leer at me as I walk by.

A different sort of fear makes me grin a little too widely. Growing up, I never had this kind of attention from men. It's intimidating and flattering at the same time.

"*Ey, Pitoune! Viens ici't!*"

A voice calls out from my left, and I've learned enough French to realize that this probably means: Hey, baby. C'mere!

Or something like that.

I turn toward the obnoxious voice. He leans against the wall and shakes his Molson beer.

"*Un autre.*" Another one.

A sweet smile spreads across my face as I slowly size him up. He might be connected—he's not wearing a suit, but he looks too young anyway.

I size up the men in the bar, completely alien to the way men are when no one knows who I am or who my father is. It's strange to feel so many eyes on me like this. I keep scanning the crowd, but deep down there's really only one guy who made an impression on me. My heart pounds, thinking about how confident Tony was when he kissed me. He knew I had an ex-boyfriend in the mob, and he didn't care.

He wanted me anyway.

The energy in the bar is warm and rowdy. I scan the crowd as I give out drink orders, stumbling through French and English to find out what they want. The hours fly by, and the bar slows down. I remember why I'm here and I peek at my phone, seeing another barrage of text messages from Rafael. My throat closes up as Tommy peers into the bar, looking surprised to see me.

"Elena, your shift ended an hour ago."

I grit my teeth and look into his unconcerned eyes. "Please—I don't want to go home. Just let me work."

The edges of his lips lift slightly and he nods. "All right." He gives me another long look and disappears into the back. I know that if I'm here when Tommy's around, I'll be safe.

What the fuck am I going to do when the bar closes?

Genevieve, the bartender, flies around me with drink orders as I scan the men sitting there. In sheer desperation, I study them. Some of them don't even glance at me. They're too busy texting on their phones. Then my gaze almost skips over him.

Tony.

The man who I slapped just a few days ago.

He's the biggest man in the bar by far and he sits in his seat, twirling his cocktail with a small smile as he looks across the beer taps, right at me. His eyes strike at me with the force of a javelin. I feel immediately warm, and my face flushes as I smile back at him.

He's not pissed.

That washes over me in a wave of relief.

Despite his immaculate suit, there's something rough about him. Maybe it's the dark hair, flying around his head as if he intentionally mussed it up—or his hooded, unflinching eyes, or the way he watches me with a thrilling confidence. I'm drawn to it like a moth to a flame.

A slow burn builds up over my face as I watch him closely, unable to sustain his heated gaze. What a joke. I slapped him when he hit on me the other day. It was one of my first few days in Montreal, and I was stressed out of my mind. He still deserved it, but he'll probably laugh in my face if I ask him out now.

The corner of his mouth lifts in a grin and his eyes flick down to my cleavage, slowly raking up my body until he meets my eyes again. His eyebrows lift and he gives me another devious smirk, one that sends a hot line of desire all the way down my back. Holy fuck, if that isn't an invitation, I don't know what is.

Then I know that he's the one I have to go home with. Just like that, my mind is made up.

My cheeks flush when I think about straddling his waist, his full mouth kissing a line down my throat. I wanted to go home with the meanest-looking man in the bar, and he fits the bill exactly. He turns his head and the smile evaporates from his face. Suddenly, he looks like a viper, ready to strike. Like he could fuck up the first person who touches him.

Jesus.

I'm startled by the transformation, and I lose my nerve for a moment. Suppose he's worse than Rafael?

Don't really have a choice. Yeah, I'm that desperate.

So how do I do it? Do I just ask him now? Apologize first?

I've never done this before. Rafael was my first, and he was the one who pursued me.

It shouldn't be that hard—just pretend you're someone else!

I grab a glass from the counter and pour a beer, blushing hard as I walk from the bar to give him a drink.

No, this won't work if you act like a blushing virgin. You need to be desirable. Be desirable.

Right. I compose myself for a moment and head for his back, trying to ignore the wildly flying butterflies in my stomach. The bar is so packed that I have to squeeze my body beside him.

My heart pounds somewhere in my throat as I take his shoulder with my left hand and slide the drink under his nose. God, this guy has muscles. I can feel them through his suit. His shoulder is rock hard.

His head turns slightly. "Who is this from?"

I smile at him, cocking my head. "Me."

His lips pull slightly. "If you're here to hit me again, think again. You got me once, sweetheart. You won't get me again." He takes a sip from the drink politely and licks his lips slowly. Damn. The way he looks at me sends shivers down my spine.

"I really—I wanted to apologize for that. It was rude, I'm sorry."

Actually, you kind of deserved it.

"Are you? Or are you just here to ask me for something?"

There are other women looking at him hopefully from across the bar, and a spasm of fear suddenly clenches my heart.

Now what do I do?

My heart pounds absurdly hard against my chest as he

leans on the bar, turning his body toward me. I'm struck by his size, and his closeness momentarily robs me of breath. His eyes watch me with an unrelenting intensity, and he smiles, deep dimples carving into his face. A swooping feeling in my stomach makes me feel weak, and I forget about my brazen plan.

"I am really sorry. I was just—really stressed."

My fingers brush his shoulder again, and he turns his head. Heart hammering, I lean closer and touch my lips to his cheek. The smell of his hair surrounds me for a moment, and then I pull back, already blushing hard.

He doesn't smile. "Look, I told you before. I can't help you."

"I know." I sit down next to him, not knowing where the hell I should start. He was all over me the other night, but now he's keeping his distance.

You did slap him, idiot.

"I—I want to take you up on your offer."

"Take me up on my offer?" He smiles, laughing through his nose. "It's called *fucking*, Elena. You want me to *fuck* you. Say it."

The word slams through me. *Fuck*. From his mouth, it sounds so damn dirty. I won't lie, the thought of going home with him and stripping off all my clothes scares the shit out of me. The man's gorgeous, but that doesn't take away from the fact that the only man I've ever been with is Rafael. I've never had a one-night stand. Never would have considered jumping into bed with a guy this quickly.

Spending the night alone might mean a death sentence. I'd much rather be wrapped in Tony's arms, with his sweat clinging to my skin. I'd rather feel his lips all over my body, and his tongue gently stroking my clit.

Jesus.

"I want you." I don't think it's possible for my cheeks to burn any brighter than they are. He raises his eyebrows. "I want you to fuck me."

"What if my offer expired?"

My heart skips in my chest as I search his face desperately. He can't—he doesn't mean that, right?

"Then I just have to change your mind."

I get up from the chair and move between his legs as his eyes, shining with amusement, follow me. My hand curls over his massive thigh. Damn, he's so warm. His warmth blazes through the slacks and sparks fly over my skin.

"What are you doing?"

I ignore him, keeping my eyes locked on his as I slowly ride up his muscular thighs, heading for the bunched up fabric between his legs. The shape of his cock is just visible.

"What's it look like? I'm getting you hard." I try to fight down a grin, but it doesn't quite work.

Laughter booms from his chest and he shakes his head at me. "Right here in front of everyone?"

"Why not?"

He cocks his head. "If my cock is out in a room filled with guys, I better be fucking a girl."

I make a sound at the back of my throat as I grab his hardening cock. It twitches in my hand and Tony lets out a small groan.

"Looks like it's working."

His face darkens as he lets out a primal growl that makes my core contract. "Any guy will get hard with a chick's hand on his cock."

"Oh—so you don't want to fuck me?"

I find the head of his cock and give it a squeeze and he makes another deep rumble in his throat. His eyes smolder with desire.

I'm in a bar, surrounded with people who can see exactly what I'm doing if I they glance over. I suspect the bartender saw something, because she keeps throwing me a big smile.

He suddenly grabs my wrist, pulling it away from his

cock. "*Enough.*"

"Sorry, did you get too close?"

"Please, I'm not that easy."

Tony's cock strains against his slacks like an iron rod shoved down pants that are too tight. He shifts his jacket to hide his boner, and then he pulls me close enough to kiss. I turned him on too well, and now he's pissed. My heart pounds in my head and I'm startled by the electricity between us.

"I don't like being teased."

"I'm not teasing you. I just thought you liked cutting through the bullshit."

A slow smile tiptoes across his face. "Not exactly what I meant."

He still won't let go of my wrist, but I don't really want him to. The noise in the bar drops to a distant rumble. I'm close enough to smell the musky scent clinging to his skin—no cologne at all, just Old Spice. My mouth waters when his thumb caresses my wrist.

"What makes you think you can just grab my dick like that?"

That's a good question.

"You didn't stop me."

His eyes crease as his lips lift in a faint smile, and warmth inexplicably floods my skin. "What the fuck do you want from me?"

I smile back, grateful that he isn't pissed off. My voice dips lower. "I want you to bring me home."

My eyes flick toward the other girls in the bar watching us surreptitiously.

"Bullshit."

His hands suddenly wrap around my waist and my heart flutters. I'm faint as his fingers stroke the exposed area just above my hipbones.

"It's not bullshit." Then I soften my voice, loving the attention he's giving me. "I want you."

"I don't doubt that you want me to fuck you, sweetheart. Every girl wants to fuck me. I just don't know what you really want."

So he's a cocky asshole, isn't he?

I move my lips to his ear, our cheeks pressed together. "Tony, we can argue about what I really want all night, or you can literally take me home right now and fuck me."

A deep chuckle vibrates through his chest and into mine. His fingernails slightly drag over the skin at my waist.

"You said you could make me forget about my ex. Was that true or are you full of shit?"

He regards me for a moment, his gaze lingering on my

lips. "Why should I give you the time of day after you slapped me?"

His tone makes me want to flinch, and I feel like an idiot for pursuing someone like him. He's a man who spends his days doing God knows what for the mob. There are scuff marks all over his knuckles and his Tough Guy attitude is too familiar. He reminds me *way* too much of the guys back home.

"Because you want me, too."

That's true, isn't it?

Then I tug his tie and lean my face forward, crushing my lips against his startled ones. I'm determined to make him want me, but I'm surprised at how much I want *him*.

Heat spreads like a fire under my skin the moment his tongue slides inside my mouth, and I dig my fingers in his hair, which is softer than I realize. God, he smells incredible, and his mouth tastes amazing. My palm spreads over his broad chest and travels down his dress shirt, to his waist. Then I ride my palm over his hardening cock, and I give him a squeeze.

He breaks off the kiss and gives me that sleepy, lustful look that sends a jolt of excitement through my heart. With a scorching look directed toward me, he reaches into his pants and pulls out a few bills, slapping them on the counter.

TONY

I don't know what the fuck this crazy bitch wants from me. One minute, I'm flirting with this hot broad who brought me a drink, and the next she's grabbing my dick in a bar full of people.

Jesus.

I didn't know what to expect when she made a beeline for me at the bar, but I was fully committed to spending the next fifteen or twenty minutes torturing her before taking her home and fucking the shit out of her. Then her hand moved up my thigh and my cock sprung to life. Heat rushed into my veins like whiskey and all I could think about was the feeling of her hands. It was as if we had fucked many times before. She surprised me. I grabbed her wrist and pulled her away from my cock, my heart pounding in my ears as my dick twitched and twitched in my pants.

What a crazy bitch.

What a crazy, *hot* bitch.

Red flags blaze at me at the back of my mind, but her hand rolls over my groin and squeezes. It lengthens underneath her delicate hands. She's a Mafia princess. I thought that she was probably uptight and boring like the rest of the girls connected with the life.

Within a few seconds of apologizing, she grabbed my cock.

So much for that theory.

Elena's pretty smile makes my heart clench again, or maybe it's the fact that her hand keeps stroking my cock. Fuck, it's hard to concentrate. Unconsciously, I slap some money on the bar and catch Tommy's eye near the back. He grins at me and shakes his head, disappearing to the back.

Go ahead and tell Johnny about this, I don't give a fuck.

I love easy pussy, and this one seems wild. What the fuck would possess a chick to grab a stranger's cock? She's either horny out of her mind or on drugs, but her eyes look clear to me.

I close my hand over my wrist and pull her body over my lap. "Hold on a second, hon."

She sighs, shifting her hips over my lap. My cock makes a loud protest that I try to ignore.

"What is it?"

"Tell me what you want."

The last time she saw me, she asked me to kill her ex.

An irritated look flashes over her face. "Do you want to take me home or not?"

Whoa.

"I'll take you home and fuck you in due time, but first I want to know what you want from me."

Her fingers brush against my neck and her lips fall against mine. She kisses me, if you can call that a kiss. Tantalizing lips and tongue brush over my mouth, barely there. It heats my chest and makes my heart pound.

"I haven't had good sex in months."

"What changed between the last time you saw me?" I say in a low voice.

"I—I was overwhelmed with personal things."

I don't buy it—not the fact that she doesn't want to fuck me—but that she doesn't want anything from me. She asked me to get rid of her ex the first time. She'll probably ask again.

Whatever. I just want to fuck her.

"All right, let's get out of here."

Elena returns from the back of the bar, all dressed up for the outdoors, but leaves her wool coat open, probably so that I can't miss her cleavage.

Nothing about this girl makes sense. She acts like an unapologetic slut, but she doesn't look like one. There's very little makeup on her face, and what little there is enhances her natural beauty. She looks like the girl next door. Innocent. Fresh.

I stiffen as she bumps against my side and slides her small hand in mine. Then I smile to myself. Definitely not a whore.

"Your place or mine."

"Yours," she says immediately.

My cock stirs when she looks at me under her eyelashes. Damn, this chick fucking wants me. It's suspicious, but my dick could care less. I take her to my car and my hand slips from hers. I open the door for her, and she smiles and gets in.

She rubs her fingers for warmth as I start the car and gives me a wide, playful grin.

I'm going to have you every which way.

I must be driving 80 kilometers per hour down these fucking streets. Her hand lays on my thigh like a hot brand. Her fingers make small movements over my thigh, driving me nuts as she slowly inches closer and closer to my groin.

Her fingers keep rolling over my cock as I drive, driving me fucking insane. I nearly blow through a red light, and she laughs. The sound of her laughter echoes in my car, and I catch a glimpse of her smiling face. Strands of her black hair cling to her mouth as she laughs, and then she slowly pulls them away from her face, and I want to keep looking at her.

Jesus. Get in control.

Finally, I park outside my brownstone. My heart beats steadily, slowly picking up the pace as it realizes how close I am to getting my cock wrapped in her pussy. Then her hand curls around my arm just as I'm about to open the door. I turn my head, and she wraps her arms around my neck and kisses me. She shoves her goddamn tongue down my throat. It's fucking hot, and my hand immediately goes for her tits. I unbutton the top of her blouse, exposing a black lace bra and her creamy-white tits. She inhales a sharp breath as I slide my hand under her bra and squeeze her. I *love* her warmth.

She leans forward with a grin and slides her hand up my thigh. A million nerve endings singe as she grabs my cock and squeezes hard.

I break from her mouth and grab a fistful of her hair. "If you don't stop, I'm going to fuck you right now in this car."

"You can do anything you want with me."

I let out a small groan as I look at the door. It's all the way over *there*.

Take her inside. The last thing Johnny needs is one of his guys getting busted for public indecency.

"Get out of the car." The voice I use surprises me, but she obeys instantly.

I get out with a little bit of difficulty and drape my coat to cover my rock-hard erection. Smiling, she walks up to me and takes my hand, leading me toward the door.

When we're at the top of the steps, my head burns with the things I want to do to this broad. Her chest flushes with color as I pin her against the door, and I dig my cock into her thigh so that she knows how hard I am. Elena's dark eyes flash at me when I take her small chin between my fingers.

"Not many girls get me this turned on."

Her tits bump against my chest as she straightens. My heart actually flips when she kisses me, and I sigh into her, moving forward, but she pulls back with a slick smile. She's got me right where she wants me.

Fuck.

"I want to be the best fuck you've ever had."

It turns me on to hear how eager she is to please me, but I really doubt she'll make that much of a lasting impression.

"What makes you think you're going to be the best? I've been with a lot of women, and I'll be with a lot more after you."

She gives me a smoldering look. "Because I want you more than anyone else you've been with."

Wow.

Her fingers splay over the back of my neck, tingling my skin as she plants another soft kiss on my mouth.

Well, fuck me.

This girl could be completely out of her mind, but I can handle her. I've fucked crazy chicks before.

Who the fuck cares, moron! Shut up and fuck her!

She tries to open the door, even though it's locked. My laughter echoes in the street, and she turns to me with a blush.

"Slow down, *ma belle*. You'll taste my cock soon enough."

When I finally approach my door, she slips between my arms. Her hot mouth descends over my neck and she unbuttons my dress shirt, and I know there won't be any bullshit the moment we step through that door. No getting drinks or making boring small talk or watching a movie. We've barely said any words to each other, and my cock is hard enough to pound nails. The keys miss the hole several times—it's hard to concentrate when her hand's on my dick and she keeps jerking me off through my slacks. Finally, it bursts open and her hands yank my coat, pulling me inside.

Normally, I like to take control, but this is so fucking hot that I just let her. The door slams shut and silence descends over us, but it's not awkward. It's simmering.

Her eyes widen slightly as she stands in my apartment, suddenly looking vulnerable. My hips bump into hers, and I sweep back her long black hair from her face. A strange feeling clenches my heart when I look at her. I don't understand it.

"You're fucking beautiful."

A switch seems to flip inside her and her hands sweep off my coat. Then they latch over my belt and she pulls me forward, grinning.

"It's my turn to fuck you the way I want, since I asked for it first."

Actually, I asked for it first, but I let her take control. I don't know how long I'll last—there won't be anything in the world to stop me from throwing her over my kitchen table if she keeps teasing me.

I pull her close to me, the very smell of her hair arousing me. Everything about her makes it so fucking hard not to act out on my urges. "I can't promise you that I'll wait for my turn."

Elena smirks in response and leads me into my living room, where there's a large mirror. She drags a chair in front of the mirror and pushes me hard into it. It makes me laugh, but I pretend to stumble backward into it. She stands close enough for me to see the stitching of her clothes, and then she rips them off. I follow the hem of her shirt as she pulls it over her creamy-white skin, over the swell of her breasts, and then I watch her toss her black head as the shirt sails into the air. A seductive smile spreads over her face as she slowly undoes the clasp of her bra. Fuck, she's good at it. I feel like I'm watching a professional strip show, except none of them ever made me this fucking hard in my life. The straps torturously fall down her arms one by one, and then the bra falls from her tits, which are big enough for me to lose myself in.

Holy fucking Christ.

"*Maddon*, you have great tits."

I'm desperately trying to keep my cool—to not grab her—

"You think so?" she says innocently, as if the bitch doesn't already fucking know.

The small, pink nipples contract in the air, and I want so badly to grab her fucking waist and fondle her tits. I want to bite her neck and her nipples and sink my teeth into her collarbone. I want her.

She bends over before I can act on it, and I stare at her tits drooping down into perfect teardrop shapes. Her leggings snag at her waist and she pulls them all the way off her small, hairless thighs. Then the black panties are next to follow, and her shaven pussy glistens in the low light.

Oh Jesus.

She plays with my belt. The sound is almost painful to my ears. I want to rip it off and fuck her, and use the belt to make big welts on her ass for taking so fucking long. I'm completely out of my element, and I'm not used to it. I'm used to ordering the girl around, getting what I want.

I'm about ten seconds away from losing all control.

My slacks pull down to my knees, and my cock jumps as she rips my briefs down. Then she straddles my waist, my cock in her fist, her tits in my face. Oh God, tits. She sinks down, right over my throbbing cock. Her wet cunt completely swallows my cock.

Condom!

I don't give a fuck right now. Elena's beautiful body rises, her tits slapping my face as she sinks back down on my cock with that incredible, wet heat gripping my cock. She moans in my ear.

"You're so fucking big. So deep—ah!"

She fucks me hard, riding my cock like I'm a goddamn bull, and I take her hips in my hands. It's overwhelming— her tits in my face, her tiny waist moving up and down. Her sweet pussy swallowing me. God, it's been so long since I've fucked a girl barebacked, I forgot how good it was.

Her lips attack mine with a passion I've never

experienced before, even in all my drug-induced, frenzied fucks. Her hands fuck up my hair, and then she yanks as she drops down hard, my balls smacking against her pussy. Then she turns my head to the side.

"Look."

I see myself in the mirror, laughing and half-dressed as a naked girl bounces on my lap, her tits slapping my face. She grinds herself on my cock as her face twists with a moan. Fuck, it's an incredibly hot sight. I could stare at her all fucking day.

"Do you like this?"

"*Fuck yes.*"

The sounds of her body bouncing on me are almost enough to make me come. She pants from the exertion of bouncing on my cock, moaning when I lift my hips to fuck her deep. Then suddenly, she lifts herself from my waist, and cold air hits my wet dick.

"What the fuck are you doing?"

"Sucking your cock."

She's already between my knees, gripping my iron rod of a cock in her hands. Her mouth slides over my length, and it's like slipping into paradise. Tight, hot, wet. Her tongue slides down my length as her mouth sucks the juices from her pussy. Fuck. Holy fuck.

My nerves scream as she moves her wet little mouth up

and down me, nearly gagging at times. The sweet, innocent Mafia princess can suck cock like a champ. It blows my mind. A growing pressure behind my dick fills me with a burning desire to fuck the shit out of her mouth, but she's determined to control everything. I get a nice view of her body as she sucks me off, and then she does something with her mouth. A stream of precum flows out of me as she uses my cock like a lollipop, the obscene, sucking noises almost too much for me. My cock pops out of her mouth and she grins at me, still fisting my dick.

"I want you to come in my mouth."

"I like that idea."

Suddenly, she climbs over my lap again and aims my aching cock toward her pussy. A delicious sigh leaves her mouth as she sinks down. Her thighs smack against mine as she fucks me furiously, her tits smashed against my face. I've never been fucked like this before—*holy shit!*

My hands curl over her shoulders and I drive my hips upward, my lips meeting hers. Her tongue, honeyed with some sweet drink, sweeps into my mouth as her teeth bite down. She's fucking wild. My heart pounds my chest like a battering ram, and then she sweeps my hair from my face and kisses me again. It's intense, almost as if I'm some kind of long lost lover.

Her cunt squeezes my cock as she sinks down hard

enough to hurt my balls, and then they tighten. It's building up—this girl's going to make me fucking come in five minutes like some kind of chump.

"I—I'm going to—"

Cold air stings my cock as she leaps off and sinks to her knees. Her hot mouth swallows me again, a ring of pressure around the base of my cock. She takes my hand and places it behind her head, and I ball my fingers in her hair.

She wants me to fuck her mouth.

I oblige the filthy slut, digging my cock inside her as deep as she'll take me—which is really fucking deep. Her lips brush the base of my balls and her tongue sweeps me from side to side, igniting a million pleasure nerves. I choke her throat. It makes me fucking insane to hear the sounds my dick makes when it moves down her bulging throat. Then I grab the sides of her head and I feel it—a hot rush of cum bursting through my cock.

My moan echoes throughout the kitchen as I bury myself deep, my manhood spurting long jets in the back of her throat. She keeps her mouth sealed against my cock and sucks every drop from me. Ecstasy shakes my thighs as I keep pumping inside her, until finally her lips pop from me. She rises to her feet and sits on my lap.

And then I feel incredibly unsatisfied.

I wanted her pussy, and I got her mouth.

She wraps her arms around my neck, still giving me that unsettling, deep stare. "Next time, you get to fuck me however you like."

A grin spreads across my face. Next time? Who said there would be a next time? But I know that there will be. She's too damn hot and willing. I know it's against my rules—I know that I'm supposed to kick her out now, but I can't help it. I want her again. And again.

"I liked what you did with your mouth." My fingers trace her lips, and then I lean forward, inexplicably drawn to her. She kisses me as though she wants me again, and then I reach underneath for her pussy and it's still soaking wet.

Well, well, well.

"I'm on birth control, by the way."

Part of me doesn't believe her, and part of me doesn't give a shit.

She squeals as I stand up with her in my arms and pivot on the spot, heading for my bedroom. "I'm going to fuck the shit out of you tonight. You won't be able to walk straight for a week because you've been with me. I let you have your fun, and now it's my turn."

Elena gives me a coy smile as I set her down on my bed, and she immediately plays with my cock. It grows in her hands as I feel the blood pulse through it. Goddamn it. How does she do that to me?

Her hair fans out behind her as she lays on her back, her knees pushed together. My eyes wander down her thighs to her swollen pussy, still wet for me.

"I want you to fuck me until I'm numb. Even when I beg you to stop."

"Yeah? You want more of this?"

She does. Elena smiles under her eyelashes.

"Go ahead and suck it like a good slut."

A faint blush tinges her cheeks as she sits up on her knees and does exactly what I asked her. I sigh as her lips pass over the head of my cock to make that wonderful, sucking noise that immediately gets my dick hard.

She's good enough to make me want to come inside her pretty mouth again. Watching her lick every drop from me was amazing, but I want *her* to get hot for me. I want her to beg me for more.

I pull my hips away from her and she looks up at me with a questioning look. Then I smooth my hand over her flushed tits and gently push her back down.

"Spread those beautiful legs for me."

They're so soft. I run my hands along her inner thighs as she opens them for me, exposing her pink pussy. My mouth waters just thinking about having her buck against my tongue.

I spread a hand over her belly as I kneel down between her legs and breathe in her scent. It's heady with the smell of us combined. She lifts her head and looks at me.

"*Tony.*"

Then her voice lifts into a cry as my mouth smothers her pussy. My tongue flicks her clit, already swollen with need, and then I lick her all the way back to the front. Her back arches and her legs shiver. She reaches out, trying to touch me, and her knees tighten around my head.

And I smile against her cunt.

"Please, Tony—please don't!"

It sounds like she's crying for the opposite. She fists the sheets, bucking madly as my chin runs with her juices. My tongue fucks her deeper as my mouth sucks her little clit, and then I pull back when her breathing quickens.

"Fuck me!"

I want to. My cock is hard enough so that I feel every painful throb of my heart through the veins in my dick. She's soaking wet and her pussy will let me glide through without any resistance, and everything inside me thinks that I'm fucking crazy for not fucking her already.

My fingers slide right through her pussy, curling upward. When she makes a sharp moan, I know I've hit the right spot. Her pussy clenches around my fingers as I tongue her clit. It's so fucking wet, and then she pounds the mattress with her fist.

"Just fuck me already! Please!"

I laugh, my breath billowing over her clit. "You want me that badly?"

My mouth makes a seal on her inner thigh and I suck until there's a bright red mark. Her face twitches as if she's in pain, and then she grabs my hand.

"I wanted you the moment I saw you."

I'm ready with a sneer the moment the words leave her mouth. She has no idea how many women I've been through. I don't give a fuck about anything, but when she looks at me like that, I believe her.

I take her in my arms—she doesn't weigh a thing—and I carry her to the living room, dick throbbing. My high-rise has a wall of glass separating the building from the outside. Elena's cheeks darken when she realizes what I have planned, but she doesn't object.

I want the whole world to see us fucking.

She slides from my waist, and I rip the shirt and tie from my body, gazing out into the cold outdoors. There are countless, glowing windows on the other side of the street. We're easily visible. Everyone's going to be able to see her tits pressed up against the glass as I fuck her from behind.

Elena hesitates as I turn her around so that she can see the faint outline of her reflection.

"This is—I—"

My lips bend to her ear. "If you want my cock, you'll bend over and place your palms flat on the glass."

My arm wraps around her tits and gives them a squeeze, and for a moment I think she's going to chicken out. She freezes.

Then she bends over obediently, palms flat against the glass. Then she waits for me, her thighs quivering. Her head lifts so that anyone looking will see the expressions on her face. Her cheek presses against the glass as I aim my dick between her slick pussy and ease in. Fuck, she feels good.

Her pussy lets me glide right in, the walls opening up for my cock. She lifts her head and gasps when I grind against her hips. I jerk her hips toward me as I pound her pussy in earnest, screams ripping from her throat to bounce all around us as I nail her against the glass. She forgets all about her embarrassment and flattens her elbows against the glass.

"Tony! Oh my God!"

Yes, that's what I was fucking waiting for. Scream for me, honey.

She's bouncing against my cock so hard that her tits

swing back and forth in beautiful, teardrop shapes. I reach under her and grope one of them as she tries to turn her head and look at me with a smoldering look that makes me want to come all over her face.

I want more of her.

She straightens her back as I tighten my arm around her waist, lifting her up to fuck her hard against the glass. Her tits press against it and I imagine the sight from the other side: two huge tits in perfect circles, the side of her face a mask of frustration and pleasure. I think I see a light flicker from the opposite side of the street, and a dark figure stands silhouetted against the light. He's facing us.

A thrill shoots up my spine as I hammer her wet cunt, her cries almost frantic now. What a beautiful sound, and it's all for me. The pressure builds up in my balls, and I see myself thrusting behind her sexy ass, arms wrapped around my woman as I claim her pussy.

Then it rips through me like the force of a bomb. My groan mingles with her shouts as I bury myself deep, and then incredible relief fires into my veins as I blast cum into her soaked pussy. I grab her throat as I thrust hard, and she twists in my arms slightly to kiss me. Her stung lips part into a small moan as I slide in and out of her.

I feel lightheaded.

I pull out of her, watching as cum slips out and runs

down her legs. Anxiety suddenly punctures my euphoria. I always use a condom. Always. How did this girl make me forget to use one?

We collapse on the couch together and she sits across my legs, nuzzling my neck.

"I've never been fucked like that in my life."

Calm settles over my limbs as I let her curl up next to me. I always hate this part—the coming down from a high that always makes me feel like a goddamn void. It's usually also the time I start my countdown to the minutes I gently ask the girl to leave, but I don't feel like I'm in a hurry this time.

I rub the back of her neck as she plants kisses on my throat, and it's more than pleasant. Something uncomfortable bristles inside me.

Fuck. I shouldn't let her stay long.

"I know."

"You're a confident guy, aren't you?"

"I am when it comes to fucking."

My skin shivers when she gives me a kiss right under my ear.

"You should be."

Elena pulls back and beams at me. The smile she gives me makes me want her again, but I've already broken my rules once. She needs to get the fuck out.

"I've got work to do tonight."

She stiffens as she recognizes the dismissal and her eyes suddenly look so sad that it's like a knife to my gut.

"No you don't."

A slow smile spreads across my face. "Sorry, hon, but I do."

Her lip quivers and I see the destruction all over her face. Her eyes swim and a tear runs down her face. I'm used to seeing chicks crying all the time, most of the time from rage, but this is different. This makes me feel bad. Not just in a general guilty sense, but in a way that makes my blood cold.

She takes my face in her hands and bites down her lip viciously. "Please let me stay the night."

There's a tugging feeling in my chest that I despise. She runs her thumb over the stubble on my jaw, pleading me with her eyes. I think about those bruises on her neck.

"Why?"

Let her fucking stay!

Elena shakes her head violently. "I just need to stay here for one night. Just let me stay here, and I swear I'll never bother you again if that's what you want."

The red flags are in flames.

The sweetness evaporates from my voice. "All right. I don't usually do this, but I'll let you stay so long as you don't give me drama in the morning."

She flinches from the coldness in my voice, but nods gratefully.

"Thank you."

The warmth from her body disappears as she gets up from my lap and pads to the entrance to gather her clothes, and I hate the sting of cold from her absence. Blood pounds in my head as I go back inside my bedroom and pick a pair of boxers. The nagging feeling in my head grows as I brush my teeth in the bathroom.

She'll give me a hard time in the morning. I just know it. She'll cry. She'll moan. She'll complain.

Fucking idiot. Shouldn't have told her she could stay.

The mattress sinks I sit down and wait for her to come inside. Ten minutes later, I stand up with a growl and search for her. What the fuck is she doing?

Then I see her wide-eyed face curled up on the couch, trembling from the cold.

What a fucking asshole you are, Tony.

It hits my gut, seeing her like that. She thinks I want her on the couch, that she's not good enough for my bed. That couldn't be further from the truth. I just don't want attachments. My shirtless reflection glares at me from the glass window, and I fix my expression, walking towards the curled up girl. She stiffens when I lay my hand on her head.

"Come."

She turns her head and notices me. "It's okay," she says in a reedy voice. "I'm fine."

"*Come.*"

My mother didn't raise me to be an asshole to girls. I take her hand and she follows me into the bedroom. I crawl under the sheets, and she follows swiftly, adding her warmth to my king sized bed.

"Thanks, Tony."

Don't thank me.

I don't want to feel anything for her, that's the whole fucking point of my 'one night' rule. I turn my back on my guilt and shut the light, imagining the grateful smile on her face in the dark.

* * *

A soft feeling on my cheek, and then lips kissing my eyes open.

It's peaceful. Beautiful. Then I look directly into her dark eyes, slightly creased with sadness.

The warmth in my chest disappears and I adjust myself under the sheets, noticing with a delayed fog that her naked tits press into my chest. My cock wakes up sharply and my eyes flare open. From the look on her face, she isn't wearing anything else.

Well, that's one way to wake up.

"Bonjour mademoiselle."

"Hi." Elena's lips seal against mine as her hand anchors over my cock. It stiffens almost immediately, and Elena pulls back, smirking.

"I didn't fuck you hard enough last night?"

"No, I don't think so."

My mouth gapes open slightly as I feel heat rolling from her body. She's not lying—I can feel her wetness when I curl my hand between her thighs. It comes back soaking.

I just can't let her leave unsatisfied.

Fuck yes.

My body rolls to the side and I yank open the nightstand drawer, fishing for a condom. Using my teeth, I tear it open and roll it over my rock-hard cock. No frills. Just a quick, hard fuck. She wraps her legs around me and gasps as I fuck her pussy, hammering her hard until she clutches my shoulders, screaming. It's different when you can see their faces clearly in the daylight. Every vulnerability is laid out in the open for me, and Elena bares it all. She doesn't hide.

Her back arches, thrusting her tits into my chest as I bury myself as deep as I can. If I could fuck every feeling away, I would. Then my legs shudder and I groan into her neck as her pussy clenches over my cock. She digs her nails into my scalp and then sinks into the sheets as the orgasm wipes every worry from her face.

I collapse beside her, breathing hard. My dick is fucking sore, and for once I'm not in a hurry to make her leave. I'm just exhausted. She curls next to me, her arm splayed across my chest.

It's a nice view. Christ, she'll be masturbation material for a long time.

The events of last night slide over my eyes like a highly graphic porn video, and I smile to myself as I stroke her back lightly. Then I remember her tears when I asked her to leave and the smile disappears. She nearly begged me to stay the night. Why?

"Why were you so upset last night?"

I tell myself I shouldn't care—I don't care, but it's a curiosity.

Elena's face freezes, but she stays silent.

"I did what you wanted. Can't you at least tell me why I had to let you stay?"

The breath hitches in her throat and she opens and closes her mouth. I start to get impatient, but I force myself to wait it out.

Let her talk.

"I needed a safe place to crash."

I thought it had something to do with the ex.

"Call the cops."

"He'll kill me before I can get a restraining order."

I won't lie, it's not uncommon to hear about a wiseguy slapping around his girl. It's frowned upon, but tolerated because no one ever sees the abuse. There's always an explanation for the bruises, even though we all know the truth. It sickens me. One of the many things I can't stand about the life.

"So your solution is to what? Fuck me? Get him jealous or something?"

"No, I just didn't want to be home."

Acrid bile rises in my throat when I look at her worried face.

"Johnny told me to keep an eye on you."

She lets out a sound through her nose. "What the fuck?"

"He just wants to make sure you don't do anything stupid."

For a moment, she looks furious and I brace myself for the hell storm that's sure to follow, but she deflates almost instantly.

"Please don't make me go back to him."

The fear trembling her voice makes me curious. It also adds a bad taste to my mouth.

"No one's going to make you do anything, but no one's going to help you either."

She says nothing for a while. "I just don't want to be with him."

A gaunt look makes her face look sunken. Her eyes are listless as they stare into mine and then drop away. She slides away from my arms to sit on the edge of the bed. There's nothing but the coarse sound of her legs moving over the sheets, and somehow it's grating to my ears.

Something goes through me when I watch her bent over back. Self-disgust, maybe. Elena bends her face into her hands for a few seconds before inhaling a long breath, and I have a sudden desire to slide next to her and wrap an arm around her, but I don't make a move. She picks up her clothes one by one and pulls them on. The misery on her face bothers me more than I'd like to admit, but there's nothing I can do for her. Nothing. If I laid a hand on him, I would get killed. Made members aren't allowed to be touched without permission.

I'm willing to fuck her, but not to stick my neck out for her.

I really am a bastard.

I open my mouth, but there's really nothing to say to her. Not when she's leaving my place, and I'll probably never be alone with her again. Though I suppose I'll see her again if she works at Tommy's bar.

"Can I have your number?"

The question startles me, and I hate myself even more when I have to turn her down.

"Sorry, but I never see a girl twice."

Disappointment floods her pretty face as she nods. Thank God, she doesn't cry.

I walk her to the door, grappling with changing my goddamn mind, and then she whirls around to grab my shoulders. Hanging in the doorway, she kisses me as though it's the last time. I suppose it is, but no one's ever made me aware of that quite like her.

Damn, she's beautiful.

Her thigh bumps into my cock as she crushes her mouth against mine. A weak feeling spreads through my limbs and I grin when she reaches around to grab my ass.

"I guess I should count myself lucky that you fucked me more than once."

I like the fact that she just brushes it off like it's nothing. She's not a crier. She's tough.

Elena's flushed lips pull into a sad smile as she steps back from me and gives me a little wave.

"See you."

"Bye."

Then I watch her flounce down the steps and walk

down the street. I keep watching her even though the cold rolls over my bare feet and makes them numb.

ELENA

Snow dusts my jacket as I walk down the white street. Heaps of fresh snow pile on the sidewalk, and it's fucking freezing. My toes are numb. The cold air stings my eyes and the white burns.

But it's beautiful.

I brush my cotton gloves over a dusting of snow, and immediately regret it when it soaks through, stinging my fingertips. I walk past brownstones, and see a brilliant splash of red on some fresh snow. It looks like juice, but it reminds me of blood.

Then I think of how beautiful it would look—my body on the snow, a halo of red around my head. The irony makes me smile.

What the fuck is wrong with me?

Everything just feels surreal. These last few months felt like a practical joke. I'm aware that I should be worried for myself. I should race down these frozen streets and ask Tommy for a gun, or hell, just keep running. Something that might give me a fighting chance at survival.

Is it crazy that last night is the only thing I want to think about?

The moment I saw him in the bar, I wanted him. Yeah, he's just another bad boy—a wiseguy who's going to chew me up and spit me out, just like Rafael did. At least he had the decency to be honest with me. You can't say that about most men. Usually, they ignore you because they don't even think you're worthy of dealing with.

I didn't care, though. It was instant fire through my veins, the moment I locked eyes with him. He had an amazing body—ripped, and he used it like a pro. He wanted me to get off. He enjoyed it.

Beyond that, I didn't really think it through. I thought that if I went home with him, at least I'd be safe for one night.

What a crazy night. My face burns when I think about how he utterly destroyed all my expectations. He was so fucking good. I felt like I was floating on clouds the whole time, but it wasn't anything more than a great night. It would always be just one night.

I mull him over, unable to cool the burn that spreads over my skin. I can't stop thinking about those eyes full of sin and his devilish smile that hints that he's nothing but trouble. Tony is the kind of bad boy I always lusted after, until I realized just how bad they really are.

Forget about him.

It would be easier to forget how to breathe.

Why am I lusting after a one-night stand when I have bigger issues?

After taking a chain of subways, I'm back at my apartment. Fear prickles all over my skin as I stare up at it.

He might be waiting for me. Right inside my apartment.

Then I finally turn my phone on and there are about twenty text messages from Rafael. I blow out a frustrated gust of white into the crisp air. He's either here or not. I'm out of options and it's hard to care anymore. I could barely get a stranger to let me stay the night, even though there's a fucking psycho gunning for me.

Maybe this is the punishment I get for being spoiled my whole life, and doing nothing to earn a single dime. I never really achieved anything. I graduated high school by the skin of my teeth and fucked around in college, wasting Daddy's money as I tried to figure out what I wanted to do with my life. I never figured it out. The next stepping stone was always marriage, and shortly after, kids. It's what they expected from me. It's what all good Italian girls did, and I have to admit that I didn't really mind settling in that role. Why did people always want to make me feel bad for just wanting a simple life?

Rafael seemed like a great candidate. My dad approved of him, which was hard enough to get, and he was Italian.

Worked in the same 'business' as Dad. It didn't even occur to me that he would change after we moved in together.

If Dad was alive, I wouldn't know what to say to him. I can't even think about him without feeling a mixture of guilt and betrayal. He sold us out, and for what? To get killed anyway.

Maybe I deserve this.

My feet are like lead as I climb up the stone steps. There's another set of footprints leading to my apartment, but I don't care. Fuck it all. My mother is a hollow shell and my own sister resents me. There's just nothing left anymore. Just a bag of money my dear old Dad left for me.

At the top of the stairs, a small voice whispers in my ear.

There's still time to make something of your life.

Tony's hands wrap around my waist and his mouth covers mine. I see that wry smile on his lips as I sit on his lap, straddling his legs. Heat rushes to my face as my heart pounds like a drum, vibrating my whole chest.

Isn't it worth chasing that feeling instead of giving yourself over to that asshole?

Too late.

My hand trembles on the doorknob, and I push it open. I know that it's already unlocked.

A scene of devastation greets my eyes. Everything

standing is tipped over—every chair and stick of furniture. There's a vase smashed on the floor, the water darkens the hardwood.

"Fuck!"

My face burns as I walk inside, slamming the door. I pick up the phone and immediately dial the emergency number.

"Someone broke into my house."

I rattle off the address, and then I carry the phone with me. It trembles in my hand as the operator tries to comfort me.

"Miss, you need to get to a safe place. You need to leave the apartment."

But I can't fucking leave. All my possessions are here, everything I bought with the thousands of dollars I brought with me. What a fucking jerk. What a loser.

Every drawer is yanked out, their contents spilled on the floor. I whimper as I step inside my bedroom. Every stitch of clothing is ruined, ripped in half, or otherwise flung to the floor in discarded piles. I bend over and touch the blouses I just bought, their colors bleeding together.

"Hello, Elena."

I whirl around, red in the face and furious. My body bumps into his leather chest and I scream, my heart rate jacked. The murderous look on his face doesn't phase me.

"Get out of my fucking house!"

I flinch at the noise of leather squeaking as he lifts his hand and touches my face. "I'm not leaving without you and my money."

"Yeah, I don't think so."

"Listen to me, you little twat. You're going to bring me to wherever the fuck you stashed the money, and then I'm taking you back to where you belong."

I shove his chest with both hands, and for a moment he looks incredulous. I don't think he ever believed I would fight back.

"*You* listen to me. *We are done* and you are not getting a cent of that money!"

It's like some kind of bizarre dance. I back away, and he advances. His hip bumps into mine until the backs of my legs hit the bed.

He grabs my face and shoves me backward. My back hits the mattress hard and I try to scramble to my feet, heart racing, but he places his hand on my shoulder and presses down. He's so strong that he doesn't have to try very hard.

Fucking asshole.

Rafael lowers his head, the lines under his eyes like dark scars. "You're coming back to New York with me, right after you give me my money."

"Never going to fucking happen, you psycho."

My face screws up in pain before the blow comes, but a soft hand caresses my face. I open my eyes in surprise.

"Ah, Elena. I missed this."

Then a violent force smashes the side of my face and stars erupt in my vision. I roll on the wooden floor, my head splitting into two. My skin burns, but nothing compares to the pain of my humiliation. I'm so fucking tired of falling—of just taking it and never saying a word.

"Where the fuck were you last night, huh?"

"None of your damn business."

"You were fucking some other guy, weren't you?"

I say nothing.

His face twists in rage. "You fucking whore!"

He aims a boot toward my ribs, but I spring to my feet and grab the closest thing—a crystal paperweight on my nightstand that I use for decoration—and I hurl it into his face. Rafael clutches his nose and screams, and I jump on the bed, bouncing toward the entrance.

It was so fucking stupid to come back here.

My feet pound the wooden floorboards as I race down the hallway. His heavy footsteps tell me that he's not far behind. My voice stabs my ears as I scream down the hall, hoping that someone, anyone will hear me.

"HELP ME!"

"FUCKING CUNT!"

A violent force rips me backward as Rafael grabs the back of my collar and wrenches me. My hands fly out in front of me, trying to grab something to break his hold on me, but he's too fucking strong. A surge of self-hatred for my weak body makes me scream, and then the side of my body crashes against the wall, shattering a photograph on the wall.

"*Arrêtez!*"

A volley of French voice makes Rafael freeze behind me, his hands still balled in my hair. "Mind your own fucking business!"

Two men stream inside the apartment, guns drawn. I flatten against the wall, but Rafael advances toward them.

Please, shoot him. Please.

"This is none of your fucking business!"

One of the cops raises his gun to Rafael's chest. "HANDS BEHIND YOUR FUCKING HEAD!"

I place my hands behind my head, trembling as they tackle Rafael against the wall. His head crushes against the plaster, he gives me a look of potent rage. It's more than that, though. He just looks—evil. There's nothing behind those eyes but ill will.

He won't stop until I'm buried in the ground.

"*Mademoiselle*—Miss, are you okay?"

The cop touches my shoulder, giving me a puzzled look. I swallow hard and let my hands drop from my head as a snarling Rafael is dragged outside the house.

"BITCH!"

I flinch at the angry sound.

"Miss, you want to press charges?"

I gaze around at my apartment, which looks like a tornado blew through it. I'd like nothing better than to see that fucker locked up, but I know that he'll just come after me once he gets out. Or his boss might do it for him.

Numbly, I shake my head. "No."

The disappointment on his face gives me a guilty squirm. "Miss, let me give you ah—*numéro de téléphone* for women's shelter."

I take the card he gives me in his shaking hands. Yeah, I might be able to live for a few days until Rafael finds a way to bribe one of the cops here and finds its location.

"Take care."

He gives me a sad smile and leaves my apartment. I look around, knowing that I should clean up, or pack, or something, but I just can't bring myself to do any of it.

* * *

The best—the only—defense I can come up with is to pretend that everything's normal. That my ex-boyfriend didn't just track me down to my apartment to kill me, and

I only just got away. If I accepted the seriousness of it, I would panic.

Panicking doesn't help.

They'll probably keep him in lockup for a day or two for resisting arrest, so that's a small comfort.

The door swings open for me as a man steps out, holding open the door. The din in the bar swallows me like a shroud, and I feel safe surrounded by so many people. I scan the mass of people, my eyes cutting through the crowd of testosterone to find the man I found last night. It's too much to hope that Tony will be here tonight, but even if he was here, what could he do for me?

My gaze passes over Tommy, whose penetrating stare eats right through me.

What the hell does he want?

He jerks his head toward the back of the bar. Swallowing down my heart, I brush past him and squeeze my eyes shut when I hear him follow. I bend down, changing my shoes in the back as I imagine him standing over me, his arms folded.

"What is it?" I finally snap.

"Your boyfriend came in here last night, not long after you left with Tony."

I didn't want to hear that. He knows where I work and he knows where I live.

I'm fucked.

"He's not my boyfriend."

His hazel eyes narrow at me. "Are you sure you told him that, because I don't think he got the memo."

The blood pounding in my head feels like a headache. It's as though there's a sledgehammer smashing my skull. *BAM. BAM. BAM.*

I swallow hard as I raise a shaking hand to my head. "I was pretty fucking clear. He's just crazy."

Tommy rolls up his white sleeves and bends down to my level, a tinge of emotion shining in his eyes.

"If he finds out you went home with Tony, he'll fucking kill you."

"W—well, he tried and I'm still here."

For some reason, his concern brings me another thrill of fear. My eyes search his desperately, but I know he won't stick out a limb for me. Yeah, he helped put a band-aid over the situation, and Rafael ripped it right off.

"What the fuck are you talking about?"

"He came to my house. I called the cops on him—"

Tommy rakes a hand through his hair and lets out a groan. "Jesus."

"I'm not pressing charges."

"Why the fuck not?"

I stare at him. "There are people in New York who

would love an excuse to see me dead."

"Well, honey, you've got to do something. He's going to come after you."

Tears well in my eyes as I shrug at him and stand up. "Do what? I don't know what else there is to do. I thought that if I—if I left New York, maybe he'd leave me alone. Maybe if I was with someone else, I don't know."

"He's going to find you, and when he does New York will be the least of your problems. He's going to kill you, Elena—"

"I *know*! You don't think I fucking know that?"

My head pounds with what will surely become another bruise. The air feels strangely thin, and I stagger toward the wall. Colors bleed together, and the room swims. It feels as though I'm drunk, but it's hard to breathe. Tommy grips my arm and squeezes hard, and the pressure from his fingers makes me feel my pulse pounding against his skin.

It's happening.

I'm panicking.

"You don't look good, hon. Maybe you should take the night off."

"Hell, no! I'm not—I'm not leaving here. This is the only place I feel safe."

Tommy's concerned face swims in front of me. "Safe? He's not going to leave you alone, Elena. Not unless you're fucking married—"

I don't hear the rest of Tommy's sentence.

Not unless you were married.

So I just have to marry someone. Simple. No, that's fucking crazy.

You have a ton of cash. It's possible.

Yes. Someone out there is willing to marry me for cash. I'm certain of it.

"That's it!"

I'm still shaking, but my vision clears and I grip Tommy's arms, almost sobbing in relief.

Tommy smiles back weakly, uncomprehending. "What is it?"

"That's—a really good idea."

"What did I say?"

"What if I gave you a ton of cash to marry me?"

He tries to swallow his laughter, and it cuts right into me like a sharp knife. "Sweetie, I've a girlfriend. I don't think she'd like that very much."

Fuck.

I turn my back to him and enter the bar, looking for the guy I was with last night. He's fucking perfect. He's a member, isn't he? He was kind of an asshole, but it'll just be for a little while. Long enough to get Rafael off my back.

"What about Tony?"

Loud, obnoxious laughter echoes down the hallway. I whirl around, annoyed when I see Tommy leaning against the wall, laughing his ass off. He looks at my serious expression and tries to keep it together, but he just can't.

"You're—you're fucking serious? He's the biggest man whore I've ever met. He'll never do it."

"Then I'll find someone else," I say in a hard voice.

"It's a stupid idea."

It is stupid. So is doing nothing.

Tommy's mirth rings in my head as I step into the bar. Immediately, I spot Tony hanging at the same spot. I hang near the doorway like an awkward mannequin, and then his heated gaze finds me.

A violent flush creeps up my neck as I imagine Tony laughing the same way Tommy did when I told him about my idea.

It is fucking stupid.

It's so dumb, it just might work.

It's not like I wouldn't make it worth his while. I was willing to part with a lot of money to place a hit on Rafael. What should I offer him?

Twenty-five grand? Thirty? What's fair?

You barely know the guy.

I'm desperate. If it gets Rafael to back off, it'll be worth it. As of right now, the only future I see for myself is in a body bag.

The only problem is that Tony intimidates the hell out of me. He reminds me of Rafael, in a way. The same allure drew me to him—the suspense, the excitement. I had to beg him to let me stay the night. What kind of asshole does that to someone? He's the only other guy I've slept with—and I had to pull all the stops to impress him. Will I be able to do it a second time? A third?

I just don't know.

My heart pounds hard when my eyes sweep over his handsome face. Last night throbs in my head, all of the images playing in front of me like a highly-colored dream.

A perfect shadow of stubble covers his jaw and mouth, just long enough to look sexy, teetering on the edge of being disheveled. Cool eyes meet mine, almost indifferently, and my guts clench. I lose my nerve. I grab a discarded rag with the pretense of cleaning something.

Then I see something that makes me want to vomit.

A woman hangs around his arm, and then sits down next to him. She's beautiful, with long highlighted hair and shining, red lips, and Tony gives her a lascivious grin that makes my insides clench. A vicious surge of jealousy rises in my throat as I gather the drink orders and pass them out.

I can't let her get him.

"Another one! *Hey! Mange de la marde!*" *Eat shit!*

A patron hisses at me as I ignore his request and disappear behind the bar, watching as she reaches forward to touch his thigh. My face heats as I watch them together.

I'm annoyed by the fact that I'm annoyed at their antics.

She whispers something in his ear, and he smiles. The bitch gets up to go to the bathroom, leaving him alone.

Good.

He doesn't see me coming. The glass he's holding obscures his vision as he sips his drink until I slide another one under his nose. Tony responds to my presence with a wide, cocky grin.

"Hey, sexy."

Hey, asshole.

My heart makes another painful thump against my chest as I take the girl's seat, forcing a smile on my face. The last thing I want is to ask him for a favor because of the way he looks at me with the widest, smuggest smile. Vivid images of his wickedly tattooed body thrusting over mine run through my head. The smile paired with his seductive eyes seems downright dangerous. He looks up and down my body, the heat from his gaze scorching through my clothes. He wears a midnight-blue suit, the stubble over his jaw rougher than yesterday's.

"I enjoyed last night."

"Of course you did."

Smug asshole.

"Your tits looked better in that other outfit."

Ah, the backhanded compliment. What a jerk.

"Yeah? Would you rather I took my shirt off?"

Amusement twinkles in his eyes. "I think every guy in the bar would love that."

"Too bad I'm only interested in what you want."

Rich laughter booms from his chest. "I've already got what I want, sweetheart."

"You should take me out and fuck me again."

So fucking blunt.

He doesn't seem to mind. In fact, his attention is riveted. There are probably hundreds of women constantly kissing his ass.

I'm different.

His eyes sear my flesh. "One night, hon. That's all you get."

"One night? Even though I made you come three times? Sounds like three nights to me." I lift my shoulder in a shrug. "You've already broken your rule."

"You were a lot more fun than most girls, I'll admit that."

I lean in, placing both hands on his thighs as my lips brush his ear. "Then fuck me again. And again."

His voice strokes my ear. "Are you begging me for more, or do you want something specific from me?"

"*Specifically*, I want your cock. Inside me. Now."

A small growl rumbles in his throat. "It's rented for the night."

My hand slides around the back of his neck. "Aren't you tired of mediocre sex?"

His eyes lighten at that, and a smile spreads over his rugged face. "Who says I'm having mediocre sex?"

"Can that girl suck your dick like I can? Can she fuck you like I can?"

Tony's smile never falters, but it darkens. His eyes are all over me.

"You're fucking crazy, aren't you?"

Lust heats his face until I can almost feel it radiating off his skin. My fingertips brush over his cock, and he suddenly grabs my arm. My heart leaps as he pulls me onto his lap and crushes his lips against mine.

It's like instant electricity. It shocks me to feel the sudden rush of blood. Then my back hits the bar counter as his tongue slips into my mouth. I cling to his shoulders because all the energy evaporates from my limbs. I kiss him back and gasp as he grabs my tits, right in the middle of this bar. Everyone can see, but he doesn't give a shit. He pulls back with a grin that sends a jolt of anxiety through my heart, and I realize I've just given myself to another monster.

He's deadly. Just look at him.

"What the fuck!"

A shrill, feminine voice makes him break apart from me, but only barely. I taste the sweetness from his tongue, and I want more.

"Ah shit."

"Putain de merde!" The tall brunette screams herself hoarse, looking mad with rage.

The whole bar turns their attention to the pretty girl, screaming her head off. They laugh behind their hands and even Tommy emerges from his office to see the commotion. He leans against the doorway, spotting me on Tony's lap, and frowns.

My face burns as she turns away from us, angry tears glittering in her eyes as she stalks away. Another man attempts to comfort her, but she storms out of the bar.

Her tears give me a stab of guilt, but it dissolves when Tony turns back toward me with a shrug, extreme indifference all over his face.

"Well, I guess that makes your decision much easier."

He takes my head in his hands. "This is all your fault."

"Yeah, but I'm not sorry for that."

Deep laughter shakes from his barrel-like chest, and my face flushes with pleasure. I've never heard him laugh before, and it fills me with warmth. My fingers play with the hair behind his neck. It's just at a length where I can curl my fingers in his strands.

"Let's get out of here."

"Don't you have work?"

"Fuck work."

He smirks at that. "Ask Tommy if you can cut out early. I'll wait."

"You better."

As I slide from his lap, I feel his hands on my ass. There are people watching us as he gives me a rough squeeze and then slaps me, sending me on my way. He winks at me when I turn around, and I feel like shrinking on the spot.

The men jeer after me as I enter the back and look for Tommy. He's on the phone, a mess of paperwork scattered on his desk. He's frowning.

"All right, I'll—yeah. Thanks, Vince."

At the mention of his name, fear stabs my chest. The high from successfully asking out Tony pops like a soap bubble, and a chill creeps up my arms.

Vincent. There's only one that Tommy and I know.

He hangs up the phone and folds his hands into steeples, looking unhappy. "Listen, Vince just found out that one of his men was detained for resisting arrest. He doesn't know why, but he wants one of us to bail him out. Whatever you're going to do, you better do it fast."

My face drains of color. "Thanks—I was going to leave with Tony. Is that all right?"

He looks like he wants to say something else, but he stops himself. "Yeah, okay."

Shit. He's getting bailed out a lot sooner than I thought.

I gather my things and head out, fixing a smile to my face when I rejoin Tony at the bar. The sooner I ask him, the better. The tension in his face dissolves somewhat when I take his hand. A dark, searching look descends over Tony's face as he squeezes my fingers.

"Are you hungry? I was going to take that girl to dinner."

Surprised, I look up at his expressionless face. "Yeah, a little."

"Great. Let's go."

"Okay."

He leads me out of the bar, holding the door open for me with a self-assured smile. God, the man exudes confidence. All of Dad's men seemed like that, at first. It took a few months for me to realize the difference between confidence and cocky assholes flying off the handle at every perceived slight.

"So what kind of food do you like?"

"Oh, anything is fine. Really."

We walk down the streets as I cling to his hand for warmth. He keeps giving me meaningful looks as we pause for the lights, and then we finally stop in front of a restaurant. Tapeo.

"Hope you like Spanish."

There's a line inside the restaurant. The foyer is completely packed, but Tony calmly pushes to the front where the hostess recognizes him.

"There's no way we'll get a table!" I shout over the din.

He gives me a secretive smile and nods toward the hostess. "Table for two," he says in his deep voice.

"Right this way, Mr. Vidal."

My jaw drops as he turns around to give me a wink.

Of course. Johnny must have all the restaurants in the city in his pocket.

The hostess takes the heavy coat from my shoulders, and I feel oddly vulnerable without it. Without it, I'm dressed in a flowing tank top and jeans, and he's in a suit. Discomfort rattles against my ribs.

It's a nice restaurant, low lit and moody. The golden

tone of the lights compliments the steel-blue walls nicely. Tony's strong hand wraps around my waist and a flash of desire trails up my thighs. I forgot what it was like to be excited for a date, to have his hands around my waist and for that small, yet powerfully intimate touch to send a thrill to my heart.

But it's not a date.

No, I'm here to ask Tony for a favor.

The hostess leads us to a table with two white, round candles. The rustic decor in the restaurant gives the place a trendy vibe. There are no tablecloths. Tony pulls my chair out and pushes me in when I sit down.

It's kind of startling to see how well mannered he is. I didn't expect it because he talks like a goddamn jerk.

Here we go.

My nerves fire up as he sits across from me and orders a bottle of wine. The sommelier whisks back with the bottle, pouring two glasses for us. I take the delicate stem in my hands and swallow a small gulp, shuddering as it spreads heat over my chest. Tony looks vaguely content, his eyes relaxed, but with the occasional glance toward the door.

I wish I could just sit here and enjoy the night like a normal person.

"When was the last time you've been on a date?" I ask

him.

"I go on dates all the time, I just don't go on second dates."

"Why not?"

He lifts his shoulder in an elegant shrug as a complicated look flashes over his face. "What's the point?"

What's the point?

"Oh, I don't know. Friendship? Love?"

He smiles at me. "I don't know if I care about any of that."

Wow.

"What do you care about?"

He grins like a devil. "Pussy. Money. Those are my two loves."

It's like a wrench inside my chest. This is going to go so badly. A man like this will never agree to marriage of convenience.

"Aren't you a charmer," I say in a very dry voice, sipping more wine.

"I never pretended to be."

His grey eyes are as dark as his face, and just as cold. It strikes me hard, and I don't know why I care. I don't care. Whatever, I'm not here to make him smitten with me. I'm here to hopefully get him to agree to marry me.

"So why the fuck are we here, huh? You got rid of that

girl I was going to bring home."

I roll my eyes at his narrowed eyes. I decide that Tony looks even sexier with a scowl on his face. "Please, don't act like you don't want me. Your eyes were all over me as soon as you recognized me in the bar."

"I don't like being manipulated, sweetheart. Just tell me what you want."

The tiny flames of the candles flicker in his unrelenting stare.

Fine, I'll tell him.

I lick my dry lips and open my mouth, unable to ask him.

Hey, guy I barely know. Wanna marry me for money?

The cutlery on the table rattles as I bump my fist against the wood, suddenly overcome with a fit of giggles. I cover my mouth as he stares back at me in bemusement, my shoulders shaking.

He swirls his wineglass. "You seem a bit stressed." Then he leans in closer. "Maybe I should have just taken you to my place to fuck the pain away."

The laughter breaks off and my skin blazes under his penetrating stare. "Yeah, maybe you should have."

"This is about your ex, isn't it?"

A wary look hardens his face.

"Yeah, but it's not what you think."

I still can't fucking tell him.

"He showed up to my apartment right after I got home yesterday. We—we fought."

He says nothing, but his eyes blaze.

"The cops showed up just in time, but he'll be out soon. And then he'll come after me."

My face still smarts where he hit me, made worse by the alcohol flushing my skin. Tony looks back at me, his face stony. "How did you end up with a guy like that?"

Now it's my turn to shrug.

"Dating opportunities were pretty thin on the ground. Daddy scared the guys away and he didn't approve of a lot of them. He liked Rafael, though."

Tony would know all about the traitorous New York boss, who was killed by his own crew for mob justice.

He leans back into his chair and swallows hard. Grey eyes flick toward my eyes and away. "I'm sorry about your dad. I know what it's like to lose a father."

Somehow I see that. Something deep stirs inside his eyes: the jagged pain of losing someone too young, or some long ago horror.

"You're the first person who's said that to me. Isn't that—isn't that funny?"

It's not, really, but he makes a valiant attempt at a smile. His hand slides over the rough wooden table and seizes my hand, squeezing it.

Why is he being so nice to me? This wasn't what I expected at all. A lump rises in my throat and my hand trembles inside his.

I bite my lip hard as images of the poorly attended funeral run through my mind, everyone's lack of sympathy, my mother, crying. It buries me.

"You should be glad I even came," Rafael said, his mouth curled. "Your father was a coward—"

"Don't you—don't you dare talk about my father like that!"

It hurt me to hear those poisonous accusations from my boyfriend. He was supposed to protect me, and instead he tortured me.

"I'll say whatever the fuck I want." Then his voice dropped to a whisper as his fingers cruelly pinched my waist.

Tony looks at me, at a total loss for words. I want to talk to him about it. I want to talk to *someone*. I want to tell him how horrible it has been. Everything had to be locked tight inside, because I wasn't allowed to grieve for my worthless, rat-bastard father.

He was always my daddy.

Bury that shit, damn it. Just be like a fucking stone.

I look into his impassive gaze as I freeze over my facial muscles. "Sorry, this is not what I—I don't want to bring you down."

"Why don't you just tell me what you want from me?"

My cheeks burn when I realize how transparent I must be, but he doesn't look angry. I open my mouth to tell him, and my guts clench.

God, this is a lot harder than I thought it would be.

"What makes you think that I want something?"

An unpleasant chill wafts from his eyes. "Cut the bullshit already and ask."

I hate that I have to look across the table into his heavy eyes and ask him for something. The men back home wouldn't have lifted a finger for me because I no longer mattered to them. The moment my dad became a traitor, I stopped existing. And they call it a family. What fucking family?

"Well, you're right. I did want to ask you something."

"Tell me."

"Uh—well…" *I was just wondering if you would maybe like to marry me in exchange for money. But don't worry, it'll only be for a little while.*

Oh my fucking God, this is going to be a disaster.

My face feels like I have a sunburn, and he laughs at my discomfort.

"Jesus, what the hell is it? Just tell me."

Yeah, just tell him.

He's going to laugh in my face.

"I want to—to pay you to do something for me."

"Okay…" he motions with his hand. "What?"

"To—to marry me. I have fifty thousand dollars in cash."

It sounds just as stupid as I thought it would, and I want to evaporate on the spot.

A strange expression suddenly contorts Tony's face. It takes a moment before I realize that he's actually *scared of me*. Because he thinks I'm nuts.

Then the irony of a six-foot something Mafioso actually fearing *me* hits me hard, and I nearly burst.

He shifts in his chair. "Uh—"

This is life and death.

"This is the only way to get Rafael off my back," I say quickly, my face a shade of fuchsia, I'm sure. "I can't get rid of him."

He looks at me as though he's concerned for my sanity.

"That's the dumbest idea I've ever heard of. It is fucking ridiculous. Marry you? Are you fucking crazy?"

His indignant tone pisses me off.

"Since you're a genius, you tell me what to do."

"Get a fucking gun and just kill him." He mimes with his fingers. *Pop-pop.*

I give him a hollow laugh. "And when Vincent finds out, then what? I'm just as fucked, and that's assuming I can actually kill him and get rid of his body."

The very idea fills me with revulsion. As much as I hate Rafael, I'm not a violent person, and blood disgusts me. I wouldn't even know how to get rid of a body.

Tony crosses his arms, thinking, and then he shakes his head with a boom of laughter. "You know, I knew there was something off about you the moment you grabbed my cock in the bar. Amazing in bed, but completely fucking nuts."

Oh fuck you.

My face burns again, this time flushed with the embarrassment of his insult. "I'm not crazy. I need to be married to a made guy, or I am dead."

"That's ridiculous."

"Yeah, it fucking is," I fire back. "It's also the only thing that'll keep me alive."

Tony plays with the silverware on the table, tapping the butt end of the knife on the wood as he looks at me.

"Fifty-thousand dollars for a few months work isn't ridiculous. It's fair."

Another snort of laughter leaves his mouth and he drops the knife. He covers his mouth with both hands, his eyes alive with mirth. I should have known he wasn't going to take me seriously.

I slam my purse on the table and stand up abruptly.

Suddenly, his attitude turns. His hands lay flat on the

table as the humor wipes from his face, and he looks at me with a paralyzing stare.

"Where the hell do you think you're going?"

"I won't be laughed at," I snarl, suddenly hating everything about him right down to his smug smirk. He doesn't know what the fuck I'm going through.

"I'm *really* not the guy you go to for this shit."

"I'm aware of that, but I'm short on time, and I'll be paying you, for fuck's sake. It's just another job."

"It's extreme."

You want to see what I'm fucking running from, asshole?

In front of the whole restaurant, I lift up my shirt, stopping just below my bra.

Black eyebrows narrow dangerously at me. "What *the fuck* are you doing? This is a nice place. You can't disrespect—"

"Look."

I point at the huge purple bruise stretching over the side of my abdomen, the dark horror that he missed in the dark. His face sobers immediately.

"He did that?" His voice sounds uncomfortable.

"There's more," I say in a toneless voice, dropping my shirt.

"That looks pretty serious."

"That's the fucking point."

"I meant that you should see a doctor."

"I don't need a fucking doctor. A doctor won't help me stay alive the next few days. You just—you don't understand what it's like. I'm scared, and this is the only thing I can think of."

Tears thicken my voice, and I hate that I can't keep it together in front of this guy.

He sighs and wipes his hand down his face. "Sit down."

Trembling, I return to my seat and ball my fists on my knees.

Tony begins talking in a softer voice. "I'm telling you, it's a bad idea. No one will believe it."

"Who cares if they don't believe it? I just need to be married, right?"

He buries his face in his hands. "What the fuck do you think this is, the boy scouts? *No*—not if people think it's fake. Besides, if Johnny found out, I'd have to give him tribute."

Shit.

"Well—"

"How do I even know you have access to that kind of money?"

I hurl him an ugly look. "Tommy is holding it for me. I have over a hundred grand American."

His eyebrows lift at that, and he takes the glass of wine, taking a huge gulp. "It's still a bad idea."

"I don't have any alternative! Do you think I *want* to marry some guy I just met?"

"People know me, sweetheart. They know I'd never get hitched."

My head perks up. "Does this mean you're interested?"

"It's a lot of fucking money, of course I'm interested. But that's a lot of—" A lump moves up his throat. "My mom—it would fucking kill her. She'd never forgive me."

I lean forward and take his hand, expecting him to rip it away from me, but he lets me smooth my thumb over his knuckles. "I'm sure she'd be proud of you for helping someone whose life was in danger."

His eyes cut me. "You don't know her, and you don't know me. What makes you think I'm the right guy for this? You think that just because we had a good time, I won't just rob you and throw you into the streets?"

My hands twist in my lap as he stares at me with that intense glare, daring me to contradict him.

"I have to have faith in something. I don't know you, but I don't think you'll hurt me."

He crosses his arms and a scowl burns on his face.

He's right. This is stupid. I don't know him, and he doesn't know me. There's no way he'll agree to do this for me. My best bet is to just run. Run far away, and keep running until Raf gets tired of chasing me.

"I'm really sorry."

I take my purse and stand up from the table, eyes blinking away tears as I walk to the closet and grab my coat roughly, sending the hanger flying.

Honestly, what did I expect?

I ignore the hostess as I barge outside and walk swiftly down the freezing streets. Fuck, it's so much colder here than New York, and it's the kind of cold that seeps through every layer. I hug myself in the middle of the sidewalk, blinking furiously and feeling utterly alone in this foreign place.

I can't even speak the language.

Nowhere to go.

My back slides against a brick wall and I huddle in the snow, hands wrapped around my knees. Part of me hopes I'll freeze—maybe it's cold enough to freeze my heart into place.

A man in a long, wool coat walks past me, his gaze flicking to me sharply before he walks on. Then he stops in his tracks and doubles back.

"Elena?"

Tony. He came after me. The way he says my name fills me with hope. I know that it's dangerous to hope, but I can't help but lift my head to look at him.

"What?"

Tony frowns at me as he walks close enough so that his boots touch mine.

"I need assurances." He gives me a shrewd look. "I don't trust you."

"I'll pay you half up front. Tommy's in on it, and he trusts me."

That was not entirely true, but close enough.

"That's not good enough."

He bends down and takes my freezing hands, and I stand up with him. It makes my heart pound to be so close to him.

"I—I don't know what else to do, then."

His hand curls around my neck and my pulse beats into his thumb. Grey eyes search my face, which grow more and more hot. "How am I supposed to trust you and let you in my home?"

"Why would I do anything to piss you off? I already have one pissed off mobster after me."

Deep dimples carve into his face.

"What if we don't get along? Three months is a long time."

"We don't have to get along. We just have to tolerate one another."

"This is crazy, Elena. It's fucking nuts."

"But it'll work, and you'll be fifty thousand dollars richer. In a few months, we'll divorce. *It won't mean anything*, I just need to have a fucking ring on my finger for a while."

He considers it, lifting his head as he stares into the brick wall. I can see the cogs working in his head, weighing the advantages and disadvantages.

"If you were my ex-wife, I could probably get a sit-down with Johnny if that asshole tried anything."

"Perfect."

He smiles at me. "There's still no way you're going to get people to believe this."

I think hard, staring into his honest eyes, and then a rush of adrenaline runs through my veins. "I'm pregnant."

A stunned silence follows my words, which Tony eventually breaks with a laugh.

"That might work," he says in an impressed voice. "Fuck, I'm going to hell."

A sigh of relief runs through my body as he shuts his eyes.

"Why me?"

He cuts through my words, as cold as the snow beneath my feet. Why did I choose him? Well, that's simple.

"You looked strong and—and I thought you were—well, you're my type."

Mischief shines through his eyes. "Am I?"

His eyes smolder suddenly and his hand wraps around my wrist, pulling me into his chest.

"Can't you tell?"

A rush of heat fills my neck as I feel his warmth and his lips touch right under my ear. My skin shivers at the contact of his lips. Everything—his hands around my waist and his breath billowing over my skin—they overwhelm me. I've never been quite this speechless around a man before, but the sensations he gives me voids all thought from my head.

"Yes, I think I can." He sears my neck with a biting kiss, one that's sure to leave a mark. I moan and tremble in his arms.

"Tony, I really don't think we should—if we're going to be living together we don't want to complicate things."

He pulls back with a steely look in his eyes. "What?"

"We shouldn't have sex anymore."

A black look descends over his face. "What's the point of having a fake marriage if I can't have any of the benefits?"

I inhale a sharp breath as he plants a kiss, breathing hot air over my neck. Damn, it feels amazing. "It's just a—a job."

"Uh-huh. And how the hell am I supposed to bring women back home if you're there all the time?"

My insides clench hard as I think about it. Fuck, I don't want to think of him with other women. The thought of hearing him with another girl in his room makes me feel slightly sick.

"We'll think of something. I can stay at Tommy's bar overnight."

He takes my face in his hands and I don't think I've ever looked into someone's eyes like this. It's like he's stripping me down.

"This isn't going to change me, understand? Don't ask me any more favors. I fuck who I want."

I swallow hard and give him a nod. "You're a great lay, and all, but that doesn't mean I'm attached to you. This is just business. We should keep it that way."

The smirk, his eyes, his thumbs slightly caressing my skin—it's hard to think with all three at the same time.

"We'll see."

"I'm not exactly *eager* to jump into bed with another connected guy, if you know what I mean."

"I'm nothing like your piece of shit ex," he says in a heated voice, eyes flashing. "As long as you understand that what we have isn't ever going to become anything, we'll be fine."

Good.

"It'll just be fun."

A pleasant growl rumbles in his throat.

"Hold on—We only just met—doesn't it take a while for those tests to find out if you're pregnant?"

Oh shit.

"Yeah, but I don't have a week."

He smiles against my neck and it sends electricity through my skin. "You can stay at my place."

"What—what if he shows up?"

"He won't."

Emotion floods my chest as I turn in his arms, cupping his rough face. "Tony, thank you." I lean into his broad chest as he hands slip under the hem of my shirt, stroking my skin. Kissing him is so much stronger than the alcohol running through my veins. I feel myself unfolding, losing myself in his smell and the taste of his mouth.

I shouldn't touch him.

He pulls back, his lips swollen. "We need to talk more about it, but right now—all I can think about is fucking you."

* * *

The door closes and the shaking reverberates throughout the entire apartment. For a moment I think about how that sound terrifies me, and Tony's huge bulk looms over me like a shadow. He just smiles at me in the darkness, knowing that I'll eventually go to him. That my heart already pounds in anticipation of his touch.

We're not supposed to have sex.

It keeps repeating in my head like a feeble whisper.

What is it about him? I know he's no good. He's cut from the same cloth as Rafael. He's a man whore, for god's sake, and yet I still find myself drawn toward him beyond all sense or logic. How can I ignore a guy whose body looks like Brad Pitt's in *Troy*?

I step into his chest, swallowing down my dread that I've signed myself a deal with the devil. He seems to notice my mood. A slick grin spreads across his face and he smoothes the hair on my shoulders, tucking a few strands behind my ear.

"What's wrong, sweetheart? Cold feet?"

His hand feels incredibly cool against my cheek, or maybe it's because I'm burning up. "No, it's just—I don't know how to act around you."

You make me nervous.

"You're paying me for my time, that's all. Fucking me is *not* part of the payment, understand? I want you to want me."

His thumb brushes under my bottom lip as his smooth

voice caresses my ears, and my palm spreads over his broad chest. "I *do* want you."

"I know."

"I just don't know if this is a good idea."

"This whole thing isn't a good idea."

"I know, but—"

His mouth descends over mine finally, cutting off my protests, and I weaken in his arms as though his kiss somehow drains me of all energy. Then he bends, reaching under my knees so that I fly into the air—into his arms like a ragdoll. My arms link around his neck, but he pushes me higher so that my legs straddle his head. I squeal and clutch his head as he backs me against the wall.

"I'm going to make you come with my mouth."

How can I resist that?

Last time, I tell myself. *It'll be the last time I have sex with him.*

His gritty voice makes my blood pound in my ears, and then his fingers burrow under my jeans and cool air stings my skin as he pulls them down. A thrill runs through me as he reaches under my shirt, finding the hem of my thong.

It seems ridiculous, but my stomach flips at the thought of him eating me out. Rafael never would have done it—he thought that it was emasculating.

Tony kisses my inner thigh and I curl my fingers in his

hair. "I'm going to lick your pussy, and you're going to love it."

The last thread of resistance breaks as soon as his dark head bends over, his hot mouth breathing over my wet folds, and then the slightest touch of his lips against my clit sends a lightning bolt through me. I arch my back as his tongue reaches back and licks.

A shrill sound escapes my mouth.

Holy crap.

I've never, ever experienced anything like this.

He lifts his head, smiling.

"That's right. I want to hear you scream. I want to feel you come when my tongue fucks you."

It thrills me to hear him talking like that. Fuck, it's hot.

The wet, hot muscles moves down my slit, taking care to flick over my sensitive clit as I try not to squeeze his head off with my thighs. His mouth closes over my clit, and I'm overwhelmed by the sensation. I look down, and his head is buried in my pussy. Eyes closed in apparent ecstasy, he sucks hard, and a small explosion occurs in the pit of my stomach. I never knew it could feel so fucking good. My fingers dig into his skull as the pounding ache between my legs grows, and I dimly feel ashamed for how turned on I am, for how my juices run down his chin. The smooth muscle slides inside me, teasing me. It's not big enough—not wide enough to satisfy the burning ache.

"Tony, please—Jesus!"

He ignores me as his hands caress my bare ass, his tongue continuing its torture as he fucks me with his mouth. I dig my fingers into his hair and pull hard, and he lets out a muffled growl.

"You're so fucking wet for me."

His finger curves into my pussy and I moan out loud as it slides into me. His tongue flicks over my clit as his finger fucks me mercilessly, and I clench my muscles, face screwed up almost in pain. I just want him to fuck me, already. *Just fuck me!*

Then his tongue slides in again and he presses his face to my pussy, burying his tongue as deep as it can go as he pinches my clit. A violent reaction rips through my body, and I cry out loud as contractions seize my body. Ecstasy rolls through me as Tony pulls away, laughing. He kisses my inner thigh and I dig my hands in his hair so painfully that he winces.

I slide down his chest, and as my hands explore his body—the rock-hard cock between his legs, I want him again. My swollen core clenches hard, and I tear the shirt away from his body. I just yank the shirt apart, hard enough so that several buttons fly off.

He laughs as they scatter loudly over the floor and his

wet lips press against mine. "You are so fucking eager. I love it."

I open my mouth, tasting myself, loving the way my musk mingles with his scent. My hands move over his ripped muscles, and I want to lick every hard bump and stretch of taut muscle.

Suddenly, he buries his hand in my hair and pulls hard. "I don't care if our arrangement isn't real, your tongue will only taste my cock." His fingers shove inside me. "Same with your pussy. It's mine, along with the rest of you. I have a reputation, and you're not going to fuck it up."

"So you can fuck whoever you want, but I can't? That's not fair."

"Nothing about the life is fair."

I curl my lip bitterly when I look at his rigid face. He's right, though. Mafiosi may fuck behind their wives' back, but the wives definitely don't do the same thing. Not if they know what's good for them.

It's fucked up.

"You want to be married to me? You have to play the game."

That's right. Play the game.

A satisfied smirk flicks over his face, and then is replaced with smoldering lust. I know that I'm just a good lay to him. He doesn't do relationships. I can see the conflict in his eyes.

"Don't get attached to me, Elena. I'll just disappoint you. Just expect great sex from me, nothing else."

"I don't know if I can detach like that."

His voice is ragged. "Try."

His hand gropes my breast, his thumb stroking my nipple as he kisses me again, and then he leads me to the huge window and turns on the light so that we light up like a Christmas tree. Everyone in the neighborhood can see us. Excitement runs up my leg when he slides up behind me, kissing my neck. A possessive arm snakes around my waist and grabs my tits roughly.

"Do you want to please me, baby?"

His lips sear my neck over and over, like hot brands. It's as though he's marking me as his.

"Yes, fuck—*Of course*—"

I can't fucking think when you're playing with my tits and kissing my neck.

"If you want to be in this house, you'll let me fuck you in front of the whole world." He squeezes my breast again. "I want them to see me claiming your beautiful body. I want every asshole looking in my apartment to be jealous of me. I want your ex to see me banging his girl." A wolfish grin smiles at me, reflected from the glass. "The fact that I'm fucking a made guy's girl gives me a bigger thrill than finding a new piece of ass every night."

He's cruel and crazy, but the hard bump digging into my ass is impossible to ignore. I turn around in his arms and I grab his thick cock, loving how his eyes lock onto mine. I sink to my knees and kiss his cock through his slacks, feeling him twitch.

It's fucking crazy. I shouldn't feed his ego, but his words have me on fire, and I'll do anything for him. I'll blow him in front of the window, and I hope Rafael sees. A savage pleasure burns my chest at the very idea.

Fuck you, asshole. You and I are done.

I tear the slacks from his hips. Without even looking at him, I slide his hard length in my mouth as his hands caress my head. The long sigh he gives me makes my pussy contract, and I reach around his muscled thighs to run my hands over his ass. I stick my tongue out, imaging that asshole watches from the ground, and I take his cock as deep as I can. I want him to see me blowing Tony with more enthusiasm than I ever showed him.

Tony lets out a volley of swear words in French that makes the glow between my legs pulse.

"*Crisse de tabarnak*...Keep going, baby!"

I ride my tongue under the ridge of his cock, flicking it over his head. The sloppy, wet noises echo in his apartment and I see myself, head swinging back and forth as his hands fist my hair. Then he moves his hips, grunting loudly. My jaws widen as he pushes all the way down my throat, and I push my tongue out so that it just barely strokes his balls. His abdomen presses against my nose as I feel him throb inside my throat, and then he pulls out so that I can breathe.

"Do you like it when I fuck your mouth?"

My chest heaves as I catch my breath, his cock rock-hard in my hands. "Yes. Yes, I do."

He strokes my head in a surprisingly tender gesture. "All right, baby. Open wide."

I grab his thighs and open my mouth obediently. He thrusts inside my mouth slowly, gradually picking up the pace. Then he buries himself inside me. I feel the thickness bulging down my throat as his hips slide closer and closer to my eyes. My air chokes off and he bends slightly, grinding his cock against my mouth even though it can't go any deeper. I clutch his thighs and raise my mouth, wanting more of him.

"Fuck!"

He pulls out of my mouth and looks down at me, raking a shaking hand through his hair. He grabs my arm and pulls me up roughly. "I need that pussy of yours now."

An indescribable look consumes Tony's face before he

crushes his lips against mine and slams me against the glass. His arms curl underneath me and he lifts me over his powerful waist. A thickness presses against my core and suddenly it yields. I bury my face in his neck as his cock sinks into me.

My legs wrap around him and he stabs my pussy with his cock, burying his face in my neck. God, it's so long and deep. I feel it sliding up my channel, widening the walls. Then he thrusts hard, and it knocks the breath out of me.

Again.

And again.

And *again*.

I moan to the ceiling as he kisses my neck. His balls slap against my pussy as his body rocks with his thrusts. My back freezes against the cold glass, but I imagine the show we must be giving to anyone looking out the window, and it fills me with fire. My flesh stings as Tony takes one of my nipples in his mouth and bites down, pulling my waist down to bury his cock inside me at the same time.

"Fucking gorgeous tits."

He throbs inside me, slowly pulsing in and out as his tongue works magic on my tits. He takes my breast in his cavernous mouth and sucks hard, flicking his tongue over my nipple. It's like he's rubbing my clit, and the ruthless pounding tightens the coils inside me like a spring. My moans reverberate in my ears, which cut off sharply with a jerk of his hips. Then he lifts his head with a manic grin on his face, and I know that every sound I make feeds his energy.

He kisses me and swallows my moans. I make several more desperate sounds, and then he bites my lip hard and thrusts. The glass groans as I'm crushed against it. His body rubs against my clit and fireworks explode in my abdomen, my pussy clenches over him and he sucks hard on my bottom lip. Then his cock makes a twitch inside me and his low voice groans in my mouth. Liquid warmth fills my pussy as he makes one last, violent shove, and another.

Then, shaking, he lowers me to my feet. I tremble on my legs and sit down against the glass, feeling like a puddle of water. Tony sits down next to me and wraps an arm around my waist, pulling me into his heated chest.

It's relaxing and comfortable, sitting here in his arms.

"So, do you think anyone saw us?"

A shaky laugh leaves my mouth as I glance down the street. "I don't know."

Now that it's over, a stab of anxiety hits my heart. We both got a bit carried away in the heat of the moment.

"I wonder if he's out there—watching."

The thought sends goosebumps prickling my flesh. "I

doubt it."

"We'll have to rectify that."

My body shudders. "Tony, I don't want to provoke him. You don't either."

"Oh, I do. It gets me off, Elena." He strokes my hair. "Fucking you is playing with fire. If he had any inkling that we were messing around, I would get killed."

I turn around in his arms and look at his strangely calm face. "Then why are you doing this?"

"Because I don't care."

He smirks, but I don't feel any of the warmth. It's like being doused in ice water.

I really did make a deal with the devil.

TONY

The cold liquid burns a line of fire down my throat. It's raw. It hurts. It used to be that the pain was enough to drown out the gnawing ache in my chest. After years and years of fucking people up, and disposing bodies, the pain vanished. Just like everything else.

I slam down shots because I want to put on an act. I want to look like a man at the end of his rope.

Tommy's bar is the perfect place to do this. There are wiseguys everywhere, and news will spread fast.

I'm already attracting looks from the other guys for keeping to myself and not saying a damn word to anyone. My eyes stare straight ahead into the blackboard list of beers on tap, ignoring Genevieve, who whispers something into Tommy's ear. I feel his stare, even if I can't really see it.

Tommy's not buying my act, but Francois and Johnny openly gawk at me from across the bar, giving me odd looks.

"*Qu'est-ce qui se passe avec lui?*" What's wrong with him?

My captain, Francois, shrugs his shoulders. I make a show of burying my face in my hands and rubbing my head. My shoulders slump and I bury my fingers in my hair, fighting to keep the laughter shaking in my chest inside me.

"I'll go ask," I hear him say.

I try not to smile as I hear his footsteps growing louder, and then a heavy hand drops on my shoulders and shakes me roughly.

"Tony, what the fuck is wrong with you?"

"I don't want to fucking talk about it."

I can almost see the surprise on his lined face. Nothing really ever gets me down, and seeing me like this must be unnerving.

Hopefully, I'm not overdoing it.

"Jesus. What happened?"

Slowly, I raise my head from my hands and look into his concerned face. "I got a girl pregnant."

The words explode in the middle of the bar, and they pretend to have not heard what I just said even though everyone's standing unnaturally still. There's no excitement. No cheers. They all know it's my worst nightmare. Men freeze with glasses in their hands as they stare at me with expressions of amusement and pity.

"Congratulations!" Francois pounds my back, laughter trembling in his voice.

I send him a heated look. "I don't fucking see what

there is to celebrate. My life is basically over and I barely know this broad."

"Don't be such an asshole," Johnny snaps. "A child is a gift from God—a fuckin' gift. You better do right by this girl, Tony. I'm serious."

I straighten myself and peer into the depths of my glass. "Yeah, yeah. I guess we have to get married. *Fuck*."

The bar explodes into cheers, and Francois flings an arm around my neck. "I can't fucking believe this. You're getting married? Holy shit—"

Johnny gives me an approving nod. "It's the right thing to do."

"Yeah, well—that doesn't mean I'm going to fucking *change* for her."

The young boss beams at me, and he bumps his glass against my empty one. "*Salute*, Tony. I'm happy for you."

"That makes one of us."

My stomach clenches as he wraps an arm around my shoulders and gives me a hug.

"I want to meet this girl. We should have an engagement party this weekend."

I look into Johnny's smiling face. "You already know her. She's Jack Vittorio's daughter."

His face goes slack as the men scream with laughter.

"*He knocked up a boss' daughter!*"

"Good thing Jack is dead, eh buddy?"

I ignore the elbows digging into my side, the hands clapping down my shoulder, the insidious laughter erupting around me and gaze into Johnny's furious face.

"You fucking moron, Tony. *You fucking dumb piece of shit.*" He slams his drink on the counter and grabs my lapels, shoving me against the bar. "What the fuck were you thinking?"

I have at least fifty pounds on Johnny, but I don't lift a finger against him. To do so would be suicide, even though it would be satisfying—so fucking satisfying.

"No one was ever going to find out."

His face contorts with rage and the laughter dissipates from the bar. "You realize, you stupid fuck, that her ex now has a legitimate beef with us? *You fucked his girl.*"

"A girl that didn't want to be his in the first place."

"That doesn't matter."

"She's carrying my kid," I say in a cold voice. "That's all that matters. We're getting married, and that's that. If that asshole has a problem with it, I shove a gun up his ass."

Murmurs of approval echo around me, and then I know I've won.

He lets go of my jacket, still furious, and jabs a finger in my face. "I want a fucking paternity test."

That might be hard to get.

"Johnny, it's my fucking kid."

"I need proof, goddamn it. Word is going to spread very quickly about this—to friends of ours in New York, and that piece of shit has been in my restaurant every day, demanding to know where his girlfriend is."

Ah, good. He's still here.

A smirk spreads across my face. "She's been with me."

He rakes his hand through his hair. "Goddamn it— *crisse de tarbanak de marde de gang des cons.* WHAT THE FUCK IS WRONG WITH YOU?" He shoves my chest against the bar again. "You have a fucking death wish?"

Maybe I just don't fucking care, Johnny. I don't give a fuck about you, or the family, or saving my own damn skin. I do what I want.

I shrug my shoulder as the heart in my chest beats like a steady drum.

"Bring me the fucking paternity test before he asks for a sit-down."

"Whatever."

I slide from the stool, ignoring the grins thrown my way as I walk out of the bar. It's bad to piss off the boss. I know that, but I can't bring myself to care. Although I'd never admit it, there's no loyalty in my chest for Johnny. The only person in my life who matters is my mother. She loves me even though I've put her through so much shit. She's the only person I live for.

A flash of emotion chips through and the blood leaves my face.

What the fuck are you doing? You're going to get killed—This is fucking crazy, and your ma will never forgive you. Ever.

Fifty grand.

With that kind of money, I'll be able to make sure arrangements for my mother are taken care of. She'll never want for anything. Then it's just a matter of waiting.

Waiting to die.

That's how all our stories end in this life. Fucking pointless, isn't it? My dad died young and I will too, because I was a moron and followed in his footsteps.

C'est la vie?

Resentment boils in my chest as I cross the street and head back to my apartment. I don't like thinking about this shit. I have everything I want, and yet nothing satisfies me. There's nothing deep going on inside me. Just spades of boredom and restlessness. Emptiness.

I've felt like this for a long time.

The urge to stride into Tommy's bar and find someone else to fuck flames inside me for a moment and then quickly dissipates. Why go to the bar when I have a real piece of ass waiting for me at home? Thinking of her brings a smile to my face. Yeah that whole 'no sex' deal we made lasted a grand total of twelve minutes. Who would have thought that Jack's daughter would've been such a great lay? I mean, holy shit. The girl gets me hard every morning. Beyond that, it's exciting. It's fucking wrong. I could get my brains blown out just for touching her.

Yeah, it's fucked up.

Energy ramps inside my chest as I climb the stairs to my apartment, unlocking the door to my apartment. A rich smell from the kitchen makes my mouth water, and I hang my coat before walking into the kitchen. Elena sits at the kitchen table and smiles at me.

"Hey."

My chest tightens as I smile back to her, and I glance at the pot on the stove.

"What's that?"

"Dinner."

Sometimes, I wonder if she's taking this role too seriously. "We're roommates, hon. You don't have to cook me dinner."

A complicated look falls on her face. "I know...it's just—there's not much else for me to do. Why not?"

I shrug at her and sit down across the table from her. "I told Johnny that I knocked you up. He wasn't very happy about it."

181

On the table, her hands shake and she nervously smoothes her hair. "He'll know—won't he? He'll come after you. I still get messages from him everyday."

"Let him try."

"W—what if you're not here and he—"

I reach forward and grasp her hand, bringing it to my lips. The last of her bruises only just healed, and I'm glad. A sick feeling filled my stomach every time I saw them splayed over her perfect skin. Fucking jackass.

"I will kill him. I would consider it an honor and a privilege."

She just melts at those words. I see her struggling to hold back tears as she clings to my hand. The poor girl is lonely as fuck. She's stuck here all day without anyone to talk to.

"Maybe I should talk to the other guys' wives. I know Tommy's girlfriend is from New York, too. Maybe she can help you plan the wedding. At least you'll have someone to hang out with."

The wedding. It sounds so strange coming from my lips like a matter of fact statement. Our wedding. To a girl I barely know or care about.

It's weird.

"Thanks, Tony. That's—that's really sweet of you."

A chuckle escapes my mouth. Sweet? I've never heard a

girl call me that in my life, ever, but she looks like she really means it. The expression on her face makes me uncomfortable. She looks at me as though I'm her goddamn savior, even though I'm only doing this for money. Part of me wants to set her straight, but I don't want to see her upset.

She gets up from her chair and walks to me, looking at me with a wide smile that makes me feel light. Then she straddles my legs and her fingers slowly rake through my hair. I touch her small waist and I think of all the women I've fucked in the past few years—how none of them even come close to her. She gets my dick hard whenever she feels like it, and the smug broad knows it. It worried me in the beginning that she was only fucking me to placate me, but after a week of nonstop fucking I know better.

She needs my cock just as much as I need her pussy.

Sometimes in the middle of the night, when I'm barely awake, I'll feel her hand on my cock. Then I'll fuck the shit out of her at some ungodly hour, and then when I wake up in the morning I'll fuck her again. And then she'll want more when I get back home. Fuck, it's heaven for my overactive cock, but I am tired as hell all the time.

"I missed you."

Elena's sigh washes over my ears as she sits down on my lap, straddling my waist. I groan as she reaches down and grabs my hardness, and then she kisses me, and I fight the urge to shove my tongue down her throat.

"Elena, we're going to visit my ma tomorrow." I swallow hard. "To tell her everything."

My palms sweat just thinking about it.

"Okay," she says, twirling a finger in my hair. "What's she like?"

"Old-fashioned, I guess. She'll be very happy to meet you."

Her brilliant smile falters somewhat, and my chest tightens a little. I know that she's not really mine, that this is all for show, but I can't help but feel a little annoyed. She should be fucking grateful for this.

"I'm just—I wonder what's happening with my mom right now. I didn't leave her with anything."

So that's what's bothering her.

Then her hand freezes in my hair and she stands up from my lap, looking embarrassed.

"Sorry, I know that you're not here to listen to my problems."

"You barely talk to me at all, hon." I stand up and my hip bumps into her waist, and she grabs a strand of her hair and tugs it. "When I come home, the first thing you do is jump on my cock. Don't look at me like that—I'm not complaining."

"I just don't know how to act around you. I don't know what you expect from me."

"I don't expect anything, doll. You're the one paying me—"

"—But I'm in your house, using your things, invading your privacy—"

My laugh cuts her off. "You're paying me fifty grand for a few months rent. I shouldn't let you use my things?" My hand snakes around her neck. "Maybe you're right. I should make you walk naked around the house."

Her watery eyes shine in the overhead lights and the laughter dies in my throat. All of a sudden, she shakes in my arms and tears stream down her face.

Jesus.

"What did I say?"

She shakes her head, trying to turn out of my grasp. "Nothing."

A small yelp leaves her throat as I curl my hand around her forearm and yank her into my chest. Fear flashes through her tears and I let go of her arm as though it burned me.

"Don't walk away from me, Elena."

"I'm just overwhelmed. Rafael keeps contacting me and I'm getting married and we're building up all these lies that we can't possibly keep straight."

"First of all, give me that phone right now."

She grudgingly reaches inside the pocket of her jeans and hands me her cellphone. I turn it on and briefly scroll through the wall of angry text messages.

When I find you I'll RIP YOUR FUCKING FACE OFF

Ur not gonna last five fucking minutes the moment I find you

I dont think you realize how much STRESS you're causing me. After everything I've fuckin done for you, you two-timing slut I will—

My fingers are so tight around the phone that I'm sure the glass is about to break.

"He sounds like a stand-up guy."

She smiles weakly.

Then I hurl the phone to the floor as hard as I can, shattering the glass. Ignoring her screams of protest, I dig my boot into the plastic and stomp hard until it's nothing but bits and pieces.

"What the hell did you do?"

"I'll get you a new phone. You don't need to read that shit everyday, it'll just make you upset." I take her shoulders in my hands and squeeze them.

"But I'll have no idea if he's planning something."

"You let me worry about that, sweetheart." I kiss her wet lips, and she releases a sigh.

* * *

Honestly, there's nothing better than starting off the day with a blowjob.

Wet, full lips wrapped around the most sensitive part of your cock, tongue riding up and down your shaft, swirling around your head.

Everything fades away. Fucking world peace could be accomplished if everyone got enough head.

Elena kneels on the shower floor, blinking up at me as hot water rains over her dark hair, which flattens to her face. She smiles at me, taking a break from shoving my fat cock down her throat. It's a perfect thing to look at. She's fucking hot, and she's on her knees sucking my cock. At the same time, it's agonizing because I can't touch her beautiful tits or that pussy always aching for me.

How the fuck does she do this to me? How?

I can't take it anymore—the wetness, the sliding, the sounds of her greedy mouth. I yank her arm so that she stumbles to her feet, and I gently push her against the glass with a growl.

"You just love how hard you can get me, don't you? Admit it."

Her lips touch my face, kissing my cheek, and I feel her smile against my skin.

"Maybe I enjoy it just a little."

Her tits flush against my chest and blood pounds

through my cock. Every throbbing beat is like a mantra. *Fuck. Her. Fuck. Her.*

Delicate hands wrap around my thick cock and squeeze as she nips my neck.

A little, my ass.

I grab her shoulders and turn her around, and then my palm rips across her ass. The sound cracks through the bathroom, sounding a lot worse from the water coating her skin. She yelps as a bright red mark blooms over her skin. Then she bends over, palms flat against the wall.

As long as she's willing, I'm going to fuck this girl every spare second that I have. Any time she's not begging at my knees or bent over at her waist is a fucking waste. Her wet hair slides in my hand as I reach forward and yank hard, forcing her to arch her back.

"You're too fucking sexy for your own good."

And too damn cocky.

Goddamn, even the sight of her tits hanging down makes my cock twitch. The curve of her back, the swell of her ass, her glistening pussy—it's an image of perfection.

My length throbs as I aim it between her lips. They spread apart with the slightest pressure, and she shudders with pleasure as I sink into her. Her legs tremble as I pull back and thrust, addicted to her warmth heat. Fuck, it's incredible. We fit together perfectly. She's snug around my dick, and I feel her pussy clinging to my dick as I pull out as if it's desperate to keep me inside.

Her palms slip on the glass as I grab her hips and thrust hard; pummeling her pussy hard enough to make her feet stumble. Still, I find myself wishing we had an audience to fuck in front of, so that everyone can see that this amazing girl is all mine.

She pushes her greedy ass against mine, taking more of my cock inside her. I grind against her ass, laughing when the bathroom echoes with her sharp gasps. The real thrill is when the girl comes. Absolutely nothing gives me a greater high than a girl becoming completely undone over my cock. It's intoxicating to have that kind of power over someone. The more I fuck her, the more of a turn on it is. She's not tired of me, no matter how many times I fuck her.

"Tony, more!"

I'll give you more.

I grasp her hips, digging my fingers into her flesh as my hips smash into her. She screams, slipping on the wall, but I hold her against me, pounding hard as she contorts her face, her tits swinging.

"Harder!"

Dammit. I can't fuck you much harder.

The ecstasy twisting her face makes blood rush to my

chest. The steam rises in the shower, scorching our bodies, and I feel almost faint. My hand reaches around, playing with her clit as I watch my cock pulse inside her. I feel the bulge moving through her.

"Come for me, baby. I want you to come hard on my dick."

"I—I am—I'm—" a wordless moan cuts off the rest of her words and she collapses on the glass.

Her cunt tightens around me and then I pull out. The pressure builds as I fist my cock and I stroke once, sighing as jets of cum blast over her back.

Elena turns around and I get a brief look of her flushed face before her arms wrap around my head and her lips crush against mine, so insistent and consuming. She bites my bottom lip and pulls back.

"I want more."

My hand snakes around her neck and I grab a fistful of hair. "How many times a day do I have to fuck you to make you happy?"

She reaches behind herself, smiling and shuts off the water. "I don't know yet."

She's either some kind of angel sent from Heaven with the mission of overworking my cock, or she's fucking the pain away.

Whatever the reason, I'm glad.

I admire the way her tits move as she reaches up and wrings out her hair, and grab two towels for her before running one all over myself. I get ready in the other bathroom while she hogs the main one. It takes her fucking long to do all the shit she needs to do with makeup and her hair, but when she's finished, she looks gorgeous.

My chest tightens as she gives me a kiss on the cheek. She wears a skin-tight semi-sheer black sweater and jeans that leave little to the imagination. I know that I barely know her and she's mostly just a hot girl that I fuck, but it makes me proud. I'm proud to show her off to my ma.

She takes my hand, squeezing hard as we leave my apartment. I watch her face, her darting eyes and her mouth, slightly parted as if she's seconds from screaming. A hot wave of rage suddenly rises inside me for that asshole who made her so afraid.

There's no one outside the icy streets and I open the car door, letting her inside first. Then I join her and we drive out of there. Silence descends in the car, and I keep sneaking glances at her.

I barely know a thing about her.

"So what's with you?"

"What do you mean?"

My hands tighten on the steering wheel. "I've never

known a girl to want it that often."

"I haven't had fun in a very long time." She gives me a curious look and her hand curves around my thigh. "You make me feel really good about myself. I—I never realized how much I needed that."

A pang of sadness hits me suddenly, and I can't help but feel that whatever this is between us—she's already feeling something a little more than lust.

Then she lets out a shaky sigh. "I'm worried about this."

Truth be told, my guts haven't unclenched since we left my apartment. I don't like lying to my ma, but for once in my worthless life I'm doing something for the greater good.

She'll understand.

I hope.

"Don't worry about her. It'll be fine."

Like hell it'll be.

I know exactly what my mother will do. She'll scream, she'll cry, she'll want to be involved in every damn aspect of the wedding.

The forty minutes to Terrebonne don't take very long at all and I pull into the driveway. We sit in the car as the engine ticks, staring at my childhood home. Even though it's freezing, neither of us makes the move to open the car door.

"All right. Let's do this."

I open the door and step outside as Elena does the same, wrapping her arms around her sides immediately. She waits for me to walk around the car, and then we walk up the path to the front door. Elena lets out a nervous sigh as I raise my fist—

The door flies open and my ma stands in the doorway, looking beautiful and put-together as always. "Hi, baby!"

I gesture toward Elena. "Ma, this is Elena."

Poor Elena stiffens as my mother throws her arms around her neck and kisses her cheeks, nearly crying in ecstasy.

"It's nice to meet you."

"Oh my God, she's so—you're so beautiful. My son *finally* has a girlfriend. Come in. Come *in*!"

Red-faced, Elena smiles and walks in the house as I take a huge breath.

Here we fucking go.

It smells wonderful in the house, but then again, it always does. It doesn't matter what time of the night it is, whenever I come over my ma insists on feeding me. Typical Italian mom, I guess.

The house looks exactly the same as it did when my dad was still alive. Same beaten up furniture that my ma refuses to replace for some reason that escapes me. It's as though she expects him to walk in any moment and find everything exactly the way he left it. A pain hits my side whenever I see a photo of him, and they're everywhere in this fucking house. When he died, it was as though my heart was ripped from my breast.

My petite mom waves Elena inside, motioning toward the kitchen. "Please, sit, sit. Tony, come here and help your mother."

Elena stands up from the chair. "I can help, too."

"No, no. Sit down and relax. Have some—oh Jesus, where are my oven mitts!"

Chuckling, I walk into the kitchen and grab the oven mitts from the top of the refrigerator. "Here."

Ma squints at me through her glasses and takes the mitts from me. "*Maddon*, I'm losing it. Tony, set the table."

I grab fists full of silverware and place them around the small table, smiling at Elena who sits as if her back is attached to a steel rod. She flinches suddenly as I drop my hand over her shoulder and squeeze it.

"Relax, hon."

Her muscles relax under my hand. She turns her head as I stroke her back, smiling at me.

"You two look so adorable," my ma says, smiling at us. "I never thought my son would bring home a girl. It's been at least ten years since he had a girlfriend—"

"—*Ma!*"

Jesus fucking Christ don't bring that up.

Her smile fumbles under my glare, and I grab a stack of plates, ignoring Elena's curious stare. My hands shake and the ceramic cracks together noisily. Ma winces.

"Watch it! Those are new!"

"Sorry, Ma."

The oven blows a cloud of steam into the kitchen as Ma takes out the roast ham and lets it rest on the kitchen counter.

"You never told me how you met each other."

I sit down next to Elena, finding her hand under the table.

Let me do the talking.

"At Tommy's bar."

Ma gets the knife out of the drawer and sticks the meat thermometer in the steaming ham. "And you two hit it off?"

Her fingers tighten around mine. They feel ice-cold.

I've done drug deals with bikers and I've never been this nervous. There's a golf ball in my throat. My heart pounds and my mouth is dry. "Well—ah. Yeah, I guess you could say that."

She frowns at me over the ham and finally sets the

thermometer down.

"Ma, could you come sit down?"

"What?" Her eyes widen. "What's wrong? There's something wrong, isn't there? I can tell."

"No, not really—"

Her mouth trembles as she tears off her glasses and wipes her face. Tears burst from her eyes. "You're going to prison, aren't you?"

My jaw drops. "*No.*"

It's a fucking nightmare. The kitchen echoes with her heart-wrenching sobs, and I take her hand in mine.

"I never wanted you to be in this—your father would turn in his grave if he knew—"

"Ma, I'm not going to jail!"

She leans over the table, her eyes blazing. There's no trust in her gaze.

I feel like such a scumbag.

"Then what is it? *What is it, Tony?*"

"I'm pregnant!"

My head snaps to a stunned Elena, whose whole face slowly burns red. She looks like she can't believe what she just said.

"What?"

The look my mother gives me makes me wish that I was getting the shit beaten out of me. I feel small. My hand drapes over Elena's shoulder and I pull her into my chest, rubbing her arm.

"We're having a baby, Ma."

She rubs her eyes and looks at me as though I must be an apparition.

"You're having a baby? Elena's pregnant?"

Elena opens her mouth and gives her a tentative smile. "Yes."

"You're going to be a *nonna*."

Her mouth trembles and fresh tears spill from her eyes. "*Oh my god*! I can't believe it!"

Within seconds, her arms fly around my neck and she squeezes until I grunt. "Ma, relax."

She dissolves into tears around my neck, and her sobbing punches me right in the chest. Elena looks at me, wearing an expression that mirrors what I feel.

I'm going to Hell for this. No redemption.

Then she unsticks herself from my neck and clings to Elena. "You're going to have my grandbaby? Oh my god, I'm so excited!"

My chest tightens as she embraces my mom back and I'm surprised to see her eyes swimming with tears. Is she acting?

My mom finally releases Elena and collapses on the chair. "Oh thank the Lord, I never thought this day would come. Your father would be so proud—he'd be so happy."

I have no fucking idea what my father would have felt. He died before I got to know him. I was eight.

"I know."

"Oh, *Tony.*"

"Elena wants to get married before she starts showing."

Ma gulps down her cries and nods. "Of course, but— Oh my God."

"I'm really sorry to dump all of this on you, Ma. We only just found out."

"Do you love each other?"

I don't even dare look at Elena.

"I don't know your son very well, but I think that he's a wonderful man—and I want my baby to have a family."

Overwhelmed, my mother presses her hand towel to her face as tears stream down her face, and Elena reaches across the table and takes my mom's hand.

"Please don't be upset."

I watch her quivering mouth and I suddenly have a strange impulse to tuck the hair hanging around her face behind her ear.

"I—I wish it were under different circumstances, but I'm not upset." She trembles and then bursts out, "Oh *bless you*! I thought I'd never see my son get married."

The rest of the evening passes slowly. It's torturous, and I feel more and more rotten as the hours go by. She dials every fucking member of my family to tell them the news, and she cries, and she gives Elena the numbers of every recommended florist and bakery and venue that she can think of. Worse of all are the constant references to my dad, and how *proud* he'd be and how she wishes he were still alive. Finally, it's time to go, and Ma stops me right as I'm about to leave the house.

She clings to my jacket. "Tony, you better raise this baby right."

"Of course I will."

"I mean it," she snaps. "I know how you spend your nights, and I don't want to see that sweet girl hurt."

"It's not like she'd know about it."

Her hand whirls out of nowhere, slapping me hard across the face. It's fucking humiliating. She glowers at me.

"What the fuck?"

"I don't want to hear any of your smart mouth. You have a responsibility to your wife and baby. It's time to grow up, Tony."

Tears glaze her eyes and the air leaves my chest.

"I didn't raise you right."

"*What?*"

"You followed in your dad's footsteps, after I did

199

everything I could to stop it."

My voice dips to a growl. "You've got to stop blaming yourself for that. I chose the life. It was a mistake. I have to live with that, not you."

"I have to live with every stupid decision you make, Tony. That's what you don't realize. Promise me you'll be good to this girl. You're not going to leave her for someone else when she gives birth to your baby. Promise me."

My eyes water from staring at her for so long. "I won't."

Ma looks at me for a moment as though she wants to believe me, and then she closes the door.

* * *

This is too much.

This is way too fucking much.

If that prick doesn't kill me, my mother will.

I slam the door to the apartment and Elena flinches beside me. Her face cringes with that disgusting emotion that I hate to see on any woman's face. She's never seen me angry.

My mother's anguished face flashes through my mind as I rip open the refrigerator door and pull out a beer. I snap off the top, glaring at Elena as she stands in the kitchen, carefully avoiding my eyes.

I guzzle down the beer and feel it add to the pool of hot, burning guilt.

"Tony, I—I'm really sorry for all this. I know it must have been really difficult. It was hard for me, too."

She's just another girl who wants something from me. Why the fuck did I ever agree to do this? What amount of money is worth ruining my relationship with my mother, the only person I care about in the whole world?

"Oh, it was hard for you? Please, tell me how it was hard for you. My own mother slapped me. She expects me to keep my dick in my pants for our *marriage*."

Her beautiful face whitens. "I like your mother, and I don't want to see her get hurt. I'm not—I'm not proud of what I did."

The heat burns down my throat as I swallow another mouthful. "I can't fucking do this."

"What? No, Tony, *please*—"

"I'm sorry, babe, but it's just not worth it. I can't do this. I can't fuck one woman for three months, I can't be a good husband, I can't do any of the things you want me to do."

She stares at me for a moment, flinching from my words. I hate that look on her face. I hate anything that makes me feel for her. An awful sound pierces through my chest as Elena tries to draw in breath. Then her body shakes and my chest caves in as she grabs my shoulders.

"Tell me what I have to do. *I'll do anything you want.* Just don't—please don't—"

The vein on her forehead looks like it's going to blow, and then the smallest tear squeezes from her eye.

And I'm done.

Be good to her, Tony.

My mother's voice snarls in my head and I wrap my arms around Elena's body, unable to stomach the look of destruction on her face.

What if I don't want to be good? I never gave a shit about being the good guy, why should I now? Because she's a great piece of ass?

"I'll ask someone else," she says finally.

"*No.*"

It bursts out of me immediately like a visceral reaction. Suddenly, blood churns in my head as I think about her fucking some other made guy. No fucking way.

Fuck, I'm stuck with this chick. I couldn't live with myself if I pawned her off to someone else. I'm not attached, but I want to possess her. She's my prize, and I like having access to her pussy 24/7.

"*I need more.*"

She blinks. "I have more money."

"I don't give a shit about your money." My hand curls

underneath her jaw and a smile spreads across my face as I think about all the things I could get her to do for me.

I thought I was being the good guy for helping her out, but I couldn't have been more wrong. Meeting my mother taught me that. It's time to stop giving a fuck about being the good guy. Let's face it, I'm an asshole. Always will be.

"You need to be mine—*completely* mine."

She hiccups. "Well, we are getting married."

I grope her tight ass and my cock stiffens in my slacks. "Yeah, but it's not a real marriage. You don't really belong to me, and that's what's bothering me."

Her eyes widen as she looks at me. "What are you saying? You want to—you want it to be real?"

"*No.* I just don't want your fucking money."

"I—I don't get understand."

"It's simple." I take her beautiful face in my hands and my thumb runs along her bottom lip. "You want my help? *Fine.* I'll take you as payment."

Her mouth opens and my brain lurches, suddenly frozen. I want to kiss her. I want to fuck those perfect lips.

"*What does that mean?*"

"It means that you're mine. Your body in exchange for being your husband." I love the way her cheeks fill with color. For some reason, it turns me on to think that the sexy minx I brought home might *actually* be shy.

Because breaking her in would be so goddamn fun.

"I hate the idea of being on loan for you."

She makes a face. "*Jesus.* Is that what this is about? The fucking money? I thought you were a businessman. Who the hell cares how you make your money? It can't be any worse than what you've already done."

A surge of anger fills my chest, hot and disturbing. In the beginning, I thought it was smart. Hell, fifty grand to fuck some chick for a few months? Why not? I couldn't see past my own dick, and I've already invested too much in this. Tommy knows about the money, which means there's a risk that Johnny will find out.

And he can't find out.

There's also the fact that the moment I take her money, I become her employee. I'm hers, when it should be the other way around.

I can't live like that.

"I don't care about right and wrong. I've just changed my mind."

Her eyes harden like dark gems. "Tell me why you want me to do this."

"It's the only way this will work. I need to be in control of you, sweetheart. If I don't feel like I'm in control, I won't be able to keep my dick in my pants. If I don't do that, then everyone will know this is a complete sham."

Elena nods and grits her teeth, looking pissed off. *"What do you want?"*

"There are things I've never tried with a girl that I'd love to try on you."

"I—like what?"

Oh, like fucking you in front of a crowd of men.

"Things that might make you embarrassed."

I sweep her hair over her neck as redness pricks over her cheeks. I think about Tommy's bar, about the thrill I used to feel getting some random chick to scream my name. It pales in comparison to the thrill of what I could do with Elena.

I'm an asshole for doing this.

It's time to embrace it.

ELENA

The sterling-silver metal egg rests in the palm of my hand, the coolness pleasant against my hand. I gaze into the mirror, and he stands behind me, his grinning face amused by my horror.

"You want me—you seriously want me to put this thing…"

"In your pussy, yes."

He's lost his goddamn mind.

Tony wraps an arm around my bare midriff, planting a kiss on my neck that makes my core heat up. "It's remote controlled and there are various settings."

His other hand snakes around my waist with the tiny remote. There's a clicking noise and then the egg in my hand vibrates violently. His thumb rolls over the wheel and the shaking increases in intensity.

"Shit."

It nearly tumbles out of my palm, and he turns it off. A strange thrill runs through my body at the thought of wearing this thing to our engagement party, where the boss of the Cravotta family will be.

Then I feel slightly ill. I stare into his happy face,

unable to believe what I'm hearing.

"*You're insane.* I can't fucking do this."

"Yes, you can."

"*Johnny* will be there, for fuck's sake! You really want me to do this in front of your boss?"

His wolfish grin sends chills down my spine, and then he spreads his hands over my naked skin and I shudder as heat burns my skin.

"Especially him, yes."

I gape at him through the mirror. Why the fuck would he want to disrespect his boss like that? "Why?"

"Because it turns me on, baby. I like the idea of you getting wet and frustrated in front of all these guys, who'll have no idea what's going on."

My skin prickles with desire as he runs his hands over my skin, his coarse cheek slightly brushing mine as his words hiss over my ear, making my heart pound.

I don't know how I feel about it—I'm embarrassed, that's for sure, and a little bewildered.

Who knew he'd be such a kinky freak?

"Where the hell is this coming from?"

Strong hands curl around my shoulders, and turn me around so that I'm facing him. A flush fills my cheeks and chest as he gives me that gorgeous, panty-melting smile. He takes the egg from my hands and his lips bump against mine. My body weakens as his tongue strokes my lips, and I open my mouth for him. At the same time, I feel his callused fingers reaching down between my legs. I widen my stance and he rubs the vibrator over my clit.

"I've been thinking a lot about you, and all the things I could get you to do for me—"

"Basically, you're an asshole."

He grins at me. "Don't pretend you don't fucking love it."

A small moan escapes my lips when he plants another hot kiss over my mouth.

"Listen, baby. *I want you.* I want you in ways that you're not always going to love, but you'll do them anyway—for me."

It's hard to think when his fingers slip between my swollen lips, curling upward as the vibrator hums over my clit.

"I want you begging me to fuck me by the end of the night."

A shudder runs through my body as he pushes the egg inside me. It slides in with little resistance as his tongue sweeps into my mouth. He pulls back, smirking.

I'm dimly aware that I should be putting up more of a fight. He's hot and all, but am I willing to humiliate myself like this for him? At the same time, I feel dirty for the excitement that shoots into my chest.

It's so fucking wrong.

"Should we test it?"

Without waiting for a response, he clicks a button and the cool metal suddenly vibrates inside me. The vibrating egg sends electrical spasms into my clit. Pleasure spikes into my core, and my core gradually throbs with a growing ache.

Holy shit.

I breathe deeply as he laughs and wrap my arms around his back. "Tony—*shit*—this is too much!"

"It's on the lowest setting, sweetheart. Is that too much for you?"

He thumbs the wheel and the vibrator increases speed like a hummingbird's wings. It's as though his tongue sliding up and down my clit, and I think about the long, hard cock between his legs, and how maddening it is that it's not inside me. Right. Fucking. Now.

"Tony!"

He chuckles and turns the vibrator off, but my legs still tremble as though weakened by it. I kiss his chest and grab a mouthful of his irresistible muscle and bite down slightly. He laughs and kisses my head.

"*Fuck me.*"

"I control your body, even when I'm not by your

side…even when we're in public."

My face burns as he reaches down and cups my wetness, sliding a hard finger over my clit. Then he pulls back and spanks my ass and a ripple of anger runs through me.

"Now get ready."

A smirk flashes at me through the mirror before he stalks out of the bathroom, leaving me there with a throbbing ache pulsing between my legs.

This is so fucking crazy.

Really, it is. I'm getting married to a man a barely know, a bad boy who had a crisis of conscience over deceiving his mother. Oh, and he's into humiliating me in front of his buddies because that apparently gets him off.

The eyeliner trembles in my hand as I imagine Rafael bursting into the restaurant with a gun. He *must* know by now, and it kills me that I don't have access to his texts anymore. He's probably murderous with rage and Tony will be at the top of his list when he finds out another guy 'knocked me up.'

Tony tells me not to worry about it, but how can I do that? My sister has my new phone number, and her scathing texts hint that she's found out about it, too.

Vince stopped by. He's looking for Rafael. He told me that you're getting engaged to some French guy in

Montreal and that you're pregnant??? What the hell is going on? BTW, Thanks a lot for the invitation to your engagement party.

Sighing, I clench my fingers around the phone. I can't deal with my pissed off family right now. No, I didn't tell her anything about the engagement, or my so-called predicament. I know that it's rude. We're Italian. Refusing to invite your family to your engagement party might as well be a capital crime.

I just don't want any of them there. It's going to be bad enough as it is, surrounded by strangers with a fucking vibrator shoved inside me.

Jesus.

How did I get from running from my ex to shoving a vibrator up my pussy for a man I hardly know?

A ripple of excitement runs through my body at the idea of a hot pulse of pleasure running between my legs the whole time I'm supposed to be meeting Cravotta family associates. I must have done hundreds of these events with my dad, and he would've busted a nut if I tried anything like this in front of his people. I choke out laughter, seizing the sink for support as I think about doing this in front of these big, scary Mafiosi. It makes me wonder why Tony would do this. Why risk his reputation just to get off?

I catch a glimpse of him shrugging on his dress shirt over his tattooed chest, a slight frown on his face. Before we met his mother, I would have thought that he was just another dead-eyed, empty shell. Beautiful to look at, but empty inside. It's a struggle to get a reaction from him. I tell him about my psychotic ex, and he shrugs as though it's hardly worth thinking about. He's unflappable.

Tony hangs in the doorway, his hair slicked back, his face freshly shaven and still moist. He looks appetizing in his black suit, the red shirt and tie making him look like a modern manifestation of the devil. His narrowed eyes radiate heat as they slip down my neck and over my curves.

He slips a casual hand into his jacket pocket and suddenly a jolt rips through my pussy. A smile spreads over his handsome face.

"Perfect."

* * *

One of the few advantages of being a woman is being able to be turned on without anybody ever realizing it. There were so many times that I sat in high school class and fantasized about the Algebra teacher bending me over his desk and fucking me hard, or sometimes I'd be trapped in an elevator with a hottie and I'd bask in his presence, imagining his mouth over mine. I'd stew in silence and feel my panties growing wet, and no one would know.

It was safe to fantasize.

It was even fun.

Tony's taken that away. He ripped the security blanket from my shoulders when he shoved that vibrator up my pussy, which is all I can think about even as I shake hands with Tony's associates with my slightly damp one.

Fucking asshole.

It hums inside me as I walk around *Le Zinc*, the restaurant Tony brought me to celebrate our engagement. He keeps a firm hand around my waist as we float from person to person.

It's a beautiful restaurant, and the live jazz band gives the place a moody, intimate feeling. I expect to see people making out—I expect to see them fucking in that darkened corner by the bathrooms—

Jesus. I'm horny as hell.

"I was wondering: Is it hard being close to me?" He slides his arm around my waist with deliberate slowness. "I can just imagine how wet your panties must be right now."

I look up and down his body, my eyes lingering right below his belt. Naked—I want him naked. I want my legs wrapped around him and that fucking irritating smile. He's just so goddamn delectable in that suit, and the vibrator keeps reminding me just how much I need him.

There's no way to get off, and people are everywhere. Tony's family and friends. People I've never met before. I should be getting to know people. Instead, I'm obsessed with getting to know the intimate details of Tony's cock.

"I'm going to kill you."

"Your pussy must be *aching*. Tell me, does every wave through your pussy remind you of how nice my cock feels inside you?" Tony's voice rumbles deliciously in my ear and I turn into his arms, my hands and face scorching hot. His quiet laughter sends a ripple of rage through me.

Fucking asshole.

"*Turn it the fuck off.*"

The violent buzzing between my legs is maddening. I'm seconds away from ripping off his clothes, and he gives me a brief, chaste kiss that only adds fuel to the blazing fire.

"Not a chance. Seeing you all worked up like this is way too fun." He takes my arms slides his hands up, and he might as well be running his hands up my legs. He turns his head. "Hey, Johnny."

Johnny? Oh fuck.

The slick Montreal boss suddenly materializes out of thin air to give Tony a swift hug and a kiss on both cheeks. A sick sensation swoops around my stomach as Tony casually slips a hand in his jacket and the vibrations magnify a hundredfold.

"Congratulations, Tony, *petit criss*."

Oh God. I'm next.

I don't even care about the fact that the last time I saw this man, he threw me out of his restaurant and denied me help. He turns to me, beaming as Tony grins behind him, indifferent to the fact that I'm *seconds* away from coming.

The boss extends a hand as my stomach tenses so hard that it's impossible to inhale.

Please don't come. Please don't.

My legs tighten as I try to still the fucking vibrator sending pleasure throughout my body, but it's cruel. It's like a knife into my flesh. I can't stop it. It can't help but build up, and up, and up.

I let out a gasp and wrap my arms around Johnny as my pussy clenches hard over the device. Tony bites his fist as he watches me come with his boss' arms wrapped around me.

"Sorry," I gasp. "I'm just—a bit—overwhelmed."

Johnny's stunned face lightens somewhat. He's not the kind of guy you touch without permission. My body trembles with the explosion, the aftershocks still singeing my nerves. Pleasure and relief flood my limbs, but the device hums against my clit, ramping it up again. I bite my lip hard. Tony lowers the speed, and I'm able to breathe.

"You all right, hon? You look a little—red."

Oh really? Is my face red? Hmm, I guess it has to do with the fucking VIBRATOR up my twat right now.

Just the thought of what I must look right now makes me shoot daggers at Tony.

Tony lets out a laugh that quickly becomes a cough. "Yeah, uh—she's worried about her ex showing up, that's all."

My ex? Oh yeah. Him.

Funny how a little toy can make you forget about violent exes.

My heart jumps when Johnny frowns at us.

"Yeah, well. I need to talk to you about that. He might show up."

"*What?*"

My hand seizes Tony's arm as dizzying shocks pound through my heart.

"You never gave me the paternity test, so now the asshole is claiming that the baby is his."

No.

The vibrator shuts off and Tony's strong, protective arm curls around my waist. I feel him bristling.

"It's Tony's. It's not his!"

Johnny turns his head with a humorless smile. "Can you prove that?"

No, I can't because there is no baby.

The bottom drops out of my stomach.

"John, I looked it up and you can't do a test like that until seven or eight months."

"We went to the doctor. He said I was a couple weeks pregnant. It fits. We only just met—"

"It could easily be Rafael's, sweetheart. Frankly, the man has a right to know if the child is his, and he has a right to be in that child's life—"

"I don't want him in my baby's life!" My voice rises to a shout and Tony squeezes my hip in warning.

Johnny's hardened face stares me down. "He has a right if he's the father."

Tony's jaw ticks as he looks back at Johnny, fuming. "John, I don't want that asshole at my engagement party. If he's showing up, we're leaving."

Disappointment steams off Johnny's face. I can tell that he doesn't approve, but he can't force us to accept a fucking audience from my ex at my own party.

"Fine. I'll let them know to bar him from the restaurant." His eyes slide to mine. "Sooner or later, you're going to have to face him."

He walks off, leaving me trembling in Tony's arms. The horror of it all buries me, until breathing feels painful. I never anticipated all this shit, but of course we should have. We were so stupid.

"*Tony.*"

Suddenly, his hand is vice-like around my arm. "Elena, get behind me."

The tension in his voice sends my heart galloping.

"*There you are, you fucking cunt!*"

A vicious voice fills my veins with toxin, and Tony throws an arm in front of me, shoving me back as Rafael lunges forward. Looking furious, Johnny seizes the back of his collar and yanks him back.

"I fucking told you to be civil," he hisses into his ear before giving him a sharp slap across the face.

Rafael's face rips to the side, and violence contorts his face. His eyes lift to John, and I'm surprised at the threat simmering inside them. "She's carrying my kid, John."

"That remains to be seen."

"If there fucking even is a kid at all," he snarls.

I open my mouth in fury, but Tony gets there first.

"*Why don't you go fuck yourself?*"

A cruel grin stretches Rafael's mouth as he appraises Tony, who is a much larger man. Unfortunately, Tony doesn't seem to intimidate Rafael.

"So you're the asshole fucking my girl?"

Tony smiles. "She's not your girl."

"Oh, I beg to differ."

"You lost the right to call her that the moment you laid

a hand on her."

His face contorts with rage. "She's mine and everything that belongs to her, belongs to me!"

"You whine like a little bitch," he snaps, finally releasing some of the anger tensing his face. "She doesn't want you. She wants me."

"Get over here!" he screams at me.

"If I see you anywhere near my fiancée, I'll cut your fucking balls off and shove them up your ass."

For a moment Rafael just stands there, quietly burning as the things he thought he had slipped from his grasp without him even realizing. I watch him suffer with a cruel sort of satisfaction pounding against my ribs. He *won't* win. Not this time. First he lost me. Now his pride is gone, too.

"You're a dead man."

"All right, that's enough," Johnny shouts. He motions with his head, and two men grab Rafael's arms, dragging him out of the restaurant.

Rafael snaps the moment they touch his arms. His voice raises to the ceiling as he screams at the top of his lungs, people glancing around in their seats. Flecks of spittle fly from his mouth.

"YOU'RE FUCKING DEAD! I'LL FUCKING KILL YOU, YOU BETTER—"

I disappear from Tony's side and run through the

restaurant, ignoring everyone's sympathetic looks as I disappear into the bathroom. My chest swells and I check every stall first, confirming that I'm alone. Then I let myself curl into a ball.

Only this once.

My back slides against the wall and I try to cover my mouth to stifle the horribly loud and embarrassing sounds. My insides feel like caving in because I'm so humiliated. Tony's mother must have seen the whole thing—and all the other wives, too. There's also the fact that we completely overlooked that Rafael might be crazy enough to claim the baby was his.

I stand up, shaking in anger as I stare into the mirror over the sink, tears blurring my vision. I want to smash that weak, pathetic thing. Who the fuck is she? She isn't Jack Vittorio's daughter. She's just a scared little girl, *too weak* to handle her own problems.

The door rattles. "Elena?"

He opens the door before I can tell him to leave and steps inside, locking the door behind him.

I look at his cool, indifferent face for a while. "What the hell are we doing, Tony?"

The bathroom echoes with his sharp footsteps, which make me flinch. He stops in front of me and my skin prickles as he brushes his fingers over my bare neck.

"What do you mean?"

"We can't possibly—we're fucked! There's no way we can keep up with these lies."

"Sure we can. We'll pay off those technicians to fake some tests for us."

He sounds so sure. So confident.

"Then what happens in a few months when I'm supposed to be showing and I'm not?"

He shrugs and laughs at me, as though I'm making a big deal out of nothing. "So we fucking say you miscarried it. It's no one's fucking business. As for Joe Jerk-off, well, he'll have to back off once we're married."

I don't know.

His lips descend over mine and I seize his neck, leaning into him as his lips devour me. At the same time, I hear a sound that reminds me of fabric—

BZZZZT.

The vibrator hums to life and my arousal returns with a vengeance as I open my mouth in a gasp. "Tony—this isn't the time!"

"This is the perfect fucking time. You need to get your mind off things, and I'll be a lot happier watching you come while you shake Johnny's hand than watching you cry."

His voice is sweet. I don't expect that, and tears thicken

my throat as he cradles my cheek in his hand. There's not a tinge of doubt in his eyes, just reassuring confidence.

"Tony, thank you for what you did. Everything that you said..." my voice croaks and those wonderful, grey eyes dent with pain.

"Jesus Christ, Elena, stop crying."

I try. My lips press together and I fight to keep the pain from bursting out, but of course it does. It's inevitable.

"It'll be all right." He wraps his arms around me and I'm swallowed by his bulk. "Please stop crying. *Please.*"

"I—I'm not upset."

I'm just happy that I have you.

The tears subside as I swallow that down. It's incredibly warm and it does make me happy. Fuck, I'm already getting *way* too attached to this guy. Even his smile gives me a high. I've never felt anything like him before.

A tentative smirk pulls at his lips when he watches me calm down as the vibrations rip through my body.

"Now get that sexy ass back outside. You need to say hello to my mother."

For all his banter, he turns off the vibrator the moment I take his hand. We leave the bathroom together and walk back into the crowd of people sipping drinks. The men slap Tony's back and smile at me.

"Jesus, what a fucking lunatic!" A man with a wide,

grinning face laughs at Tony's stony face.

"Fucking Yanks."

I flinch at that remark and turn away from the men to sit down alone at the long wooden table set up for us. The table is already laden with Italian appetizers: *salumi* and cheese, freshly cut country bread, and olives. The men start jabbering away in rapid French, all of it sounding so alien to my ears.

I'm lost here.

A chair scrapes back and I look up to see a pretty girl with dark curls and voluptuous curves sitting across the table. Her round eyes soften when she looks at me.

"Hi, my name is Melanie. I'm Tommy's girlfriend."

Oh.

She speaks with a strong New York accent. This must be Tommy's girl. I take her hand and shake it. "I'm Elena."

My head glances at the tall, lean form hanging around the group of men. Tommy must not be able to understand a word, but he doesn't look like he gives a shit. I'm trying to gauge how much she saw, and my hands shake underneath the table.

"I guess you saw what happened."

My face flushes as she nods her curly head.

"Yeah." Her eyes lower to the table.

A wave of depression suddenly hits me as I think about how I must look to these people. What a mess. I'm just an ex-Mafia princess with a ton of baggage, who got knocked up by a notorious man-whore. How ridiculous I must look to her.

Oh who the fuck cares? Look at him. He doesn't give a fuck.

Tony glances over occasionally to find me, and when he does his smile gives me instant heat, like a hot drop of pleasure down my throat. No one will dare say anything disrespectful to him about me. Insult a made guy's wife, and you might as well make plans for your funeral. That's the way this world works.

"It's a bit embarrassing."

"He made a fool out of himself, not you."

The honesty shining from her eyes makes me feel a bit better.

"So you're from New York, too? What brought you here?"

Her cheeks burn suddenly, and she looks at me almost guiltily. "It's a long story."

My guts turn to ice. After all the shit that went down with my father, Tommy had to leave town. Obviously, his girlfriend followed him. There's guilt all over her face, and the way her eyes avoid me tell me that she knows a lot more about it than I do.

Fuck, I've barely thought about it.

"I know Tommy was part of the crew that killed my dad."

Melanie's face drains of color. I almost expect to see blood pooling at her feet.

"It doesn't matter anymore. I just want to move on, you know? Make a better life for myself."

"I'm basically in the same boat." She smiles painfully at her boyfriend, who sits down next to her. "We've been here a few months. It was hard at first, but we're getting the hang of it. Enough people speak English so it's not really a problem."

A rattling sound fills me with horror. The fucking vibrator hums inside me, banging against the wooden chair. It slipped out too far, and everyone can hear the noise. Tommy frowns, looking for the source of the sound and I tighten my legs, stifling it.

I'll fucking kill him.

Tony joins me at the table with a knowing grin and slides his arm across my shoulder, kissing the shell of my ear as my core seizes. His fingers gently rake over my skin, playing over the strap of my dress and I'm consumed with an image of him tearing off my clothes. Every small movement he makes on my skin reminds me of sex and the pulsing ache between my legs, which desperately needs something long and hard. Meanwhile, I'm pinned to his warmth and there's not a thing I can do—*sex, sex, sex*. There's nothing else in my mind.

I give him a sharp look that he completely ignores.

Fine. Two can play that game, baby.

I let my left hand fall casually to my side, and then I slowly inch it under the table. There's no tablecloth. The whole fucking world can see what I'm doing, but I don't give a shit. My hand falls over his hard knee and I gently squeeze his thigh, stroking.

His muscles stiffen under my hand, but his speech doesn't falter.

"What venue were you thinking for the wedding, Tony?"

"I'm not sure. I like that one place we went to for Francois, with the gardens?"

A man down the table nods. "Yeah, that's Parc Jean-Drapeau."

My hand inches up his slacks and excitement runs through my veins as my fingers just barely touch the bulge between his legs.

Tony coughs and his hand drops his fork to slip into his jacket.

Holy fuck. It's pressing right up against my clit and the speed triples. I look down the table, trying to distract myself from the lust pounding through my veins. It's like a dirty whisper in your ear, constant and nagging.

You want to fuck him. You won't last through the night if you don't take his cock, and let him fill you up completely.

My fork clatters against the ceramic plate. All the food is delicious, but I can't taste it. I can't taste anything but the slightly salty skin of his cock when I imagine taking him in my mouth. I'm grabbing his cock in plain view. All the guy next to him would have to do is look at Tony's lap, and he'd see. My face flushes with heat when Tony grabs my hand and pulls it away from his lap.

"You're giving me a hard-on," he hisses.

I smile sweetly. "That's the point, isn't it? *You fuck with me, and I fuck with you.*"

His eyes blaze as my hand returns to his lap, fingers curling around his thickness. I squeeze and feel him twitch in my hands. He stares at me for a little too long, and then there's laughter down the table.

I let him go, convinced they saw us, but it's only Tommy, laughing at someone's joke. Relief flows over Tony's face and he gives his head a little shake. Then he leans over.

"Come with me."

"Right in the middle of dinner?"

"Stand the fuck up before I drag you."

I recognize that look smoldering in his face, and my insides leap with excitement as he excuses himself. He awkwardly positions his jacket to hide his boner, and I laugh to myself as he gives me a severe look.

My chair scrapes the floor as I get up after him, weaving around the tables as he quickly heads for the back of the restaurant. There's an enclosed glass room with sheer curtains for private parties, and Tony holds open the door for me.

"Get in."

I look inside. There's no one in there, but the table has already been set and there's a little card sitting on the long table: RESERVED.

"Tony, what—?"

"*Get in.*"

The sound of his voice makes me hesitate, but it's not just that. He looks pissed. Darkened eyes narrow at me as I pause near the doorway, and then he places a hand on the small of my back and pushes me inside roughly. The glass door rattles as he follows me inside and slams the door shut.

The breath catches in my throat as he takes several furious strides toward me, and my back bumps into the table. Then his hand buries into the back of my head and suddenly his harsh whisper cuts across my ear, the sound remarkably like steel.

"I don't ever remember telling you that you could grab my cock in public."

A small hiccup of fear cuts off my gasp when his hot breath billows over my neck. "I was just returning the favor."

I wince as his fingers tighten around the strands of my hair.

"I think you're a little fucking confused about your role, here."

"Yeah?"

"Smartass."

His hand suddenly wraps around my neck, the other one still pulling my hair, and he spins me so that my back is against his chest. I see myself in the highly reflective glass, chest pulsing under the flimsy dress he picked out for me.

"You do what I say—when I say it. That was the agreement."

My derisive laugh echoes in the empty room. "I'm pretty sure the agreement was that I pay you fifty thousand—"

"I told you. I don't give a fuck about the money." The hand lightly grasping my neck slides down my chest, and then he takes my breast under the dress. Electrical shocks run straight to my pussy as he grabs my nipple between his forefinger and thumb and squeezes. "I want you, and I'll take you as payment. How many fucking times do I have to say it?"

A sudden thrill clenches my core as the words pulse in my head.

I want you.

His fingers splay over my breast, making the breath catch in my throat before he slides his hand to the other one, groping it.

What the hell does that mean? He doesn't want the money anymore?

"But this is just—what about—?"

"Shut up and listen to me."

The gruffness in his voice steals the rest of my words, and for a moment I'm stunned. Who the hell does he think he is?

His thumb circles my nipple, teasing the sensitive flesh, and then his tongue touches my neck. It's hot and cold, like flesh on fire. His mouth closes over the skin and he sucks hard.

"You're my fiancée. That means you're mine, and you'll do as you're told."

I think he's forgetting that this was all an arrangement. My lips pull into a smile and he notices, biting down on my neck hard. The sharp pain makes me yelp.

"Or what?"

Then he grins. "Well, you might just get what you fucking want, that's all."

I'm yanked back as Tony pulls me behind the table, reaching out with an arm to sweep the candles and silverware from the table. They fly off the table, bouncing and clanging noisily over the floor, and then he places a broad hand on my back, pushing me over the table.

"Tony!"

Desperate hands seize the edge of my dress and tug it over my back, exposing my ass to the air. I flatten against the table, the curtains only partially obscuring us from the outside.

Fucking hell, I can see the party from here. All they would have to do is glance over.

"Tony, this is crazy."

"You grabbed my cock in the middle of dinner. What, did you think I was going to ignore that?"

He can't be fucking serious.

But my mind heats at the idea of him taking me right here, where they can see me. It makes me wonder. This was all supposed to be temporary, but we're already breaking down all the rules we set for ourselves, and now he doesn't even want my money?

What the hell is this, exactly?

"I hate to break it to you, but I'm not your fucking slave."

"No, but you're not a fucking princess, either. You don't get to do whatever you want anymore. Understand?"

Scorching hands scrape at my thong, pulling it all the way down my legs. The fabric shivers against my skin, and I moan when he gives me a stinging slap across my ass.

"I asked you a question."

It's not like I'm a stranger to being dominated like this. Rafael loved to 'put me in my place,' but usually that involved beating me into submission. A real man doesn't need to ask. She submits to him because she wants to, because his very presence makes her clit hum. Tony's different.

He's a bad boy, but I know he'd never raise a hand to me.

Well, you know what I mean.

Another hard slap burns my sensitive flesh as the blow reverberates through my body. I can't really think about the pain, everything hones in on how exposed we are. Jesus Christ, I can see them in the distance.

The ringing sound of his palm against my flesh snaps me out of it. I focus on his hand, splayed over my ass. He rubs the burn gently and I feel the warmth of his legs against mine. No one ever spanked me like this. Rafael's hands were always about inflicting pain, but Tony's caress soothes the slight burn.

"I can do this all fucking day."

SLAP!

My body jerks on the table as another blow rips over my right cheek. "Yes—yes, I understand."

He chuckles, the deep sound filling my chest with an angry glow. His hands roll over my curves, never ceasing their movement. It's an incredible feeling.

"I never thought I would want to fuck a woman as often as I fuck you. I'm convinced you've laced your pussy with cocaine to get me addicted."

I smile against the wooden table, and then his fingers curve over my hips and slowly descend to my pussy, which still hums with the vibrator. My shrill gasp echoes in the room as his fingers deftly reach inside, pulling the vibrator from my pussy. He rests it against my clit and then there's a click. Suddenly, I'm moaning against the table, rolling my tits over the hard wood as it makes my clit scream for more. I arch my back as his laughs wash over my ears. My lip bleeds as I bite down. Electricity shoots into my pussy, making it seize over and over.

He rolls the vibrator up and down, moving it in circles around my clit. It's torture. It's maddening. I need him inside me. Now, before I scream out loud and alert the whole place to our shenanigans.

I reach behind myself, touching his leg, feeling the hardness of his muscles before finding his long cock. My fingers slide down his length, feeling the throb beneath the fabric, the cleft of his head, and the slight wetness seeping through his slacks.

With a gritty sort of growl, he pulls his slacks down and I feel the meaty warmth of his cock pressing against my ass.

"You want this, baby? You want my cock inside you?"

"Yes, goddamn it!"

"You're going to have to say it louder."

"But—!"

But they'll hear us!

They're right there, eating dinner. All it would take is one shout, and they'd turn their heads, seeing us partially obscured by the curtains.

"I don't give a fuck about what they think. You should that realize by now."

No, he doesn't give a fuck about anything.

The hand playing with my pussy presses the vibrator against my clit. Severe shocks rip through my core, making it clench madly. I grab the edge of the table, and even the hard surface of the wood against my tits is enough to make me roll my eyes.

"Oh my God…I'm going to come."

He takes the vibrator away, and the blaze reduces to a smaller fire. It's still burning hot, but I'm no longer on the verge of exploding.

"Tony, please fuck me!"

My voice echoes loudly in the room, and he chuckles. I can almost imagine him shaking his head.

"As my wife, you'll have to learn to satisfy your husband."

"Whatever, just fuck me!"

The laughter booming from his throat pisses me off. I want to turn around and grab his lapels, and *force* him to fuck me.

"I need you to scream."

His cock plays with my pussy, the hard length sliding along my lips. I stick out my ass, trying to grind on him, but his broad hand stops me.

Scream? Scream what?

He doesn't make it hard. The vibrator returns with a vengeance, and he slips it inside my wetness, pulsing it against my clit, pulling out and rubbing the sensitive area, and then back inside. It's agony.

"FUCK ME!"

The scream rips from my throat, and then my cheeks

flood with shame as I see people at the table looking around for the noise.

Oh fuck.

But I forget all that the moment he flings the toy away, gripping my hips to position himself. The broad head of his cock pushes against my entrance and then he slides in, my walls tight around him. He sighs as though he stepped into a warm bath, and then he digs in hard, knocking the air from my chest. It's almost painful, but I'm so intent on clinging to him that I don't give a shit.

I hear the grin in his voice. "I'm going to hammer your cunt so hard, you won't be able to walk straight."

And he does. My arms fly out, trying to seize purchase as he thrusts hard enough to throw my body forward. Solid hands wrench my hips backward, and every time his hips connect with mine in a loud *smack*, I groan out loud.

"Who owns you? Say it."

A choked off scream rips through my throat as his cock throbs inside me, pounding so hard I can feel the pain rocking through my body. Then he pulls out and turns me around so that I'm flat on my back, face to face with him.

For the first time, I see him as he really is. He's not some guy I just paid to do a job for me. He's Tony Vidal, a man who always gets what he wants, a wiseguy who has decided he must have me.

My legs hitch over his shoulder as he thrusts inside me. He leans over, my legs screaming as he seizes a fistful of my hair and kisses me. His hot, urgent tongue swallows my protests, chokes off my moans, and I realize how much I've been craving this. All this time we've been fucking, it was good, clean fun, but it was empty.

This is completely different. It's dirty and angry— reminding me of home in a twisted way. I need to feel like I belong to someone. He bites my tongue as I scream into his mouth, but he keeps rutting me hard as if he fucking hates me. I love it.

He's fucking a new feeling inside me, something that makes me kiss him harder. I'm surrendering to him.

His cock pulses inside me, and I cling to his neck, moaning as he utters a groan and his legs slam hard into the table. Then I clench around him, feeling the explosion rip through me. Tenderness clenches my heart as he pulls me upright, wrapping his arms around me as his cock fills me with his essence.

My hand smoothes his lapels as his chest rises and falls, and I curl my fingers around his neck, gazing into his eyes, wrinkled with happiness. I feel lucky to have him. I'm growing more and more infatuated with him, or maybe it's the glow of the orgasm making my heart pound harder when he gives me a gentle kiss.

"You've never fucked me like that before."

"Did you like it?"

Then it's my turn to lean in closer to whisper in his ear. *"Do it again."*

* * *

It starts off like a small spark. Yellow bursts of light flinging out into space, only to disappear almost immediately. Over and over again, until it catches. Just one little flame, fairly easy to snuff out.

That's what I've got. A little flame. It quietly warms my chest as I watch him get ready for his work. There's no denying that I've got it pretty bad for him. I don't know where it came from, but all of a sudden, I'm attached. Pinpricks of fear spread over my skin as I think about his work and the kind of trouble he might get himself into.

I like him, and I don't know what to do about it.

His gaze meets mine through his bathroom mirror as notices my stare. "What is it?"

My face flushes as though he can tell what I'm thinking by watching my eyes, and I shrug. He hesitates for a moment, and continues shaving.

"I'm going to my place to pick up a few things."

He bends his face into the sink, washing his face before drying it off with a fresh towel. The light switches off and bathes him in darkness.

"And what if that shit stain is waiting for you there?"

Gentle hands cradle my face as he walks to the bed. Sometimes it hurts to see the indifference on his face. He rarely ever comes to life, except when he's thrusting between my legs.

"Well, we're engaged. He can't touch me."

"Yeah, except there's the problem of the fucking baby. Anyway, that reminds me."

He pulls something out of his pocket. A small, black box. My heart thumps hard against my chest, even though I know it's just for show. Even though it's not really for me.

Tony takes my hand as he opens the box, revealing a beautiful white gold ring with a princess cut diamond. He takes it out of its snug confinement and slowly slides it on my ring finger.

"Like it?"

Like it? "It's—it's beautiful. Where did you get it?"

He smiles at me. "Don't worry about it."

Probably stolen, then.

It dazzles in the light, all the diamond cut shards in the band sparkling as I turn it to catch the beams.

"Is it weird that I'm much more excited about this than I should be?"

"It's just a ring, Elena."

The frost in his voice dampens my happiness, and I feel myself slam hard into the ground. Back to reality.

He doesn't want to get married. Stop this right now.

Then he stoops down slightly and kisses the top of my head. "I'm glad you like it."

Ready for work, he heads to the front door and I follow him. He gives me a nervous smile as he glances at the ring on my finger.

"See you later, I guess."

The fabric of his jacket feels abrasive in my hands, but I pull him toward me anyway. I smell his aftershave on his slightly damp cheeks and I turn my head, crushing my lips against his. He smiles against mine, laughing at some joke in his head, and I slide the palm of my hand down his slacks, anchoring over his cock. He groans.

"Do all broads get wet over a diamond ring, or is that just a stereotype?"

I don't know what it is.

"It's you. You make me this way."

A grin lightens his face as he gently takes my hand away from his cock. "Stop getting me turned on before I have to leave."

"It's your fault for giving me this right before leaving."

His eyes twinkle with mischief. "Hell, you're right. I

should at least get a thank you blowjob."

"When you come back," I promise.

"Fuck." He eyes my mouth with a carnal look that he somehow stuffs it down.

I take his chin, my insides fluttering as I give him a soft kiss. His eyes stay closed when I pull away, and when they open I think I can see something flicker inside them.

"Bye, Tony."

My words seem to snap him into action, and he mechanically leans forward, kissing my cheek. He lingers a little bit too long, but he still turns away to leave.

And a wild happiness lifts me up into the sky as though wings decided to sprout from my shoulders. I dress for the cold and make my way to my apartment, stuck in that content fog. God, I'm becoming one of those people. Those blissfully unaware people walking down the street that I used to want to strangle, because the happiness that everyone seemed to have always escaped me.

It was always: hide, be quiet, keep your head down and hope for calmer waters.

I unlock the door to my apartment, my spirit falling as I see the mess all over the floors. There wasn't any time to come back after Rafael destroyed the place. For a moment my arms wrap around my body and a chill runs through me as though there's an open window somewhere.

You shouldn't have come here.

My limbs freeze even though my heart hammers against my chest. The horrific thought hisses in my ear in a harsh whisper.

Leave. Now.

I watch myself take a step toward the door. My hand reaches for the doorknob. I turn it. It's locked. I must have locked it without even thinking. Then it takes me an eon to unlock it, the brass locks moving in slow motion. Footsteps echo hollowly in my heart. They're hard and fast. A pressure squeezing down on my shoulder amps up the terror, and my voice lifts to the ceiling. Another hand clamps down hard over my mouth, cutting off the scream.

No. Oh God, no.

"You keep coming back here," the dark voice says. "It's almost as if you want me back."

He pulls me into his body, his achingly familiar contours jutting into me. Then he takes his hand away from my mouth as something cold bites into my neck.

"Make a sound, and I'll spill your dirty Vittorio blood all over the floor."

That seething undertone in his voice makes my blood harden into ice. That deadly calm terrifies me more than anything. It means that he has nothing to lose and he's not afraid to slit my throat.

Tony warned me. What the fuck was I thinking, coming here alone?

"Get off me!"

His arm tightens around both my arms like a python coiling around my body, slowly squeezing me to death. "Why should I?"

Rafael drags me further into the apartment, and my feet follow him backwards.

"What are you doing?"

Arms pinned to my side, I'm fucking helpless. Every pause makes the knife cut into my throat, and something warm tickles down my neck. It's only until he drags me into the bathroom that I see the line of blood.

"Rafael, I'm engaged. He will fucking kill you!"

The door slams shut and he hurls me away from him. I slip on the tiles and fall on the toilet seat, gazing up at Rafael's disheveled body.

He points the knife at me. "I'll fucking kill you. We're going to find out once and for all whether you are pregnant."

His black jeans swim in front of me and the flat of his blade slaps my cheek. "I know it's not beyond you to lie about something like this. You come from a family of rats."

Burning, caustic rage explodes in my chest. "You just

can't stand the fact that I've found someone else. That I left *you*."

 I expect the blow, but it still hurts when his palm rips across my face. I catch myself almost immediately, gripping the edge of the toilet seat. He slams the knife on the counter and grabs a long box from a plastic bag.

It's a pregnancy test.

My eyes burn as I take the box from him, shaking.

What the fuck am I supposed to do? I know what it's going to be negative. I take my birth control pills religiously. It was a lie to make people would believe our very abrupt, out of nowhere marriage.

Rafael takes the knife, his eyes simmering. "Take off your pants. Do it."

He expects me to do this now? In front of him?

"At least give me some privacy."

"What's the matter? Are you afraid what it'll say?" He smirks at me knowingly, giving the cheek where he slapped me a little tap. "Oh, I already fucking know you're a piece of shit liar. I just need proof."

"Then what? I'm still Tony's fiancée."

He leans in, his narrowed eyes almost gleaming with red as he presses his shaking lips to my ear. "You won't be when Johnny finds out you paid Tony off with money that should've been given to Vince."

A hole gapes inside me as though all my organs were sucked out by a vacuum. Dad never told me how he got the money, or where it was from. I never considered that it might not be entirely his, and I know Johnny. He doesn't give a shit about me.

"Take off your clothes."

Tears burn down my face as I look up at him, wanting to spare myself the humiliation of taking this test in front of him, but the knife doesn't waver from my face. I stand up and pull down my jeans and panties in one swoop, opening up the toilet seat and sitting down before he has a chance to look.

Then I rip open the packaging and grab the pregnancy test. It looks like a thermometer. I take the cap off and tear the foil from the applicator, and then I just stare at it.

"Do it."

I don't have a choice.

Even though I know what it'll say. Even though I know it's hopeless, I point it toward my body and I relieve myself, jaw clenched shut. Then Rafael takes it from me.

"We have to wait three minutes. Here, do another one."

To my astonishment, he shoves another box in my hand as he prepares a line of coke on my bathroom counter, cutting it with a small mirror before snorting the line. Jesus. No wonder he looks like shit.

I wonder if I could just charge him right now—or maybe I should just grab my cell phone. It's in my back pocket, sticking out. A few quick movements, and I'd have Tony on the phone.

Not before he'd drag that knife across my throat.

I take the second test and give it to him. My stomach turns as the seconds tick by, and I see the cocaine coursing through Rafael's system. The knife taps impatiently against the sink, and then he looks down at the test.

The knife clatters against the sink—an ugly sound that makes me flinch.

He clenches the edge of the sink, his head hanging down, staring at the test results. It's maddening.

"What the fuck?"

He says it in a soft voice that terrifies me, and I don't know why it does. The second test—he grabs that, too.

"Oh my God."

A shaking hand covers his mouth, and his head turns toward me, his eyes swimming with tears.

Tears.

What in the fucking fuck?

I can count on my hand the times I've seen Rafael cry. The first was when he hit me while my dad was still alive, when he was petrified for his life. The second is now.

"I'm so sorry, Elena."

His words slam into my chest and I grab my jeans and panties, pulling them up as I walk over and push him aside. I look at the pregnancy tests. That positive, pink plus burns in my eyes. The other one has two pink lines.

Pregnant.

I'm actually pregnant.

WHAT THE FUCK?

I can't scream it out loud, because Rafael's arms wrap around my waist, burying his face in my neck.

"I'm sorry, I didn't know."

His apologies are thick with tears, but I don't feel a thing. Pregnant? How the hell is this possible?

Has to be a mistake. A false positive.

I can't entertain the possibility that this might be true, that I might be pregnant, because how much of a disaster that would be? Assuming it's Tony's, he'd flip the fuck out. He doesn't even want to get married. What'll his reaction be when he finds out I'm carrying his child?

How am I supposed to bring a baby into my fucked up life?

A smooth hand cradles my belly, and a wave of revulsion rises inside me. I shove Rafael's body away from me.

"I fucking told you!"

Regret flashes over his lined face. "Baby, I—I didn't know. This changes—*holy Christ*, I can't believe I'm going to be a father."

The fucking arrogance.

"What makes you think it's even yours?" I seethe, enjoying the hurt transforming his face.

He raises his fists and my back hits the wall. He's close enough so that I can feel his breath billowing over my face. "Don't fucking push me, Elena."

"Do you actually think that I would allow you to be in my child's life? Look at you! You're a fucking junkie."

His nostrils flare. "Our child. And I'd like to see you make me stay away."

"A few minutes ago, you were willing to slit my throat!"

His face pinches together. "I made a mistake—"

"—I would be dead, along with the baby. You're not fit to be a father!"

"FUCK YOU!"

I scream as he punches his fist through the dry wall next to my head, cowering as bits of plaster rain down. Rafael steps back, looking at his bloody hand in mild shock as he backs away from me.

That hole in the wall could've been me.

"You're fucking *crazy*. Stay away from me!"

"Elena—"

He reaches forward with an apologetic hand, but I smack it away. He has the balls to look at me with a wounded face.

"I won't tell Tony about this as long as you leave Montreal tonight. We both know he'll have every reason in the world to kill you after this."

Before he can respond, I sweep out of the bathroom, eager just to get the fuck out of this apartment and mull over everything that happened.

My chest feels incredibly tight, and the moment I step outside I gasp for air.

The tests could be false positives. Don't freak out yet. Find out for sure.

But I just know that I am. I don't know how or why, but some kind of sixth sense tells me that I'm carrying a child and I should be thankful that I am.

Otherwise who knows what he would've done to me.

I can't think about it until I know for sure.

Using my phone, I find the nearest hospital and walk through the doors, blinking at all the French signs. An hour later, I'm staring at a nurse as she congratulates me on my pregnancy. It's positive. I'm pregnant.

"How effective is this test?"

"Up to 99%. *Mademoiselle*, do you want me to schedule a prenatal appointment?"

As I stare into the nurse's happy, young face, tears well up in my eyes. I can't be fucking pregnant. There's no way—I take those pills every day.

But you might've forgotten a couple days. During that first night with Tony. You were upset. The pills were at home. You didn't take one.

Fuck, that's right. I might've missed a few days—shit, what was I thinking?

This is such a mess. I don't want this baby—

Get an abortion.

It burns in my head, the forbidden word blazing, almost tangible on my lips, but I know that I can't. The very idea fills me with horror. Not because it's a sin. I don't know—I just can't do it. I can't snuff out a life.

The nurse tries her best to comfort me, and sends me home with a thick envelope of pamphlets and forms and numbers of doctors I need to see and how am I going to tell this to Tony? How, exactly, am I going to break this to him?

I play with my cell phone, miserably contemplating phoning my sister about the news. My thumb hovers over his name.

I just can't do it.

I don't want him to hate me, too. So far, he's the only person in the world who gives some semblance of a shit about me.

He's the father of your child. He should know.

Not yet, I whisper desperately to the voice. *Not fucking yet.*

* * *

"Where were you?"

The question slams down on my shoulders the moment I walk through the door.

I didn't expect him to be back so soon.

Tony walks into the foyer, dark hair tousled and his smoky eyes narrowed in suspicion. The moment I see him, it's like a little jump to my heart. It's like my body knows that he's the one who got me pregnant.

I take his hands and look into his gruff face, which demands for an answer.

Tell him.

I open my mouth.

He deserves to know.

"I went out for a bit."

"*Where?*" The heat in his voice makes me flinch. "I kept calling you, and you never answered. I thought something might've happened to you."

You're a coward.

My body feels tense, like a taut rubber band. I'm stretched way too thin, and any moment I'll snap. Pressure builds behind my eyes: the baby, the wedding, Rafael, all of it. It's one giant clusterfuck, and now he's giving me a hard time.

"Well, *I'm fine.*"

In seconds, he's in my space, hip bumping against mine. Eyes narrowed in disapproval capture my gaze. It's hard to look at him without feeling incredibly guilty.

"Are you giving me attitude?"

"Yeah, maybe I fucking am."

He doesn't deserve this. I know that, but I'm pissed and there's no one else to blame but him. Because he did, after all, get me fucking pregnant. I'm pissed. It was never supposed to be like this. I never wanted to get knocked up from a one-night stand. How fucking trashy is that?

He laughs as I try to push him away and catches my elbow. "Good. I like a girl with attitude. Makes it all the more satisfying when I shove my cock in her mouth." He runs his thumb over my bottom lip, giving me a look that makes me smolder against my will.

I can't help but want him.

"You promised me a blowjob, and I intend to get it."

His sweet breath heats my face, and I lean forward, irresistibly drawn to his mouth. I kiss him, and my chest heats up as he deepens the kiss, tongue sliding in my mouth. Damn, I love his fucking body. But—*no!*

I push his chest gently with my hand, and he gives me a puzzled look. "What's wrong?"

I'm pregnant.

It hangs over my lips, but I desperately want to keep it a secret. This marriage might as well be real now that I'm pregnant, and I have no idea who this guy is. No idea at all, and I'm having his baby.

"I don't know you, and we're getting married in a week."

"I don't know what to tell you," he says with a grin. "This was your idea, not mine."

A sharp, desperate gasp echoes in the room as I imagine the white dress, the ceremony, doctor visits, and all the while, dealing with my ex. Meanwhile, I'm pregnant and he has no idea. There's not an inkling of suspicion in Tony's eyes that I just might be developing feelings for him.

"I can't do this anymore. This was a mistake—a stupid, *stupid* mistake!"

The pressure on both my shoulders increase and suddenly I collapse into a chair, Tony's fierce face in front of mine.

"Oh no you don't. You're not fucking backing out now."

I bristle under his gaze. "Says who?"

"Aside from the fact that it's a piss poor idea, because that lunatic will follow you wherever you go, *I say so*. We already told everyone about it. It's too late for last-minute regrets."

I rise to my feet defiantly, and he pulls my waist toward him. "I want to know the man I'm marrying, even if it's not real."

He rolls his eyes. "What difference does it make?"

"It'll make me feel better."

Then his arms drop around from my sides and he gets his coat from the closet, handing out mine.

"Where are we going?"

"We're going out."

Now it's my turn to roll my eyes. "Why?"

"To get to know each other."

TONY

The silent white stones lean out of the grassy knoll like strange growths. There are hundreds of them. Faceless tombstones, some of their words unintelligible through countless years of wear and tear. I'm walking over bodies. A cold, clammy feeling flattens my stomach as I climb the hill, Elena not far behind me.

"You brought me to a cemetery?"

Nothing can disguise the fact that one of these days—sooner rather than later—I'll be sleeping under the ground just like Dad.

"You wanted to know me."

I slap my hand over my father's tombstone.

VITO ANTONIO VIDAL

BELOVED FATHER AND HUSBAND

(1956 - 1995)

Three lines of text and a hole in the ground. That's all you get for a lifetime of service to the family. Your kid gets to watch you get buried, gets to watch his mother cry every goddamn day for the rest of his life.

I never wanted to be like him. I never wanted to join the Mafia.

Her eyes pinch together as she reads the inscription, and I suddenly wonder why the hell I brought her here. What does it matter whether she knows me or not?

But she wants to know me—she asked. I never let anyone get close enough to ask me questions. I'd get naked with them before I'd let them ask me a single goddamn thing about myself, not that any of them cared.

All I know is that I just can't keep this inside me anymore.

She takes a cautious step forward and touches my chest. "How did he die?"

"He was big time. A captain. He became a huge target during this war between several biker gangs in the city. The family backed *Les Diables*, which made all members targets of the Machine MC. One day, they just popped him. I was eight."

The pain of that loss still smarts, but it's duller now.

"I told myself I'd never join the life. I didn't want to go the same way my father did, leaving behind a wife and kid."

With a small push off the tombstone, I turn away from Elena and walk down the hill. Her footsteps trudge behind me, and then her arm curls around mine. It's as if the landscape brightens. I don't feel as fucking bad when she's around.

Christ, I've really changed.

Gradually, though, I'm shutting down. The closer and closer we get, my insides twist and bunch together. My skin freezes—I haven't been to visit her in years.

Then finally, I get there.

It's a small, modest tombstone because her family didn't have any money. I scraped together what I had and paid for her funeral and burial. Elena stands shock still in front of the stone, her lips moving silently.

MARIA ELIZABETH DESBIENS

(1985 - 2002)

"She was my girlfriend. And she was the reason I joined."

Elena's mouth widens, and I don't blame her. I've such a shitty reputation for sticking my dick into anything that moves, it's hard to believe that I had a girlfriend. That I was once in love. That we were going to—*fuck*. It doesn't matter.

Nothing matters.

"She was killed. I went to the boss at the time and asked him for vengeance. He would only give it to me if I joined their ranks. So I did."

And I regretted it ever since.

I think she can see it in my eyes. Fuck it, I don't care about holding back anymore. I don't want to do this anymore. The killing, the violence, the pain I inflict everyday numbed me to every feeling, good and bad. Following my father's footsteps was never something that I wanted. I joined because I was young and stupid, and it's a mistake I have to live with for the rest of my life.

Maybe if I turned off everything, I'd be fine.

But I can't become yet another one of the dead-eyed assholes I work with. I just don't have it in me. Part of me is ashamed to admit that.

"So you never wanted this life?"

"Don't tell nobody."

She smiles weakly, her eyes shining with pity. I don't need that—I don't want it. It's my fault. The decision to join was mine. I'm just having a hard time living with it. Pussy and booze just doesn't cut it anymore.

"How old are you?"

"I'm 33. I like to drink Irish whiskey. I love French onion soup and I can't stand Tim Hortons. My favorite color is blue. Christmas is my favorite holiday, and I love skiing in the winter."

"What about—"

I grasp her shoulders and that seems to silence her. "None of that shit tells you who I am, Elena. Don't you see? It doesn't *matter*. You'll find out who I am."

I release a long breath, feeling the tension exhale out of

my lungs. "So what about you? I told you my big secret."

Elena shrugs, looking at the ground. "I'm 27. I don't have anyone and I don't really know what to do with my life. I hate raw tomatoes—"

"What?"

"I hate tomatoes."

My jaw drops. "You're Italian."

"I know." She narrows her eyes at me.

"You hate tomatoes? Seriously? That's like saying, 'I hate onions.' What the hell kind of—"

"You don't think I've gotten shit from my parents my whole life because of that? I hate the texture, but I don't mind when they're cooked in stuff. Anyway, my favorite color is pink and I have two siblings that I don't get along with. When Dad was boss, it was like having a big family. That's all gone now."

I'm still reeling over the shock of a full-blooded Italian hating tomatoes.

"Who cares?" I rasp finally. "They whacked your dad. You don't want anything to do with them anyway."

"I know, but they were all I had."

Her eyes are like two dark pools, and some of her sadness reaches inside me when she meets my eyes. Really, we're not that different. Both of our families were destroyed by the mob, and yet we're still indebted to them.

"What would you have done if you weren't in the life?"

My lips pull into a bitter smile. "I have no fucking clue."

I never gave it a thought, because this is all I know. Even if Johnny allowed me to leave, what would I do? I have no skills.

Her face breaks into a watery smile. "I guess we're both hopeless."

We descend the hill in silence, my head full of troubling thoughts. I don't know anything, I just know that my chest tightens when she smiles at me, and my desire for her is out of control. The wedding doesn't really bother me as much as it should anymore. I *like* the idea of her becoming mine.

"Elena, this wedding is happening," I tell her as we reach my car. "*Capiche?* I'm not stopping it for anything."

Her eyes burn with questions I'm not sure I can answer. She opens her mouth, protesting—

"Look, it doesn't mean we're *in love* or any of that shit. It just means we understand each other. You need my help, and I need your smoking-hot body."

Her cheeks flush as I wrap my arm around her waist. She wears a thin cotton dress underneath her coat, and I told her not to wear panties. It must be cold. Hell, it's the middle of January.

My hand curls around her bare thigh, pushing the dress higher and higher up her legs until she hisses through her teeth.

"Tony, we're in a parking lot."

Since when do I give a fuck?

"No one can see what I'm doing to you."

My body blocks her from view, but a thrill leaps inside me at the thought of someone catching a glimpse.

"Why is it that you always want to share me?"

Even though it's cold, her legs feel like a furnace. My fingers run over her smooth skin, over her shaved mound, and then I just graze her pussy. It's wet for me. She's always fucking wet for me.

"I would never share you. I'm showing off what's mine."

She attacks me the moment I slip my finger inside her. The smooth walls wrap around my finger like a glove as she throws her arms around my neck and moans loud enough to let the whole parking lot know what we're up to. My cock stiffens in my pants when I hear how turned on she is. Elena arches her body against mine and crushes her lips over my mouth. Her hand drops down and seizes my cock, and it's like an electric shock. Blood pounds through my dick and I bury my fingers in her wet cunt, curving inward as she moans in my mouth.

"You belong to me, baby. Just look how wet you are."

Heavy brown eyes stare into mine. "You belong to me, too."

I grin at that, but she's right. There's no denying that this girl has me, hook, line, and sinker. No one else captures my attention like her. No one gets me as hard as she does.

"I'm yours, but more importantly, *you're mine*."

I twist my fingers inside her, knowing how close she is based on her rapid breaths. Her face flushes and she bites her lip, trying to contain herself as I keep finger-fucking her.

She unzips my pants in one swift movement and yanks my briefs down. We couldn't be more exposed, but she looks at me with that desperate look that I'm addicted to.

"I need you."

Yes, she does need me.

The cold air bites my cock, but I hitch up her dress and guide my cock to her steaming pussy, which feels like a hot bath. I sink inside her, my face buried in her tits. Jesus it's so warm and tight. I glide inside her, thrusting deep as she squeezes around me.

"There's—there's someone coming!"

My teeth graze her perfect tits. "Let them watch." Smiling at her horrified face, I take as much of her as I can in my mouth and suck hard, digging my cock as deep as it'll go.

Her fingers wrench my hair as she lets out another guttural sound.

"I need you to come, baby. I can't get off unless you come."

Out of the corner of my eye, I see a couple standing unnaturally still in the parking lot as if they can't believe what they're seeing. Awesome.

She blushes hard. "I—I can't!"

"I can do this all day." I thrust hard, her body arching up my car.

Well, no. I couldn't. I'd blow a load before long, because she keeps squeezing my cock while it glides up her slick walls. Another harsh cry tears from her throat, rebounding through the parking lot, and the couple in the distance turns around. I see them holding a cell phone.

"They're calling the cops. Better hurry."

I slide my dick out of her pussy as she rakes my shoulders, and then I bend to my knee, pulling her dress over my head. Her slightly swollen pussy contracts when she feels my breath over her wet skin. Then I roll my tongue over her clit.

She makes a sound as though she's in pain. It must feel amazing in the cold to have something hot and wet engulf you. Her hips grind against my mouth as I fuck her with my mouth, sucking her juices inside me, using my fingers to pound her hard. I have three inside her, curving into that bed of nerves that makes her legs shudder. I want her as close to the edge as possible. My mouth closes over her clit and sucks hard as my tongue runs along her wetness.

"TONY!"

I stand up, her dress flattening against my body as I bury myself back inside her throbbing pussy. She clings to my shoulder and cries as she comes hard around my cock. Somehow, one of her straps falls down her arm and her bouncing tits pop out of her dress. I grab one, digging my fingers into her flesh as her nipple hardens against my palm. My fingernail pinches her nub as my hips grind against hers. The friction builds up and my balls tighten. I'm overwhelmed with the smell of her around me. She's all mine for me to do whatever I want with.

She yanks my head toward hers and her tongue slips into my mouth. I bite down hard as my cock explodes, filling her pussy with my cum. She kisses me blindly, just as crazy for me as I am for her. A flash of red and blue make my heart thump hard against my ribs. I bend down and yank my pant back up as she slips to the pavement. Then I give the couple in the distance a sarcastic wave.

"Enjoy the show?" I bellow out to them.

Elena yanks on my jacket. "Let's go."

Chuckling, I turn back toward her. I gather her beautiful face in my hands and I plant a soft kiss over her red lips, smoothing my thumbs over her cold cheeks. Aftershocks of pleasure run through my body as she slips her hands around my waist.

And I don't want her to let go.

* * *

The hushed whispers of the congregation echo through the cavernous church. I stand at the altar, hands flexing at my side. That hair-raising, unnerving song I've sat through so many times begins as a slow line of profession moves down the aisle. My stomach clenches as everyone's gaze turns back. Elena's sister appears in a champagne-colored dress. I've already forgotten her name, but I felt a strong surge of dislike when I shook her hand. She has an upturned, snotty look to her face, and seemed to be annoyed at the fact that she had to come all the way here.

Ma's already sobbing in the front row, and I try to avoid looking at her as the small procession moves down the aisle. My chest tightens as the wedding march increases in crescendo, and I think about how wrong this is—how I loathe these boring as fuck weddings, and how we should have done it in my Ma's backyard—tradition be damned. I could give a fuck about religion, and having all these eyes on me isn't pleasant.

A sliver of white moves into the room and everyone's head turns to look at my bride to be. My chest swells as she walks down the aisle in a white dress that clings to her body, showing off just enough skin to make my breath catch in my throat. The neckline dips down in a V, exposing her neck and just a hint of cleavage. Her hair is pulled up into an elegant bun, dark, smoky makeup around her eyes and light lipstick. She looks beautiful. So beautiful that my heart clenches when she reaches me.

This is it.

No turning back.

I want to reach around her head and let her hair fall to her shoulders. She doesn't look like the girl I saw in the bar—the girl who gives me so many hard-ons throughout the day that I worry my dick might fall off. I only half-listen to the priest as he prattles on and on in Italian, and I wonder why the fuck we always have these ceremonies where we can't understand the fucking words. He repeats them in French, and then in English.

To have and to hold, in sickness and in health. Blah, blah, blah.

It doesn't feel real. All of it is wrong—the church, the

music, her hair, my future sister-in-law, with a sour look on her face. Elena's trembling face.

I kiss her anyway as cheers explode in the church.

I'll make her mine in my own way, when she won't have that terrified look on her face. When I say the words, I want to mean them.

We just have to get through this bullshit.

Her hand shakes in mine as we walk down the aisle, and I smile back at Johnny's beaming face. He can't resist pounding my back as I walk past him. Sunshine pours over our heads as we leave the church to the limo waiting for us. I hold the door open for her and she bends her head as she steps inside.

"We'll meet you there!"

A wave of exhaustion hits me as I join her in the limo and shut the car door. She looks at me with the same frightened expression she had on the altar, and I catch a glimpse of her left hand, which gleams with the ring I gave her.

She turns her perfectly manicured face toward me. "I need a fucking drink."

Good thing there's champagne in the limo. I fish it out of the ice and pop open the cork, tilting the foam into a tall, skinny glass for her. She holds it daintily while I pour one for myself.

What should I toast to?

Elena seems to consider her glass before her cheeks flush and she extends it toward me. "I forgot—I'm pregnant."

I take it from her, grinning. "No one's here to see you except me."

She shakes her head. "I don't want to risk it."

Risk what? I take it from her and take the bottle of sparkling cider instead, filling her glass with that instead.

"To us."

A weak smile flickers on her face as she bumps her glass against mine and drinks. "I can't believe we actually did it."

She shoots me a guilty look that makes my insides flip. We both said we would keep a distance from each other— we wouldn't let feelings get in the way, but it already feels different. That small little band around her finger marks her as mine. She's an extension of myself—my reputation, my pride, even my life.

No one can fucking touch her while I'm alive.

"I can't wait to see that piece of shit's face when he sees my ring on your finger." My arm wraps around her waist and I pull her over my lap, running my hands over her bare arms.

"It's not official until the marriage is consummated."

Her voice is like a caress over my cock. It hardens between my legs, throbbing to life when she gives me that steamy look.

"Fuck, you're right. No matter how many times I've filled you with my cum—"

Elena's cheeks, already rosy, darken in color. "*Tony*, the driver!"

I grin as I glance at the partition in front of us.

"Do you think he'd mind if I fucked you in his backseat?"

Her eyes widen. "Tony, *no*! We still have the reception. Don't you fucking dare mess my hair!"

"I don't give a shit what your hair looks like."

"Well, I do, and that's one thing you're going to have to learn as my new husband. How to compromise."

Laughter shakes from my chest as her face burns with fury. "Compromise?"

"*Yeah*. You know, doing things you don't necessarily want to do for the sake of getting along. Meeting each other halfway?"

It sounds like hell. How many times have I heard guys bitch about their wives demanding that they attend their father's birthday party, or their sister's baby shower?

"But you're my wife. Aren't you supposed to fuck me whenever I want?"

"Yeah, it doesn't work like that. This ain't the fifties." This time she grabs my jaw and gives me a slow, burning kiss.

I pull back from her, breathing hard.

"What's the point of being married, then?"

The dress sighs as she lifts her shoulder in a shrug. "Responsibility toward one another. Did you even listen to the vows?" she says with a laugh in her voice.

"I was too busy thinking about how I was going to consummate the marriage."

The car rings with her laughter, which is a relief to see. Elena doesn't smile often, but when she does it makes my heart pound.

I pull her into another kiss, sliding my hand under her dress to grip her smooth thighs. Her hand grips my abs over the dress shirt, and then over the bunched up fabric where my cock grows. Fuck. I fist my hand in her hair. She makes a complaining sound, but I don't give a shit.

"I've got all the cards, and I'm not sorry for it. I'm not going to compromise. I'm not going to change. You picked me, remember?"

Her mouth trembles. "I didn't know this would happen."

"Well, neither did I, hon. I didn't expect your pussy to taste so sweet."

"*Don't talk to me like that.* I'm not just your fucking plaything."

That word makes my blood scalding hot. She's not just a toy. Not anymore.

"No, you're my wife."

She lays a hand on my neck and heat flares across my skin like a sudden burn. I can't believe how sudden it is—like an allergic reaction bursting all over me. It's automatic, now. I have no control over my body. She launches herself at me, so quickly that I'm convinced she's fighting me, but then she crushes her fiery lips against mine, and I free my cock from my slacks. I rip the pins from her hair and pull her tresses down until her beautiful, wavy brown hair spills over her shoulders and she shakes her head with a relieved sigh.

"I didn't wear panties."

I almost laugh out loud.

"So considerate."

My hand strokes her inner thigh, inching closer until I discover that she's right. My fingers brush over the smooth skin joining her leg to her hip. She didn't wear panties to her own wedding. Jesus.

I palm her pussy and stroke the line of wetness gathering between her legs. It's glides over my fingers as she inhales sharply. The sound of her juices sliding over my fingers makes blood pound in my ears, and every small sound is amplified. The blood rush starts in my head, running to every surface until I can feel my lips burning. Every fiber of my being wants her. I fist my cock as a bead of precum rolls down my shaft, and she raises her hips silently. Her eyes burn with the same need.

She sinks down, her soaking wet cunt almost immediately swallowing my cock. Her heat wraps around me and instant bliss floods into my veins, pounding through me. It's much more intense now. All I can see is her. All I can feel is the blood rushing to my cock. She wraps her arms around my neck and kisses me feverishly, and I marvel at the fact that something as simple as a kiss could make me so goddamn hot for her. I grab her shoulders and thrust into her as the car drives on, laughing when the driver slams the privacy screen over the partition.

"Tony, we're going to be there soon."

"Like I give a fuck."

Elena shudders in my arms, feeling my thick cock slamming inside her. I lift up her dress, bunching it in my hand so that her bare ass sits on my legs. Fuck, it's a sexy look. I grab both cheeks and lift her, watching as my thick cock slides out of her, shining. I hammer her hard, loving how she gasps at the force of my thrusts. Then I spank her ass so that the sound cracks in the limo, which has finally stopped.

Panic fills her gaze. "Tony, we're here. They're going to open the door!"

Buried balls deep inside her, I throw her dress back over her ass just as Johnny opens the door. How the fuck did he beat us here?

He takes one look at our disheveled appearance and his face cracks with a wide grin. Elena's face burns like the setting sun, and she hides it in my neck.

I feel no shame.

Johnny shakes his head. "Couldn't wait till after the reception?"

"Fuck that."

Laughter booms from his chest as he shuts the door on us, shaking his head as he walks to the sidewalk.

"Oh my God, I'm so embarrassed."

"You are?" I turn her face toward mine and thrust hard. Her blush deepens. "Cause if you are, I'll stop."

There's no fucking way I'll stop.

"No, don't."

"That's my girl. Focus on me."

"But—" She turns her head, distracted by the group of people waiting outside.

"Forget about them, hon. Trust me, they wish they

could be in my shoes. Too fucking bad you're all mine now."

With her face buried in my neck, she lifts her hips and grinds my cock, making me gasp. It's so sudden, and then she's lifting her body and she moves between my legs. She kneels in her wedding dress and takes my wet cock in her hands. I fist her hair.

It's so fucking wrong.

Her lipstick smudged, she takes my cock deep in her mouth and I rut her. Her lips close, making a tight seal as I pulse in and out of her mouth.

All the way. All the fucking way.

She's my wife, and I'll make her drink every fucking last drop. I make her swallow my cock. It bulges down her throat as she kneels on the floor of the limo, taking her husband in as deep as she can. Her lips squeeze against my balls. Holy fuck.

My cock releases hot jets of cum as I keep her head there, her tongue swirling around my head. I groan and pull out, pulsing a few more times as more streams burst from my head.

A tightening feeling in my chest almost feels painful. My hands brush the strands from her face as I lift her up with my other arm. I pull her over my lap and give her another kiss. It's soft and electrical shocks keep making my breath catch in my chest.

I've never felt like this before.

Her lips move and we break apart. "We should probably get out of the car."

My eyes flick toward the crowd of people waiting for us, and I suppress a laugh. "I guess."

"Jesus Christ, I'm a mess."

We both do what we can to fix our appearances, and then we step into the wintry air. They howl at us the moment we leave the limo, Francois, Johnny, all of them clapping their hands. It doesn't bother me. We're married. Married people have sex. Who the fuck cares?

Elena does. She shoots me a heated look as we walk to the reception hall, which is a beautiful place. Glass windows everywhere, and a garden surrounding the outside. Elena gazes at the high ceilings and mouths a "wow."

As soon as we walk in the room, the guests stand from their seats and applaud us. Elena's hand twitches in mine as we take our seats at the sweetheart table. My mother beams at me from the table with my aunts and cousins, and I feel another twist of guilt.

The evening drags on. They clink their silverware against glasses and I bring Elena's burning face in for a quick kiss to appease the assholes. I see all the attention wearing on her. She smiles at me, but there's a tinge of fear trembling her lips. Or maybe she's just overwhelmed.

This isn't what I wanted either.

Tommy joins us at the table, dressed in a dark charcoal suit and wearing a smile on his slick face. "Hey, guys. *Congratulations*," he says in a sarcastic voice. "Biggest scam anyone's ever pulled."

The big glass of wine in his hands sways dangerously. He looks unconcerned when I rise to my feet.

"*Shut the fuck up.*"

"Why should I? Doing this behind the boss' back is really fucked up."

"Tommy, you promised."

He glares at her. "I didn't promise to keep this from John. You shouldn't have put me in this position."

Heat builds up in my chest. "I didn't take any of her money, so you have nothing to worry about. As far as you're concerned, it's real."

Not believing me, Tommy's smile widens and he slowly sucks in his lip.

"Don't be a fucking jerk, Tommy."

"I just got to Montreal. I really doubt the boss will make me a member when he finds out I kept this from him. I know the baby isn't real—this whole marriage isn't real. The fucking money you're going to collect from everyone, the gifts—You don't think this is wrong?"

Fucking New York piece of shit asshole.

I don't like the way he looks at her. My teeth grind together, and I imagine smashing my fist against that fuckhead's jaw. Condescending prick.

"Mind your own goddamn business."

"She made it my fucking business when she asked me for help."

He's unyielding, like many guys in the life. The guy doesn't make a move unless there's something in it for him.

"I'm made. *You're not.* It's my word against yours, asshole."

He doesn't even blink. "It won't be when I show him that bag of cash."

I shove his chest in a sudden rush of rage. "Maybe I'll just put a bullet in your fucking head."

"*Tony!*" She makes a grab for my arm, but I pull it out of her reach.

Tommy seethes with cool anger as he takes another sip of his drink. I ball my hands into fists, waiting for him to hit me back, to give me an excuse to beat the shit out of him.

Instead that dead-eyed fuck grins at me. "Enjoy your night."

Asshole.

He backs away and I watch him slink back to his table. Elena sits back down painfully, as if there are pins in her seat. I sit down next to her and slide my arm over her shoulder, still simmering with anger.

"Hey, don't worry about him. He's just drunk."

"He looked pretty sober to me."

"Forget about it."

She shakes her head, looking troubled by his encounter.

Through the DJ's music, there's a loud crash and a bang. It's probably a waiter who dropped something, but I still raise my head in search of the noise. A drunken man stumbles into the room, hair swinging around his face. I recognize that puke-stain from his heavy Brooklyn accent.

Motherfucker.

"Where the *fuck* is she? No, don't fucking—don't touch me!"

Elena stiffens like a board when his voice carries over the music, and her face blanches.

"Stay here. I'll take care of this."

I massage my fists as I get up and stride toward Rafael, stumbles from table to table. The guys all turn around in their seats to watch him, cruel sneers on their faces. Even I've never seen something so pathetic in my life.

"You better only be here to congratulate me."

My sudden voice next to his ear startles him. The guy looks like shit, and he smells like it, too. It's like he bathed in bourbon before throwing on his wrinkled suit. His hostile face turns right toward me.

"Where the fuck is she?"

"You're going to have to be more specific." I enjoy needling this asshole.

His face contorts with rage. "My fucking girl—she's carrying *my* kid."

There's something about his face that just makes me want to punch his goddamn face in, or maybe it's the arrogant, cutting tone. The way he fucking looks at me.

"Who the fuck do you think you are? You think that because you put your cock inside her a few times, that makes her yours?"

Dipshit takes his jacket off, hurling it on the floor as he rolls up his sleeves.

He rolls up his sleeves.

Cute.

I could take this guy in one move. As far as I'm concerned, it's not a fair fight.

"You fucked my girl—!"

"Be a man, for Christ's sake. She doesn't want you."

He throws his head back in laughter, his greasy hair sliding in front of his face. "Oh, you think she fucking wants *you*—that she's not using your stupid ass?"

A flash of rage sends my fist smashing against the side of his face. He drops down like a stone, howling. I can't fucking believe the balls on this guy. I'll beat the shit out of him if he says another word.

"Maybe you don't fucking get it. *We're married.* Stay the *fuck* away from my wife!"

"Fuck you!"

He doesn't fucking learn, does he?

My shoe launches out, connecting loudly with his ribs. How the fuck did this asshole get in five yards within my woman? What the fuck did she see in him? A low groan leaves his bloodied lips as I beat the shit out of him. He's nothing to me. With one arm, I grab the scruff of his jacket, half-dragging him through the hall as he screams.

"PIECE OF SHIT!"

I let him go. His head smashes on the floor as my fist whirls across his face. Dazed eyes rolls in his head as I straighten, rage simmering under my skin.

"You want more, you fucking scumbag?"

"F—fuck—"

Hands grapple at my arms as I lay another hard kick right beneath his ribs. Rafael gives a horribly, rattling sound as the air leaves his lungs, but I don't give a shit.

"Tony, stop!"

Voices scream in my ear, but my mind is consumed with the girl I never saved. I wasn't there to protect her, to stop them from hurting her. My fists rain down on his face until I hear his nose snap, and blood gushes from his face. The hall erupts in cheers even as two strong arms grab me, pulling me away from him. I could beat him to death. Crack his fucking skull open with my bare hands.

"I'll fucking kill you!"

"Hey! Tony, stop it!"

Male voices scream in my ears for me to stop as I stare at the barely moving body on the floor. A fresh surge of energy flows through my limbs and I strain against the guys holding me back. I just want to finish the job—get rid of this asshole permanently, no matter how many witnesses there are, no matter if he's made. I just want him dead.

"Tony, what the hell are you doing?"

Ma's shrill voice joins the medley as she shoves her way through.

"Oh my God!"

Ah fuck.

Luckily, Tommy wraps an arm around my mother's shoulders and steers her away. Rafael's groans echo in the reception hall as my chest pulses with rapid breaths.

Fuck, I almost killed him.

Three guys pick him up off the floor and he stands on shaky feet, nose dripping with blood.

"The next time I see you, I'll put a bullet through your fucking head. I don't care who you are."

Johnny screams an order in French and they drag him out of the hall. He gazes at Rafael's limping form, running his fingers through his hair. "He's a made member."

He's the boss. Don't rise up. Don't yell.

"He got what he deserved."

Johnny blinks at the gruff tone in my voice. "I'm still the fucking boss." He jabs my chest. "You will not fucking kill him, do you understand? He's off fucking limits!"

"To hell with the fucking rules. I'll kill him if he harasses my wife again."

He grabs my jacketed arm. "I know you're pissed, but he's not just some fucking jerk-off. He's a member. *We don't kill other members.* Especially when she might be carrying his child."

I shrug off Johnny's hand, not caring how bad it looks. Then I stalk back to the sweetheart table, my insides broiling, but Elena isn't there. She's fucking gone.

Blood rushes to my head. Where the fuck is she? My eyes scan the hall for a flash of white, but I don't see her anywhere, and then I notice that one of the doors leading to the softly lit garden is ajar. I wrench open the door, heart pounding as cold blasts over my face.

Blue light illuminates the shrubs and the dirt paths leading into the garden. I take one at random, my breath frosting out in front of me in white clouds. Then I see her blindingly white dress, glowing in blue light as she sits on a park bench, her hands swallowing her face.

Something goes through me when I see her upset like that. It's painful, like a splinter digging into my heart. I take off my jacket and approach her, wrapping her shoulders. She jumps when I touch her, and my heart clenches as her tear-stained face turns toward me.

Some fucking wedding.

"He's gone, Elena."

Brown hair shifts in front of her face as she bows her head. "However long that'll last."

The dark tone in her voice bothers me and the look she gives me feels even worse.

Fire blazes in my chest. "What's that supposed to mean?"

Red-rimmed eyes stare back at me as she presses her lips together, refusing to respond. Then she finally croaks out.

"I don't have any choices anymore. *You* control everything. The moment you want a divorce, I'm fucked. I'm finished."

I grasp her chin, watching the tears slowly pooling in her eyes.

"He'll always be there, waiting. Won't he? I'll never be free of him."

"He won't, Elena."

"Oh, come *on*, Tony!" She pulls away from my grasp. "Let's just stop deceiving ourselves. You're not the type of guy who'll be happy with this forever. You'll get bored of me. You'll want someone else."

The sounds she makes make my chest feel like it's caving in. My arms wrap around her because I can't fucking stand it. Is she right?

"I won't let him hurt you. If things don't work out between us, I'll take care of him."

Her eyes widen. "You'd be killed."

"The way I see it, I'm dying either way."

One of these days, I'll get shot. That'll be it.

"I'd rather die protecting you than from a botched drug deal."

Her voice softens. "Tony."

"Stop it. I don't want to hear any more of this shit from you. Understand? You're my fucking wife. Act like it."

"But—"

I pull her head closer. "I'm not going anywhere. You're

stuck with me whether you like it or not."

She looks away from me and bites her lip. "I—I have to tell you something—"

I recognize that look and sigh. "Whatever it is, it can wait. I want to salvage what's left of this wedding."

Nodding, she gives me a weak smile and a pat on the hand, and I feel another surge of anger. This should be a happy day for her—fuck, for both of us.

No one should cry on their wedding day.

* * *

These places always give me hives.

I walk through the woods with Johnny and his underboss, Pierre-Luc. Twigs snap under their feet as they walk behind me. I ball my hands in the sleeves of my leather jacket. How many times have I driven out to a deserted place in the woods to get rid of some poor prick's body? It's perfectly devoid of people. Too cold for hikers, but the ground is no good for digging a hole. Frozen.

The New York boss is meeting us here and so is that fuckface, Rafael.

We'll solve this shit once and for all.

My mind focuses on the girl—my *wife*—waiting for me at home, who has no idea that this meeting is even happening. The wedding band feels tight around my finger—I'm still not used to it, but it's not suffocating.

She's mine. I wanted her the moment I laid eyes on her. Had to have her. I had to fuck the Mafia princess, just had to stick my dick in her. Then it was an addiction. I had to have her again and again. There was never a girl who made me want to break my no repeats rule. I don't know what the fuck happened, but somewhere in between all the fucking, I felt for her. There's no way I'll allow that piece of shit to hurt her any more than he already has.

It all depends on this meeting.

The New York boss waits for us under the shade of a tree. He's a tall, skinny guy with wavy black hair and a short black beard. Beside him, shit-for-brains stands. His face looks like someone took a meat tenderizer to him and I can't resist giving him a small smirk.

"Hey, John."

"Vincent." He gives the New York boss a short nod and turns his smooth face toward Rafael. "I'm glad your injuries are healing."

Rafael curls his lip and looks like he's on the verge of a nasty retort.

"Can we get this over with so I can get the fuck out of here?" Vince looks anxious as he addresses me. "Both of you have legitimate beefs against each other."

My throat burns. "What the fuck did I do except defend my pregnant wife against this psycho?"

Rafael's face twists into an ugly, almost grotesque, grimace. "Your pregnant wife is carrying my kid."

"I have to side with Tony, Vince. They married as soon as they found out about the pregnancy and as soon as that happened, that asshole showed up at their reception and started screaming threats."

Vince runs his hand over his harried face and gives Rafael a very unpleasant look. "I told you to leave her the fuck alone."

"She's pregnant—"

"I don't give a fuck! I gave you a fucking order, and you hit her again, didn't you?" His hot eyes bore into Rafael's face, and then he laughs and looks away. "You fucking deserve this beating."

Wow, I didn't expect the New York boss to turn on his own guy. Things are looking up. My hand strays toward the gun I've hidden in my jacket.

"Vince, I know I fucked up, but this is actually *real*. I'm going to be a father. I saw her pregnancy tests."

Wait, what?

I face the prick. "The fuck are you talking about?"

"I went to her house. I—I thought that it was a scam, but I made her take some tests, and they were positive." He turns toward Vince and speaks in a trembling voice. "All I want is to be there for my kid. I just want to be a part of his life. I should at least be allowed to go to doctor appointments with her."

Vince crosses his arms, looking unmoved. "*No.*"

The air leaves my chest and I look around for something to grab. He's lying. He's full of shit. Has to be.

"When the fuck did this happen?"

"A couple weeks ago." He gives me a nasty grin. "I guess she doesn't tell you everything."

Grabbing the gun from my waist, I aim it toward Rafael's mangled face as heat pounds in my head.

"Tony, what the fuck are you doing!"

I never lose my cool like this. I'm not the explosion guy, but there's something about Rafael that brings it out of me. I hate that motherfucker.

"I'm going to fucking kill him."

Vince already has his gun out, aimed at my chest. "Jesus Christ. Calm down. You don't want to do this."

"Actually, I really do. He disrespected me. He's going behind my back and seeing her without my permission."

The fact that he actually got her while I wasn't around is the worst part. A stab of anger extends to her, too. She never told me.

"A wife you only have because you think you knocked her up. I don't see why I have to respect you or that bitch."

"SHUT THE FUCK UP!"

Johnny shoves my arm as I squeeze off a shot, which blows a fist-sized hole into a tree. He wrenches the gun from my hand, screaming his head off as Vince shoves his gun into his pants.

"Jesus *fucking* Christ, you goddamn moron." Vince says savagely as Rafael stands strangely still, indifferent to the fact that he almost died. "Here's what's going to happen. You leave them the fuck alone. You're done with them. Come back to New York and forget about Elena."

"That's *impossible*."

"Until paternity is established, you leave them the fuck alone. Tony, does that work for you?"

No. Not by a long shot.

My insides simmer as Rafael looks at me with a wild, desperate rage that I can't look away from. I don't trust him to stay away, not even to protect his own life. My hand inches toward the knife I've strapped to my waist, because I'm convinced he's on the verge of doing something drastic.

"Whatever."

"Vincent, this is bullshit!"

The New York boss finally loses his temper and whirls around, his jacket whistling in the air as his fist cracks across Rafael's jaw.

"You're a real pain in my ass, Rafael. Piss me off again, and I'll kill you."

Even as he moans on the dirty snow, I can't look away from him. The whining, the moans, it all sounds so fucking fake to me. The steely vengeance flashes from his eyes and I just want to end him right there.

There's nothing more dangerous than a man with nothing to lose.

ELENA

Swirls of coffee steam rise in the air in wonderful spirals as I blow air across the rich, dark brown liquid. I take a sip and my tongue curls, loving the sprinkle of spice. I smile at Melanie, who sits across the table. She called me up on the phone and wondered if I wanted to go out for coffee. All Tony's doing, probably.

"So, what's married life like?"

I shrug my shoulder. How the hell should I know? The whole thing is a farce, except that there really is a baby growing inside me.

I still can't fucking believe it.

Call it karma or cosmic justice, but this was the last thing I wanted. What would Dad say? My insides clench as I think about the horrified reaction on his face. He probably would be glad that at the very least, I'm marrying the guy who knocked me up.

And then what? For the life of me, I can't picture what my future is supposed to look like. I have this kid, and then what?

Two words: single mom.

It's a pretty bleak future, but somehow it makes the lies

a little more forgivable. Lying to them was hard because it was really like inheriting a second family. There were so many gifts and hugs and kisses on the cheek, and everyone was so friendly.

'Course they are. You're his wife. If you weren't married, they'd tell you to fuck off.

"Everything happened so quickly."

Even the ring on my finger feels foreign, as though I'm in someone else's body. Though, of course, we're supposed to keep up with this charade and I'm supposed to be—what? It's not exactly a girl's dream to marry the guy who knocks you up.

"I can't even imagine what you must be going through."

"Honestly, I just want a good bagel from home. The ones here—they're not really the same."

"God, I know!" Melanie happily seizes on the topic and we spend time reminiscing about home.

"And what the hell is with the kissing? It's a bit weird, isn't it?"

"Nah, I'm pretty sure it's a French thing. Like shaking hands. I think they call it, *la bise.*"

I click my tongue and let the French roll over my tongue. "La bees."

She laughs at my poor attempt and I throw a napkin at

her. The door opens and a gust of cold air make me clasp my mug of hot coffee.

"Oh, hey Tony."

I look up in surprise to see my husband giant form standing over us with a very dark look on his face. He ignores Melanie's greeting.

"Get up, you're leaving."

"I just got here. What's your problem?" I shoot Melanie a look, silently apologizing for his rudeness.

"We need to fucking talk," he says in a voice that bears no argument. Then he turns toward Melanie. "Sorry about this."

Melanie waves him off, looking slightly disappointed as I stand up.

"I'm sorry, I don't know what's wrong with him. We'll do it again sometime."

"Yeah, sure."

An impatient rap on the glass makes my muscles tense. What the fuck is his problem? I follow him outside.

"You were so rude to her," I tell him the moment the door swings shut. "What the hell is wrong with you?"

He grabs my wrist and drags me to a secluded corner, his lips white and shaking. "I'll tell you what's wrong with me. *You're a fucking liar.*"

"What?"

The acidic tone cuts me to my core. I don't know what he's talking about, but the vicious look he gives me makes me swallow down bitter guilt.

"You were pregnant with that jackass' kid the whole time, weren't you? He told me that he made you take pregnancy tests." He searches my stunned face. "Well, is it true?"

"Tony, that's not really—"

"*Jesus.*"

His eyes fracture in pain and he turns away from me as though he can't stand the sight of me. I feel like the worst human being on the planet.

I have to tell him.

"Tony, I have to tell you what happened."

"Fucking save it," he hurls over his shoulder.

I step in front of him and block the way out. The furious look on his face scares me—that hint of a predator that I saw in the bar lifts his head and glares at me—and I swallow hard, hoping he won't just brush me aside.

"Trust me, you want to hear this." I take a deep, shuddering breath. "It was the day I went to get some of my stuff. Rafael was waiting for me, and he had the tests. He wanted to know it was true." I swallow hard as Tony gives me a venomous look. "They were positive. I didn't know I was pregnant."

"Tony—it's your—it's your baby."

"*What?*"

He stands there, his white face suddenly bloodless like the snow under his feet. The silence is deafening between us. The traffic from the street muffles to a distant murmur as my heart beats in my head. My mouth opens and closes. Why the fuck is this so hard?

Please don't hate me.

I talk in a very small voice. "I—I forgot to take my pills, my birth control, the first…couple times we were together."

"You what? You forgot to take your fucking pills?"

I nod shamefacedly and he swears so loudly that it echoes down the alley.

"I don't believe this."

"It's real. I've been to the doctor. I—I'm sorry, Tony."

His hands tremble as he rakes them through his hair, looking anywhere but me. He doesn't want to acknowledge it. I don't blame him.

I'm sorry I got pregnant with your kid, who you obviously don't want. I'm sorry I entered into your life at all.

I'm just sorry.

"When were you going to fucking tell me?"

"I know, it's just—there was so much shit going on, and I was afraid to tell you," I force myself to raise my voice, "and I just want to say that you don't have to do anything—you don't have to be in it's life. I totally understand."

He seizes his hair and pulls, shaking his head. "I cannot *fucking* believe this."

My heart stalls. I knew it—I knew he'd be like this, but it's still like a spike to my heart.

"I'm sor—"

"I don't want this!" he explodes. "What kind of fucking father can I be? I'm not fit to be one *at all.*"

Tears spill down my cheeks. "That's not true."

"How the fuck would you know?"

He looks at me with the air of someone being clubbed on the head. He's right, isn't he? He's a Mafioso. *I'm just waiting to die,* he said.

"You're a good man. I know you don't like to believe it—"

Wild, strangled laughter cuts me off. "I'm sorry, sweetheart, but you are dead wrong about that. You don't know me. You don't know a *thing* about the life I lead."

"Actually, I do. My dad was a boss, remember?"

That shit-eating grin is back on his face as he pins me against the wall, nudging my thighs open with his leg. I always feel so small when he surrounds me like that. It's not just his size. It's his presence: overwhelming and intoxicating at the same time. The energy between us shifts as he takes my waist in his hands, as his knee grinds my pussy. It's electric. My heart pounds, and I can't breathe as he leans in closer.

"Yeah, I know all about you Mafia princesses. Daddy would have never showed you the dark side of his business. You only saw the clothes, the jewelry, the charity gala dinners—"

"I'm not an idiot, Tony. I read the papers, and I was smart enough not to swallow every lie he tried to feed us."

"Reading about it in the paper," he sneers. "Last night, I spent eight hours torturing some poor fuck with his head trapped in a vice. Do you know what happens to someone's head when it's crushed? The eyes pop out."

A cruel mask slides over Tony's face, and it occurs to me that he might be right. That I might not know this man at all. Darkness swirls in his eyes, but they're the same ones that dented with pain when told me that he never wanted this life for himself.

"Why are you trying to scare me?" My voice grows stronger. "What exactly are you trying to accomplish, here? The baby's coming whether you like it or not."

"I'm trying to make you understand that I'm not a good man. I shouldn't be in any kid's life. I'm nothing but a bad influence."

"You don't have to be in its life."

The thigh nudges me again, and a ripple of desire moves up my body. The things he says makes my stomach cave in. Pressure builds up behind my eyes, and I'm pissed off, too. I don't believe that he'd be a bad influence. He's the one who saved me without asking for a single dime in return.

"I'm going to be in the kid's life. I just don't know for how long." He touches my face gently as another tear rolls down my cheek. His other hand curls around my waist, smoothing over my belly. His gaze softens for a moment. Then suddenly, he pulls my arm and I scramble after him in the streets.

"Tony, where are we going?"

We stop in front of his car and he opens the door, pointing inside.

"Get in."

During the car ride home, Tony keeps a stoic silence that I think is a front for his barely constrained panic. I study the tic in his jaw, the way his eyes focus on the streets without ever once glancing at me, and I wonder what the hell he's thinking. I wonder if he'll just end things between us.

Can I blame him?

When we get home, Tony dissolves into nervous

energy. I show him the test results from the doctor, the missing pills from my birth control, and it all crashes on his head. The paper trembles in his hand. I can't tell whether he's furious or terrified.

"It's really mine?"

My arms wrap around my middle as he looks at me under his dark locks. "I'm positive."

He lets out a long exhale and collapses into a chair in the kitchen. The test results sit on the kitchen table, and he stares at the paper as if it'll magically turn negative if he looks at it long enough. I can't stand the sight of him like this.

Shaking, I leave the kitchen to sit on the sofa in the living room. I try to imagine raising a kid in this place, and then in my mind's image I see Tony's face, contorted with rage as a shrill cry wakes him up from sleep. He didn't ask for this. Is it fair to expect him to take responsibility? Should I do everything because it's my fault? Is it my fault?

Heavy footsteps creak over the floorboards and finally come to a rest where I sit. His hand drops on my head, smoothing my face. I turn my head, and he grips a fistful of hair. It's painful.

What the fuck?

I find his face, and open my mouth to tell him to let me go, but the expression on his face stops me. His smile is more like a dark grin, and his eyes simmer with unbridled lust.

My throat closes.

"Get up."

He tugs my hair and I follow the pressure, standing up as he weaves an arm around my neck. My blood beats hard into his skin. His mouth hisses over my neck like a knife.

"You're such a slick little rat, aren't you?"

"What?"

His hips shift, digging his rock hard bulge into my back as he pushes me forward, toward the bedroom.

"Your plan was to get some asshole to fill you with his cum. To get you knocked up."

His hand drops to my chest, groping my tits through my shirt.

"No fucking way!"

Hot lips graze over my ear, his soft voice adding a hot line of desire all the way to my pussy.

"Except, I'm not just some asshole who's going to let you leave with my kid. I'm going to give you what you want, baby."

My back hits the bedroom door and it flies open, banging into the wall. My heart pounds into my throat as his lips touch my neck, stinging my skin as he sucks hard. I don't know what the fuck he's talking about, but every movement on my skin is like a trail of fire.

He turns me around so that his heated lips are against mine. "I'm going to fuck you and fill you with my cum every day, and after our kid is born," he touches my belly and I feel a small thrill in my chest, "I won't stop until I get you knocked up again, and *again*."

The breath catches in my throat. "I—I thought you didn't want kids."

"I always wanted kids. I just didn't want them while I was in the life, but that ship has fucking sailed. I'm going to have the family I always wanted, and you're going to give it to me."

Tony, I love you.

My heart swells and beats a little faster as I realize how true it is. I want to tell him. Maybe it's because he's embracing this fucked up situation with open arms, or maybe it's because he makes my panties melt without touching me.

I rip off my shirt and Tony's eyes watch my tits as he reaches around, undoing my bra. It slides down my arms and then I bend over to slide the jeans and soaking panties from my waist.

"Such an obedient wife." Tony's grin stretches over his handsome face as he slides a hand over my pussy, sliding his finger over my clit. My legs shiver. "You really are made for me."

A low growl reverberates in his throat as he runs his hand up my waist, cupping my tits as his forefinger and thumb pinch my hard nipple. I arch my back as he touches the sensitive flesh and I reach up, grabbing his rough face to kiss him. It's hard because he's so much taller than I am, but he bends his neck and his soft lips seal against mine. It's like having the flu: the shaking weakness, sensitive skin, the heat burning your skin. That's what he's like. Then I know that I'm bound to him for as long as he wants because he makes me feel like this. Because I love him.

I'll do anything for him.

Maybe there's a part of him that knows that. He pulls back with a very satisfied smirk, as though he already knows how bad I've got it for him.

"Get on the bed and put your hands over your head."

I lie on the bed, my core pounding in anticipation as he rummages through the nightstand and pulls out heavy, silver handcuffs. He's never used them on me. It gives me a strange thrill to feel the cool metal burning against my skin as it clicks around my wrist, and then on the headboard behind me. He removes another pair from his nightstand, grinning like a devil as he tightens them around my ankles and attaches them to rope that he has tied around the legs of his bed.

Tied up and helpless, I watch as he retrieves another instrument from his nightstand. It looks like a purple, U-shaped vibrator.

Oh fuck.

"You need to be punished first." His face hardens suddenly.

"For what?"

"Don't give me that fucking look," he snaps. "You didn't tell me that your ex ambushed you at your apartment. We're married, now. No more fucking secrets."

He's right.

Then he clicks a button and the vibrator hums madly in his hands. I watch him as he walks between my legs with deliberate slowness, and then I feel one of the arms sinking inside me. The other one slides over my clip, holding me in place like a paper clip.

I buck madly in my restraints, my heart rate jacked as both arms stimulate me. Pleasure rolls through me, slicing and zapping, and Tony smiles as he sits on the edge of the bed, fully dressed. Eventually, he lays beside me.

"I like having you like this. Easy access. Or I could just jack off to you all day."

"What are you trying to do?" My voice bursts out of me into a growl.

He laughs at my rage and reaches out, touching my leg. The slight touch sends a jolt to my pussy, like an electric current.

Oh God.

My mind screams out for more as his laughter rolls over me like hot drops of rain down my back. It infuriates me to see him smiling sweetly as I jerk and twist on the bed, pleasure riding up my pussy. It jack-knifes into my core mercilessly. My chest feels like there's a lamp hanging over my naked skin, burning. And then I feel it rippling through my core. My orgasm clenches my pussy hard as I gasp into my arm, avoiding Tony's face.

"Aw, did you come? Poor baby."

His fingers dig into my thigh as shockwaves run through my body. Slowly, he inches his hand up my thigh. It's slow and torturous, and the vibrator doesn't let up. Within seconds, my heart hammers against my chest and electric shocks of desire slam into my pussy. Tony smiles as I let out a shrill gasp, and then a moan as he envelops my pussy with his hand, muffling the sound of the vibrator for a moment.

He leans over me, the heat of his body pressing into my side as he gently wipes strands from my face while his other hand massages me. He applies pressure to the device, and I arch my back as he suddenly hits a sensitive spot. A slow grin spreads over Tony's rugged face as he presses down. Another searing, spike of pleasure jolts up my pussy and his warmth is tantalizingly close. I think of his naked body, the weight of him when he's deep inside me. I want his thick cock pulsing inside me, feeding the ache that burns for more.

"Please, Tony. I can't stand it—ah!"

Another orgasm painfully clenches my core, making the handcuffs rattle as I seize my limbs. Tony just smiles at me, planting a chaste kiss on my cheek that feels erotic. Anything from him feels erotic right now.

"That asshole made me feel like a fucking chump." He slides his hand back to my ass and holds it firmly, giving me a forbidding look. "You should have told me he went after you. I would've killed him."

The look in his eyes along with the vibrator's erotic massage makes me let out a thrilling gasp. The dark pools are filled with deadly calm, but suddenly they flash with vicious retribution.

"You're mine, and he disrespected me by meeting you behind my back. And he never faced any consequences. That's your fucking fault."

"Tony I'm really—I'm sorry—"

"You made me look weak in front of them. Do you know what that does in my line of work? Now they're think I'm some kind of moron who lets his wife two-time him." His eyes blaze and his fingers gouge into my flesh.

The vibrator keeps buzzing, maddening me as Tony's harsh voice cuts into my ear. He's pissed, and for good reason, but I don't fucking care. All I care about is the pain between my legs. It's building up again. Jesus Christ. No!

My moans shake from my chest as yet another painful grip seizes my cunt, and a wave of pleasure is quickly extinguished by the vibrator's incessant buzzing. Tony's hand suddenly smacks my ass, and the vibration from the blow adds to the maddening ache inside me.

A finger lifts my chin so that I'm staring into his eyes. My heart clenches suddenly as I meet his gaze, and I want so badly for him to kiss me.

"You will not do that again."

The voice he uses sends a stab of pain to my heart.

"I won't."

"Good," he says, his harsh voice blowing over my face. "This is not an equal relationship, hon. You do what I say for your own fucking good."

A blaze of anger rears up inside me at those words. What the fuck is he talking about? "Fuck you. I do whatever the hell I want."

"That's all in the past, babe. You're not a princess anymore, you're mine. Mine to play with, mine to fuck, mine to protect. Say it."

Heat burns my face, but then he crushes his lips against mine, devouring my lips as his tongue plays inside my mouth. His hand grabs my neck with a slightly firm grip, almost as if he meant to hold me down and claim me as he said he would. His fingers spread over my skin and drag down my chest, over the swell of my breast as he finally grabs the entire thing and squeezes. A small groan vibrates from his mouth as I arch into his touch. Everything about him drives me mad. Half of the time I want to slap him as much as I want to fuck him. He pulls back, a confident smirk playing his lips as he watches me struggle.

Who am I fucking kidding?

"I'm yours."

"Say it all."

I purse my lips. He will *not* make me say it all. Then he reaches somewhere and touches a button on the vibrator, and it suddenly triples in speed. Oh fuck. Fuck. Something thick and hard—I need it now. My muscles clench hard over the device as it teases, never quite delivering what I exactly need.

"I'm yours—Tony, please!"

Soft laughter rains down on me as he turns the device off and slides it out of me. My legs tremble as I hear the sound of his clothes hitting the floor in muffled thumps.

He climbs over the bed, the mattress squeaking as he crawls over me. His entire body is bared to me, but I can't touch him. Instead, he touches me. It's all a lesson. He's in control, not me.

A single finger rides up my stomach, between my breasts, and up my throat. Then his hand curls around my neck and I'm bursting with frustration.

Fuck me, already.

"You still can't fucking let go, can you? What do I have to do to you, huh?"

I open my mouth to speak, but he silences me with a finger.

"No—not a fucking word until you submit to me."

His weight bears down on me, and his cock flattens against my stomach. Long, thick, impossibly rigid. A low whine leaves my throat as I imagine what it'd feel like. Fucking hell.

Restrained, but not immobile, I shiver as he wetly kisses my throat, his stubble scratching my skin. Then another kiss bites the base of my neck and I gasp as he makes a sucking sound. His lips smile as he pulls back and looks at it.

Another hickey. Goddamn it.

"I will not fuck you until you tell me what I want to hear."

His knees nudge my legs, making them open wide as he begins to rock his body, sliding his cock up and down my aching pussy.

This is ridiculous. I'm Elena Vittorio, not some—not some mob wife for him to order around.

Then his tongue darts out, teasing the very tip of my hard nipple, which contracts at his touch. It's a searing sensation—a direct line to my arousal. He watches my reaction, smiles, and then he takes my breast in his mouth, biting down hard. I let out a gasp of pain, and his teeth withdraw. The wet, strong muscle teases my nipple, playing as he closes his mouth over it and sucks.

Oh God.

"Tony, please."

He bites the nipple hard and it's like another searing shock, and his cock is right there, rubbing against me. I'm ready for him.

He grabs my face, his words almost hostile. "Say the fucking words."

"Tony, I—I'm in love with you. I'll do anything."

Shock ripples through his face for a moment and he pauses, his face horribly frozen. Then he grunts and moves his hips, burying his face in my neck as he slides right in. Finally, his cock slides inside me and he thrusts hard. It feels like home, and my heart still pounds so hard that it hurts, because I told him that I loved him.

He didn't say it back.

He didn't.

I lift my legs as he fucks me mercilessly, pounding my aching pussy as he breathes harshly in my neck. Feeling him throb inside me is like paradise. I can't remember the last time I felt so connected to someone. He's the father of my child. I love him just for that.

Then he comes hard, his cock ramming me so completely that I gasp in pain, loving that deep groan that growls in my ear. His hot breath steams my neck as he pulses inside me, the wetness flooding my pussy. He pulls back and kisses me hard as he thrusts deep, our sweat mingling together as he breaks our kiss to pant against my lips. There's something different shining in his eyes as he smiles at me. I've never seen it before.

"Thank you, Elena."

The voice is so weak that I'm surprised it's coming from his chest.

"For what?"

"For making me care about something."

* * *

It's different between us.

I can't place it, can't put a finger on it.

It's enough just to sit in his lap and hear his voice

rumbling through my back. I've never felt so at peace with his arm around my waist, his chin over my shoulder. Maybe it's because he's so big, but I always feel safe in his arms. He plants an occasional kiss on my neck, and I glow inside. I flip through a catalog of baby-related shit we'll have to buy, and Tony tenses underneath me.

It's still not real for him.

"I just don't know," he admits in a low voice. "I don't know if I'll be ready."

I turn around in his lap, confronting his slightly worried gaze. It's not like him to be insecure, but how can anyone be secure about this?

"I don't even know if I'll be ready."

He lets out a short laugh. "If you're not, we're definitely fucked."

"It's normal to be scared."

He winces at the word. "I just don't want to fuck it up."

Gentle fingers brush over my belly and a light flickers in his eyes. Tony stands up with me in his arms and I slip down his waist, clutching his chest as he pulls a wad of cash from his jeans. He counts a small handful of bills and hands them to me. There has to be at least a thousand dollars in there.

"I've got to go. Use it to buy some of this shit. Go with

one of your girlfriends."

He hurriedly plants a kiss on my cheek and my heart squeezes as he gives me a wink and walks down the hall.

"Where are you going?"

He only smiles at me. *Ah. Fine.*

"I'll be back late."

TONY

"I'll be back late," I tell her.

If I come back at all.

My finger rests over the trigger of my Glock as I close the door and descend the steps of my apartment. Purpose floods my veins as I walk toward my car. I unlock the door and slide in, starting the car. The car roars as I pull out of the parallel parking and drive toward Montmartre, away from my home in Plateau so that I can meet that stupid fuck, who still texts Elena.

It wasn't all right when she was my girl, but now that she's my wife—my *actually pregnant* wife, I need to end that douchebag once and for all.

He needs to die.

My mind was made up the moment I saw that fucking look of entitlement on his face at the sit-down. He insulted me, and my blood boils just thinking about how he made me look like an asshole in front of my superiors.

I'll kill the piece of shit, and I won't be quick about it, either. I'll take my goddamn time and listen to him whine and bitch and beg me for his life.

And that means going against Johnny's orders.

Hell, it's not like we haven't killed wiseguys before without permission. Guys get killed all the time. You get a bunch of hot heads in a room with guns, and some of them have arguments and before you know it, one of them is dead. Once, a made guy from the Algiere family called Pierre an asshole while we were playing cards, and the crazy fuck shot him in the chest. Just like that—BAM— and he was gone. He was a made guy. We had to bury him where no one could ever find him. No body? No proof he was murdered.

It's that simple.

I stop the car and park, looking for a male form on the street as I get out of the car and duck behind the pork store.

I recovered the SIM card from Elena's phone after I smashed it, and I use it to keep tabs on that motherfucker. The violent shit he sends her makes me sick to my stomach to read, but mostly it's just like dumping a gallon of gasoline on fire. I've been dying to beat the piss out of this asshole for weeks. My fists are *aching* for action.

My fingers fly over my cellphone as I slide in the SIM card, ignoring the fresh wave of violent text messages. Shit, I should be allowed to whack him based on what he says here:

Your fucking boyfriend is dead, you dumb bitch

I will be in my son's life. You can't stop me.

I grin to myself. *My son's life.* Dumb fuck.

A cold feeling pricks over my bare skin and my head snaps up. A nauseating, vulnerable feeling slowly grips my insides, and I don't even bother hiding my gun. I shove the cellphone down my pocket and hold the gun with both hands, glancing down deserted, white streets.

The gun slips in my cold, clammy fingers and I tighten the grip as I search behind the line of cars on the street. I don't know why the fuck I feel like this.

Like I'm about to be jumped.

Maybe there was a flash of something—chrome. There it is. Just out of sight, peeking from the end of the block. The throttle of several motorcycle engines guns through my chest and I dive behind my car without thinking as explosions crash around me. The bikes scream down the street, and I know I'm going to die. Outnumbered.

I'm going to fucking die just like my dad.

No.

I hurl myself over the hood of my car and aim at fleeing chrome. *Pop. Pop.* Something slams into my right shoulder, numbing my arm as the bike goes down in a shower of sparks, rolling over the man.

I'm hit.

The sounds of screeching tires barely register in my

head as I wheel toward the next one, determined to take as many down with me as I can. If I die, they all fucking die. A bearded old fuck with a 20-gauge shotgun in his hands aims at me, and I fire at his face before he can touch the trigger. The back of his head explodes with pink mist, showering the pristine, white snow. It's almost beautiful.

Another punch, this time to my leg, and I crumple to the ground. This time, I don't get angry. I get really fucked scared. My mind fills with images of Elena—Elena's belly growing bigger, Elena with the baby, rocking it to sleep as her long, beautiful hair hangs over the crib. And then a single cry screams inside my head: My wife—my baby!

Is this what Dad thought before he went?

The blows rain down on my head. They flatten me down until I can't think—I can't think of a single word except this phrase running in my head, and panic that I've never known floods my lungs, or maybe it's blood. I can't breathe.

I can't—

ELENA

Shopping bags weigh down my shoulders as I descend the stairs to the metro. Melanie, also bogged with wildly swinging bags, follows me.

"Thanks for coming with me." I sigh as the white strings of shopping bags slacken around my shoulders as I slide into a plastic seat. Melanie gives me a similar look of relief as she sits down, the shopping bags crowded around our legs.

"No problem. It's probably the closest I'll ever get to having the same experience." She gives me a kind of a sad smile as I look at her. "Tommy's not really the fatherly type."

Thinking of Tony, I smile. "Yeah, that's what they all say."

I shoot off a quick text to him, telling him that I'm heading home just as the subway lurches forward. My phone buzzes and I read his response:

Dinner better be fucking ready when I get back home.

I snort to myself when I read that. He's joking, right?

It'll be ready when it's ready. We just got done shopping.

The message comes back frighteningly quickly, as if he's watching the screen, just waiting for me to reply.

You'll have it ready when I get home or you'll get my hand across your face. Or a belt.

The hostility in the message runs right through me like a sword. What the hell is with him? Cold horror ripples through my stomach and I don't hear the roar of the subway, or Melanie's chatter in my ear.

Then another text pops up on the screen:

It's your choice.

They're the same words Rafael used to hiss in my ear.

Oh God. No, please don't let that mean what I think it does.

The phone clatters to the floor.

Dimly, I hear Melanie's reproving yell. "Elena!" When I make no move, Melanie picks it up for me. "What's wrong?"

He fucking got him. *He has Tony.* Why else would Rafael's voice come out of Tony's phone?

"Oh my God."

"Jesus, what's wrong?" Melanie's whitened face turns toward me.

Panic spikes my heart as a horrible image of Tony's bloodied body flashes in front of my eyes. No, I can't lose him. I cannot fucking lose him!

"We have to hurry—I have to go home, now!"

"We're on our way," she says in a bewildered tone. "Will you tell me what the hell's going on?"

I look at the subway map, the French names blurring as tears spill from my eyes. Three stops. Three fucking stops.

"Something happened to Tony."

"What? I didn't see—" she looks at my phone and reads the texts, biting her lip. "I—don't see anything suspicious—"

"It's the sort of thing my ex would say. He has Tony's phone, which means that—" I can't bear to finish the sentence, but my voice chokes off in a sob.

He's probably dead.

"Whoa, don't you think you might be overreacting?"

I stare at her as impatient rage fumes in my chest. "No, I'm not! I know my ex and I know Tony—this isn't the way he talks to me."

I stand up as the door hisses open to my stop, but Melanie grabs my arm and forces me down.

She flinches when I glare at her. "What the hell are you doing?"

"We're not going to your apartment!"

People filter out of the car as I struggle with her. "Let go of me!" I snatch my arm from her grip.

"*Listen to me.* If you're right—"

My voice rises in a snarl. "I know I'm right."

Her hand reaches out and closes over my wrist, her fingers biting me. "Then he could be waiting for you there. It's too dangerous."

She's right. I don't stand a chance against my ex. He's probably just hoping I'll take the bait and run back home.

The door hisses shut and for some reason the image of a coffin lid closing for the last time burns in my head. A wave of crushing despair slams into my shoulders from above, like a heavy weight. My knees strike the ground. The car echoes with my sobs as passengers give me concerned looks.

Melanie's gentle hand falls on my head. "*Hey*, you don't know what happened. It could be a prank or—or something."

My eyes burn as I stare at the phone screen, the words bleeding as my eyes well up. I know exactly what happened. That bastard found Tony and probably took him by surprise, and by now he's probably—*he's gone.* Thrown in a ditch somewhere or buried. Jesus—the pain in my heart feels like it's going to kill me.

No, I can't accept that. I sit down and gulp down air as my lungs contract. Melanie grips my shoulder hard and whispers in my ear all the bullshit that she thinks will help me feel better.

"We'll find Tony. Tommy might know something."

Melanie gets on the phone with her boyfriend as I shake in the seat, staring ahead but not really seeing anything. The phone is hot in my hand, and a wave of nausea overcomes me when I look at it. It's contaminated. It's an extension of the man who did nothing but abuse me for months, and now he's extinguished the only light in my life.

Fucking hell, get a grip on yourself.

Trembling a bit on my feet, I walk out of the car with Melanie fast on my heels. Shopping bags bounce against my legs as I hurtle up the stairs. A silver Mercedes rolls against the curb and Tommy's anxious head leans toward the window.

"Get in."

Melanie opens the trunk while I shove the bags inside, and then I climb in the backseat as Melanie joins him in the front.

"Tommy—have you heard from Tony?"

He gazes at me from the rearview mirror. "No, sorry."

"We need to find him. I think Rafael might have—" the breath hitches in my throat and I swallow hard, clearing my throat, "—might have done something to him."

Tommy's eyes widen as he pulls away from the curb

and drives us away. "What makes you say that?"

Melanie gives me an anxious look as I pull up the text messages. "The texts he sent me are not from Tony, they're from Rafael."

It boils my blood to see him raise his eyebrows as though I'm being overdramatic. We stop at a light and he seizes the phone, scrolling through them. Then he shrugs.

My heart sinks.

"I don't see what's the big deal—"

"Tony would not talk to me like that!" I snarl at him.

"Actually, Elena, I've known him for longer than you have. This doesn't really surprise me."

My nails dig into my palms as he hands me back my phone. A powerless feeling throbs in my chest. Tony's out there, somewhere. Injured. In pain. He needs me to fight for him.

"Tommy, I'm telling you, Rafael kidnapped him. I need your fucking help!"

Suspicious eyes from the mirror narrow at me. "Elena, you're overreacting. If anything, he's drunk. Men are jerks when they're drunk."

"No, I'm telling you, that's not it."

"Tommy, just bring her to the fucking bar," Melanie finally yells.

He gives her a dark look. "Fine, but you might not like

what you see there."

"Meaning what?"

A fleeting look makes my insides crawl.

"He could be there with another girl."

Melanie slugs Tommy's shoulder with her fist, a very angry look on her face.

"Jesus, woman! I'm fuckin' driving!"

"Don't be such an asshole!"

"*I'm not.*"

I don't listen to them bicker. The irritating noise falls to the background and the only sound is my heartbeat in my head, pulsing loudly. What should I do? I know in my heart of hearts that something went terribly wrong when Tony left the house. Tommy isn't likely to help me, but maybe John will listen.

What if he doesn't think the texts are proof, either?

Then I take matters into my own hands.

I'll find Rafael.

I'll kill him.

There are other options besides the Mafia. Tony told me all about the bikers in Sorel-Tracy, which is northeast of the city. Their headquarters is a huge concrete bunker that you can see from the highway. The family is allied with them. Maybe they'd be able to help me.

Tommy parks the car and I immediately get out of the

car, looking through the darkened windows of his bar for Tony's shape. Even though I'm sure he's not there, I can't help but hope. Tommy rolls his eyes at me as he opens the door to the bar for Melanie and I. In the late afternoon, the bar has only a few early drinkers, and none of them are Tony. I wheel around, and Melanie fixes her boyfriend with a death glare.

"He's not here. *We need to do something!*"

His Adam's apple bobs as he looks away from Melanie's heated stare. "Look, this doesn't prove anything. The man could be anywhere—"

My scream of frustration cuts his voice off and I rush past him, heading for his office. Swift footsteps follow me into the back and I yank open drawers beside his desk, looking for my money.

"What the fuck are you doing?"

He grabs my shoulder roughly and I whirl around, tears blinding my eyes.

"I want to withdraw ten thousand dollars."

An unpleasant grimace spreads over his face. "Why?" he says, placing his hands on his hips.

"What the fuck does it matter to you? It's my money!"

"I know that fucking look—it means trouble for me. You're planning to do something stupid—"

Behind him, Melanie clutches her sleeve. "Just give her

what she wants!"

"What she wants?"

The incredulity in his tone sends a hot wave of heat up my throat.

"Don't pretend like you actually give a damn about Tony."

"Fuck you. He's my baby's father. Of course I care about him."

Even Melanie gives her boyfriend a scandalized look. "Jesus."

He looks back and forth from Melanie's face to mine, smiling at our outrage. "You realize that they made this whole thing up, right? There's no baby. She lied so she could get her ex off her back. It's all bullshit."

Tommy's angry voice rings out in the small room. Tears streak down my cheeks as his sadistic voice slaps my face. I feel it burn as though he actually struck me.

"It *was* in the beginning, but it's not anymore."

"Oh, right."

"I'm pregnant with his kid, right hand to God."

He sneers at the earnest tone in my voice and Melanie makes another violent movement toward her boyfriend.

"If you hit me again, I'll tie you up right here in this office and spank your sweet ass until it's raw."

Her face burns brightly. "You are being a complete

asshole."

"No, I'm not. You don't know this girl. She came here a month ago and told me about her plan to marry a wiseguy so that her ex would leave her alone. Fifty thousand dollars, wasn't it?"

He turns to me with a genial smile that makes my stomach twist. "It was," I say in a strong voice, "but—"

"—But you don't give a shit what happens to me if Johnny finds out about this scam, do you?"

I ball my hands into fists as bitterness gathers in my mouth. My tongue curls against the revolting taste.

"It's not a scam."

He gives me a very ugly look. "Whatever you say, sweetheart."

I've lost all fucking patience.

"If you won't help me, then just give me my fucking money!"

I can't bear looking at Melanie's confused face as Tommy wordlessly gets a paper bag and opens the wall safe. He drops bricks of cash in the bag and then slams the door shut. He walks back to me with a deadened look in his eyes, and maybe there's a sliver of something else. That I better watch my back because the man who helped me out and felt sorry for me is gone.

I stuff the paper bag in my purse and turn around to

leave.

"Elena, what about your things? They're still in Tommy's car."

"I don't care," I say in a hoarse voice. "I need to find him."

My feet fly down the bar, ignoring her protests. I run past the patrons and burst outside, thrust into the freezing cold that only feels like a mild distraction. The restaurant where Johnny always hangs out burns in my mind: *Le Zinc.* I jog down the streets, determined to talk to Johnny before I make my last, most desperate move to save Tony.

Through the pristine windows, I see Johnny seated in the back, flanked by his guards as he picks through his lunch. I yank open the doors and am confronted by the hostile hostess, who recognizes me immediately.

"*Mademoiselle*, I must insist that you leave—*Tarbarnak!*"

I ignore her completely, walking swiftly past her to weave around tables, almost bumping into several of them as I make a beeline for Johnny, who raises his head when I approach. Once again, his guards throw their arms across my chest, knocking the wind out of me.

"For fuck's sake, let her though. She's Tony's wife."

The venom in his voice is barely constrained, and I sense a certain amount of revulsion in his gaze. If my status as Tony's wife is the only reason why Johnny tolerates me, I might be in trouble. Still, he frowns when he sees my tear-stained face. I sit down across from him, legs trembling.

"What's wrong, *ma belle*?"

"Tony! He's missing I—I think Rafael has his phone."

I show him the strange text messages, and Johnny's sculpted face betrays no emotion. He gives me a blank look.

"You think Rafael is using his phone? Why?"

"He wants him dead. Obviously, Tony got jumped or something, and—"

"And what? Tony is a big boy. He can handle your pathetic, junkie ex."

"These texts aren't like him." Heat boils in my chest as I watch him study his nails. "Don't you fucking care?"

A dangerous look crosses his face as my voice snaps over him.

"Do I care about one of my men going missing? Yes."

"Then why aren't you listening to me?"

"I did listen," he says in a bored voice as his black eyes slide to mine. "Tony isn't missing. If he doesn't show up for a couple days, then I'll worry."

"A couple days? Are you fucking kidding me? I've just told you that I've reason to believe that Rafael kidnapped my husband."

"Reason? I don't see no reason." His eyes sear into mine. "I see a paranoid, newly-wedded wife. Your husband works round the clock for me. You're going to have to get used to him not coming home some nights."

This is not about that, you stupid piece of shit!

Johnny rolls a cigarette on the table with slim, deft fingers and picks it up.

"I'm sorry that you're upset, but I really don't think there's anything to worry about."

I'm seized with an urge to lunge across the table and yank him by his striped, blue tie—to make him look at me with a modicum of respect and not just as the fucking Vittorio scumbag's daughter.

Then red sparks fly as he lights up, looking at me across the table with supreme boredom.

He won't help me. No one will.

The enormity of my responsibility lays across my shoulders like a dead horse. I can barely rise from the table. Johnny gives me a fleeting look.

"You're making a big mistake."

Smoke drifts across his emotionless face. He doesn't laugh at me, or smile, or give any indication that he thinks I'm being ridiculous, but he doesn't reassure me, either.

I'm coming, Tony.

* * *

The concrete fortress stands like a sentinel over a ruined city. Crumbling infrastructure surrounds the place like rot. Urban decay. The triple barbed wire fence looks daunting, and I have no idea what to expect when I drive Tony's car to their gates, which open when I roll the car closer.

My heart jumps as the gates groan. They swing inward, and I catch a glimpse of dirty, leather-jacketed men, their arms covered in tattoos. Some wear bandanas or baseball caps, others have long, flowing beards. They lack the professional, clean vibe of the mob. Even the guys look different. They're definitely not Italian, that's for sure.

They're also armed to the fucking teeth.

A surprisingly semi-groomed man walks to my window and taps on it with his shotgun. There's a patch on his leather vest: President. Right above it: *Les Diables* MC. I know next to nothing about biker gangs, only that I wish I were anywhere but here.

Tony needs you.

I roll down the window and the President, whoever the fuck he is, bows his head. He peers at me over the rims of his Ray-Bans and spits out the toothpick he worries in his mouth. The sides of his head are shaved and there's a long star gouged into the side of his face. He gives me a long, searching look.

"Qu'est ce-que vous faites ici?"

I don't understand a word. "I don't speak French. I'm Elena, Tony Vidal's wife."

"Carlos. President of *Les Diables*. I know your husband."

"You do?"

Hope lifts my spirits as he steps back, motioning for me to get out of the car. I get out and step into the compound, which looks like a series of bunkers lined up in rows. There's a giant ranch house, which Carlos leads me to as his *friends* escort us there. My skin shivers as he opens the heavy door to the house, which looks more like a saloon as I approach it. It's well lit inside and there's a bar with pool tables and booths. Scantily clad women dance suggestively around poles. Even stranger, there's a woman holding a squalling baby near what looks like a canteen. It looks like some kind of depraved community area.

Carlos leads me into his office, and a couple other men slide into seats behind me as I sit across from his desk. He sits down and adjusts his jacket.

"What can I do for you?"

What do I want them to do? I want them to find Rafael and kill the fucker.

"I want Rafael Costa dead. Can you find him?"

He grins at me as the shock on his face fades. Then he

leans back. "You're a piece of work, aren't you? Johnny called ahead and told me that you might pay me a visit. I'm sorry. Much as I'd like to help you whack an Italian, I can't do it."

"Then—what about if you helped me find my husband? I think Rafael kidnapped him—I *know* he kidnapped him."

The men behind me shift in their seats. It raises the hair on my neck.

Carlos gives me a shrewd look. "If that's true, why are you coming to us?"

"Johnny doesn't believe me. Look, I'm willing to pay you five grand right now if you agree to go looking for Tony. You'll get another five grand when you find him."

He rubs his chin thoughtfully. "Seems like a pretty good deal."

He's probably trying to hold back how much of a steal this is. Ten grand to find a missing person? Unheard of.

"If you find him and he turns out to be fine, joke's on me, okay? But I think Rafael has him against his will and I need your help finding him."

I reach into my purse and pull out a few of the bricks of cash. I let them fall over the table. His gaze flicks to the men behind me.

"All right—"

"And I want a gun."

His grin widens, exposing a row of silver teeth. "I don't think so. No."

"But—!"

"I'm not giving Tony's wife a gun."

Fine. I can probably get one myself anyway.

I extend my hand. "Deal."

We shake hands and he keeps my fingers in his grasp for a moment.

"I don't usually get involved in mob business, but your husband was always a decent guy, not like the pricks we usually have to deal with. I'll get some people on the streets to look for him right away."

"Thank you."

The weight lessens somewhat, but then Rafael's cruel face twisted in malevolence haunts my mind. I touch my belly and another stab of panic hits me.

He's the only person who ever made me feel like I was worth a damn. My sister—my Mom, they basically left me to be consumed by my ex the moment Dad passed.

I walk outside with the bikers, who escort me back to my car. Nothing feels any better. I've someone on my side, but I don't feel any closer to finding Tony.

It all comes down to him. Rafael. It's the fault of his stupid, male ego that couldn't accept that I'm a person who made her own fucking decisions. I was never real, just a prop in his life. I was just the boss' daughter. If he was with me, maybe his career would advance. Maybe he'd be made *capo*. Who knows, maybe he'd succeed my dad as boss. But none of that ever happened. All that work he put into courting me was for nothing, because Dad's dead. My value is completely gone, and now I've left him. Why couldn't he just leave me be?

Fuck him. *Fuck him.*

My hands clench my cell phone as if it's his neck and I have a glorious vision of his eyes bugging out as I cut off his airway. *Let's see how you fucking like it.*

I drive back to Tony's apartment, because I don't care about confronting Rafael at this point. Once I'm there, I find a gun in Tony's nightstand and I pop open the safety. My dad taught me how to shoot when I was a kid. I pace back and forth in the place with it in my hand, my head steaming with images of Tony lying on some rotten floor, dead. A scream suddenly tears from my throat as sobs shake my chest. I can't stand it—I can't fucking stand this inaction. Hours tick by slowly, and I resist the urge to call Carlos, over and over. No, sorry, they still haven't found him.

I take my cell phone and stare into the glowing, blue screen. My thumb hovers over it.

Tony, come home. I'm waiting for you here.

The response is almost immediate: **All right, I'm coming.**

I want to smash the fucking screen and feel the shards of glass dig into my hand. My vision sears with red as I grab the pistol in my purse and wrench open the door to outside. My finger tenses over the trigger as I step out, just waiting for one hint of that fucker's face. I'll wait for the asshole.

That's right. Come for me, Rafael. I'll get rid of you and I won't give a flying fuck about it.

Energy roars through my veins like too many caffeinated drinks. I feel more alert than I've ever been as I hurry down the steps and hide behind a garbage bin just off the side of the brownstone. It's tall enough so that I have to only slightly bend my knees.

The streets are too cold for anyone to mingle outside, and I desperately rub my fingers together to keep them from getting numb. I need to be able to shoot him. Just point and shoot.

My heart feels as though it's on the verge of explosion. Even though I want to fucking kill him, I'm scared. It's so fast and painful against my chest that I feel dizzy with the rush of blood to my head.

It'll be a fucking miracle if he doesn't spot me, but I'm

counting on the fact that he'll be so anxious to see me that he won't be careful. He'll just run up the steps, ignoring the sides of the apartment.

From the glow of the streetlights, I see a dark, lean figure walking across the street with his hands deep inside his pockets. He looks both ways and hurries across, wet boots shining as he crosses the slick street.

This might be it.

I extend my arms just like my dad taught me, following his shape as he walks up the steps to my apartment, but I still can't make out his face.

Fuck!

Time slows down. His gait lengthens. He raises his fist to the door, and all the while a clear voice whispers in my head. It knows exactly what I need to do.

Wait till he turns. Then shoot.

The porch light flares on, and his haggard face slowly turns away from the brightness, wincing. He looks across, directly at me—and I recognize him in an instant. Half of a second—that's all it takes for me to make up my mind to kill. My finger trembles. A blast explodes from the nozzle of the gun and Rafael screams into the night. It's so fucking loud that it startles me.

Then he disappears.

Wait—where the fuck did he go?

There's a noise through the thick, cold darkness. A moaning sound—someone full of pain.

Oh God, I hope I didn't hit someone else.

The maddening thought briefly seizes my head before I see Rafael's shaking body, slumped over and partially hidden by the bars.

I fucking got him.

Heart pounding hard, I stand up from behind the garbage bin as Rafael topples backward, his body crashing into the steps as he slides down.

Yes!

I run around the side and almost run into Rafael's heaving body. He blinks rapidly as I aim my gun right at his rat face.

"You shot me?"

I did. There's a nice, clean hole buried in his shoulder. In the darkness, his leather jacket just looks wet.

And yet there's no outrage in Rafael's eyes. He can barely process what just happened.

"I can't believe you fucking shot me."

"*Where the fuck is my husband?*"

I aim the nozzle between his eyes so that he can't miss it. His eyes widen and he spreads his white hand against the snow.

His demeanor shifts when he realizes that I'm dead

fucking serious. "Your husband?"

"Want another one? Don't waste my time, you *prick*. Where's Tony?"

"Oh, Tony." He gives me a nasty grin and shrugs despite the pain in his shoulder. "Fuck if I know."

"You have his cell phone. Any more lies, and I'll shoot you again."

The gun trembles in my grip and Rafael seems to finally understand how unhinged I just might be.

"Look, he's probably already gone."

"Gone? What do you mean, *gone*?"

He raises an eyebrow. "I'm sorry, but I had to get rid of him."

"Don't!"

It rips from my throat in a scream that the whole neighborhood can probably hear. That's it—Rafael just confirmed what I knew all along, that Tony is dead. He's gone.

The world dissolves away like sand. It's all grey and flat. Suddenly, I feel the cold. Like an oppressive fog, it envelops my body. Blood rushing to my skin feels like a thousand painful pinpricks. My eyes burn, but I can't cry. I barely have the strength to hold the gun, and really the only warmth is glowing in my belly. Because the kid still matters. Because it's all I've left of him.

He's gone. *He's gone.*

I can't take it. I want to scream with the grief howling inside me. I want to destroy every shred of light left in the universe, because the only one in my life is gone.

"I was never going to let anyone come between us. Help me get up, and I'll forgive you for this."

He brushes aside Tony's death as if it was a minor inconvenience. He strains to sit up, and I aim the gun at his forehead.

I hate him.

I've never hated anyone so fucking much, not even the bastards that killed my father.

"I loved him," I scream in a shrill voice. "I loved him more than you could ever fucking fathom!"

"*I* love you," he says in an angry voice. "I did everything I could to get you back, and now that I have you back I'm never letting you go."

"You don't have me. You never had me."

The gun trembles in my hands and a thrill runs through me. I've never killed anyone before, and I'm about to see what it feels like. Will I feel anything? Will there be regret?

He shakes his head. "Baby, you don't have it in you."

"See you in Hell."

I pull the trigger as something crashes into my side. Sparks fly on the pavement as the bullet glances off the ground. I fall down, heart hammering. The wind is knocked from my chest and I wheeze.

What the fuck?

"Jesus fucking Christ."

Another man's voice growls in my ear as he yanks me upright, and I'm so bewildered that I can't find words as he picks me off the ground.

"Is he—is he dead?"

The man holding me by the scruff of my neck snarls in my face. "I don't fucking know. You're not supposed to touch him!"

"*I'm not dead.*"

Rafael's voice sounds strange, yet still very much alive. A surge of rage rushes through my limbs, and I try to shove the man aside.

"Let me kill him. I want to do it. Step aside!"

"No!"

He takes me bodily and forces me up the stairs, leaving Rafael behind.

"Give me that fucking gun."

He twists it out of my grip and shoves me into my apartment. Then I finally get a good look at him. He's one of the men I saw at the *Les Diables* fortress.

"Did you follow me here?"

"Good thing Carlos asked me to, because otherwise

you'd be in deep shit." He looks behind himself and sees Rafael, still sprawled on the pavement. "Fuck."

Fury rustles my insides like black tar. I should have killed him a long time ago, but now it's too late and Tony's gone.

"I need to make some phone calls to take care of this. Try to escape, and I'll tie you up."

He shakes his head at me as I cross my arms and sit down with an angry sob.

A strange feeling goes through me as I sit down. It's like a long, drawn out howl. The worst grief I've ever felt in my life squeezes my chest and I just collapse over the kitchen table. My sobs echo through the house, loud enough to disturb the biker from his phone calls. He steps outside, slamming the door shut. Then there's nothing but the echo of my grief and the resounding fact that I failed.

TONY

Pain. Searing, hot pain. It drags me out of whatever coma I was in and I hear a loud, scraping sound.

I'm *not* dead.

Huh.

My eyes flare open and there are at least six guys in what looks like a basement. All bikers. Not *Les Diables*. Their colors are different. One turns around, and I see the letters sprawled over the black leather: POPEYES MC. The Popeyes. Holy fuck, I can't believe I got jumped by a group of disillusioned *Les Diables* fucks.

The same disillusioned fucks who killed my dad during the biker wars. They say some things come full circle. They seem to be right.

My chest swells and the pain in my shoulder and abs stab me suddenly. Fuck, I need to get out of this alive. Elena needs me. I have a wife and a baby on the way, and I can't just fucking die. Not now.

It doesn't escape me that that fucking cunt hair is behind all of this. He hired these fucks to kill me, only they're taking their sweet ass time—why?

"You're awake," the man sitting on an empty crate says unnecessarily.

"Do you know who I am?"

"I do. The only good Italian is a dead one."

The others laugh like sheep.

I glare at all of them, trying to size them up. "So why are you taking orders from one?"

He drags a lead pipe over the cement floor and grins nastily. "Because this one has a lot of fucking money."

"All you dumbasses are going to get killed the moment Johnny gets wind of what happened to me."

I strain my biceps against my restraints. Coils and coils of rope bind me to the chair. My hands are beet red from the lack of circulation.

"We want to know where the money is. The hundred grand you have stashed away."

The basement echoes with my hollow laughter, which cuts off into a groan. The lead pipe smashes over my knees, breaking at least one of them. For a moment, I debate sending these fucking morons to Tommy. They won't get within five yards of him.

"You'll have to kill another made guy to get to the money. Does that sound worth it to you?"

That part is a lie, but they look at each other. The leader, an old man with a long, grey beard looks at me with wrinkled eyes.

"Vidal," he says, rolling the name from his tongue.

"Vito Vidal. You're his fucking kid, aren't you?"

My lungs heave as fire burns beneath my skin—I just want to smash this old fuck's face in. He knows my dad.

They shot him down in the streets like a fucking dog.

"Listen, we're just here to get you to back off from the girl. Elena Vittorio. She's Rafael's, end of story. All you have to do is say that you'll stay away from her."

"Don't talk about my wife."

"She's the one who hired us."

Their lies make me laugh. She loves me—she told me so right before I left. My chest burns when I realize that I never said it back. She just took me by surprise and I didn't have the balls to say it back. She and that baby are the only things in the world that matter to me, and God help the man who tries to take them away from me.

A bead of sweat rolls down my face as he slaps a sheet of paper—a certificate of divorce that Elena (supposedly) has already signed. Seeing her fake signature sprawled on the paper sends a jolt of pain to my heart, even though I know it's bullshit.

I look up into his faded brown eyes.

"Go fuck yourself."

He shrugs and pulls it back toward himself. "Doesn't matter. We'll get your signature one way or the other."

A man fists his hand through my hair and taps my face

with a pair of filthy pliers.

"Open up."

Pull all my teeth, you sons of bitches. I don't give a fuck. I won't sign that shit.

I open my mouth and he sticks it inside. The rubber chafes against my lips as I taste the metal in my mouth. He grips the very back molars and then I know it's going to hurt like a bitch. He twists hard and I feel the bone crunching in my mouth. Delicate tissues snap as it grinds in my head and my tongue is drenched with blood. I grip the edges of my chair and fight the urge to scream as pain rivaling my gunshot wounds tears my mouth. He yanks with a sickening, wet sound and my bloodied tooth swims in front of my face. My mouth swells immediately and dark blood gushes from my lips. I spit it out as the pain throbs, almost as if there's still something stuck in there.

Fucking bastards. I'll fucking kill every last one of them.

The old fuck lays the contract there as though I'll sign it, and I spit at it. A splatter of dark blood hits the paper.

"You know, you must be the only guy in the fucking universe who's fighting so goddamn hard to keep his wife."

The guy with the pliers presses a gun to my damp head. "Sign it."

"No."

I can't believe this—I fucking failed her, Elena. My beautiful wife is going to give birth to our kid without me, and my heart squeezes to think of her. I don't give a shit about myself, it's all about her.

The door slams open and four quick blasts cut down the Popeyes where they stand. The one holding a gun to my head wheels around, screaming, but a blast from a shotgun knocks him the fuck down. My vision swims as I see *Les Diables* bikers swarming in the small room. The old fucker is still alive. He raises his hands. Kevin, one of the guys I recognize, raises his gun to his head.

"Wait," I say to him. "I want to do him."

"Let's make this quick."

Relief floods over my body as they cut through my ropes. I wonder what fucking God I have to thank for this. So many questions run through my mind, but I'm just glad that my ass is saved. I stand up, a little shaky on my feet, but Kevin hands me a gun.

"Wait," the old fuck begs. "Just wait a second. The Italian was the one who put us up to this. He never said to kill you. We weren't going t—"

BAM.

His head explodes into fragments of skull and brain matter, which vomits out the back of his head. His body lands with a loud thump to the floor.

The bikers hardly blink an eye.

"Thank you guys," I say through my swollen jaw. "How the fuck did you know I was here?"

"Thank your wife."

My wife?

I grasp his tattooed arm and he gives me a once over. "Jesus, we should get you to a hospital."

"I need to see my wife first."

"She's fine. I got one of my guys watching her."

"I'm going home to check on my wife. You can either help me or not."

My heart thuds, blood sluggishly pulsing from my wounds. Fuck, I feel like I'm going to pass out. Only sheer willpower puts one step in front of the other. I burst out of the dank room and almost trip over the couple bodies strewn on the floor. Julien gives one of them a fierce kick.

"Good thing we found this place. Looks like their stronghold. Pathetic fucks."

I don't know where the hell I am and it's pitch black outside. Jesus, how long was I out?

I pile in the van waiting for us, and the Vice-President steps outside. "Hurry the fuck up before the cops get here."

Everyone shoves themselves inside the van and I close

347

my hand over the wound in my side, which throbs with increasing intensity. It's like a stabbing pain that's impossible to ignore or distract from. Pain, pain, pain. My mind flashes with words like: searing flesh.

"He doesn't look too good."

"I'm fucking fine," I roar, my voice punctuated with pain. "I need to see her first."

"You're lucky she hired us."

Hired? What the fuck is going on?

The pieces fall together when we stop in front of my house. Johnny's car is there and a needle of pain goes right through my heart. She must have asked him for help, but he wouldn't give it to her.

One of the bikers hurries out of the van to help me climb the steps, but I shove him out of the way.

"I can do it myself!"

"Tony, you have two gunshot wounds."

I'm fine—I just fucking need to see her. I need to make sure nothing happened to her. I palm the door, and a bloody handprint smears as I push it open.

"Elena!" I yell into the apartment.

Footsteps run toward me, and then I see Elena's widened, red face and my heart clenches.

"Tony! Oh my God, you're—you're hurt!"

She rushes toward me and I wrap my arms around her

waist, an incredible wave of relief crashing over me. My eyes burn suddenly and I dig my fingers into her clothes, willing myself not to cry out.

Anything could have happened to her.

Her chest shakes against mine as she succumbs to tears, clutching me so fiercely that I grunt in pain. She pulls back, tears burning red paths down her face as she touches my jaw tenderly.

"Jesus, what did they do to you?"

"I love you, Elena."

Her lips tremble with a spark of happiness, and I feel it grow inside my chest.

"I never got to say it before they took me, and it was all I could think about."

My vision swims and I stumble backward. Elena looks horrified.

"Okay, he needs a hospital." I recognize Johnny's sharp tone and feel a sudden surge of anger toward him.

His strong arm slides across my shoulders, his hand anchoring under my good one as he lifts me upright and we make our way outside, into his car.

"You're driving me, boss? I'll get blood all over your seats."

Elena opens the passenger door for us, her face white. "Get in, Tony."

I slide inside and she takes the backseat. God, I'm tired. I just want to fall asleep, even though the leather is fucking freezing against my back.

Johnny gets inside and starts the car. It screams as we peel out of there.

"Want to tell me why my wife was forced to go to *Les Diables* for help?"

A guilty look crosses Johnny's face. "I'm sorry, Tony. I didn't think anything happened to you. I didn't—"

"You didn't believe my wife." My voice cuts across his and resentment bleeds into my chest. The bullet wounds throb with my rage.

"She didn't exactly come to me with much proof."

"Seemed to be enough for the bikers."

"She paid them—"

"Of course she fucking did, because my own family didn't think I was good enough to protect. You would have just left me for dead—"

"That's not true. If I had known, I would have put guys out on the street."

"You did know. Elena told you."

He lifts a hand, shrugging as he turns the wheel and takes a left turn. "Nothing she showed me caused me any concern."

"She's an extension of myself, and you didn't believe

her? Why the fuck would she lie about something like this?"

"I thought she was being paranoid!" He glowers at me, his young face creased with anger. "I apologize. I didn't think that fucking moron had the balls to go after you again after Vincent's warning."

Whatever.

I groan as the pain in my abdomen feels like it's twisting inside me, like a sharp blade digging in my flesh. Elena utters a gasp and threads her fingers through my hair.

"We're almost there," she says in a thick voice.

It feels good to have her hands on my skin. I sigh as she caresses my hair and Johnny gives us a strange look.

"All right, we're here."

He slams the brakes and men in white coats dash outside to meet us, rolling a stretcher between them. Johnny opens the door for me and Elena holds her hands to her face, trying to look brave for me.

"Is he—is he going to be okay?"

"I don't know, ma'am."

They roll me on the stretcher and I let out a stream of curses as my body flattens on the bed.

"White male, late twenties, multiple gunshot—"

My mind drifts as they wheel me into the hospital,

Elena keeping pace with them. She squeezes my hand.

* * *

"He's not in this hospital. I've my guys searching everywhere for him, but looks like the bastard was smart enough to avoid going to one."

A female voice, distracted. "What does that mean?"

The grim male voice booms out. "It means he's biding his time. Fuck, maybe he bled out and died in a ditch somewhere. Anyway, I still can't go to Vincent with this. There's no proof linking him to the bikers."

"I don't fucking believe this!"

Something heavy slams against a metallic object that rattles loudly. My eyes crack open and I feel strangely restricted. My chest pulses and I feel the strict bandage over my shoulder. An ice bag sits against my cheek, freezing the skin.

My eyes slide over to John, who stands next to my wife near the window.

"If you won't kill him, I will."

They both start when they realize I'm awake. A slow smile pulls at Elena's lips as she approaches my bed and kisses my forehead. She takes the bag of ice away and looks at me through warm eyes. Perfect love and trust shines through them.

Johnny looks at me, unsmiling, pulling me irresistibly to

the present.

"My hands are fucking tied, but I can't ignore this. We'll take care of him."

"Fuck that, I want to be the one to kill that motherfucker."

I rip the blanket off my legs and attempt to sit up. My side screams in pain, and Elena pushes me back down. "Don't be stupid. You're in no condition."

"Fuck my condition."

Johnny grins at me. "Did your wife tell you she shot that asshole?"

What the fuck?

Elena lowers her eyes when I glare at her. "What the fuck is he talking about?"

"I thought you were dead."

"Elena, what the fuck happened."

She flinches at my tone. "I wanted him to come to me so I could kill him. I almost did."

Holy shit.

"Are you out of your mind? Someone could have seen you. You could have been hurt."

Her eyes glimmer with angry tears. "I had to do something!"

Johnny looks at my wife with a bit of grudging respect. None of the other guys' wives would have had the balls to do what she did.

She's crazy.

She's mine.

"Nothing can be done until we find the guy. Just rest, Tony."

Just rest. Easy for him to fucking say.

A familiar voice yelling down the hallway makes my guts seize.

Oh fucking no.

"*Where's my son?*"

"Mrs. Vidal, your son is talking to Johnny."

A muffled voice from outside is cut off by my mother's angry retort.

"I don't give a damn about that man. Get out of my way!"

"Mrs. Vidal!"

"I'll go. See you later, Tone." Johnny gives me a short wave before heading outside. Part of me wants to call him back.

"Oh fuck."

Elena's hands freeze in my hair as my mother bursts through the door, looking as though she's aged several years.

"Oh my God. My son! My beautiful son—what happened?"

Elena steps away from the bed as Ma comes barreling for me. I brace for the impact as she throws her arms around my neck and squeezes.

"I'm just a little banged up, Ma."

"You were shot! Who did this to you?" She speaks in a low, gritty voice, as though the neighborhood kid beat me up.

"Don't worry about it."

Her face screws up in anger and she swells like a bullfrog. "Don't worry about it? Why don't you tell that to your wife and baby? How the hell are you going to raise this kid if you're getting shot—"

"Ma, *relax*."

Her mouth trembles as she falls silent, her eyes wrinkled in pain. "Tony, I love you but you are destroying yourself."

Her seething voice cuts me deeper than the wounds burrowed in my body. I never wanted this, and I can't get out.

"You know I can't leave."

"Try. For their sakes."

Elena's worried face meets mine, and I watch her flatten her shirt over her belly. The one that has my baby growing inside her. Sadness clenches my heart and I let my head fall back on the pillows, blinking rapidly. The thought of leaving them crushes my heart. For the first time in my life, I'm afraid. I don't want to die.

Ma's face hovers over mine, and she seems to understand the turmoil in my head.

"It's different when you have a kid, isn't it?"

Yeah, it is.

ELENA

My hands smooth over Tony's sculpted arms, tracing over the intricate tattoos inked on his tanned skin. He closes his eyes as if it soothes him to have my hands on his skin, and then he takes my hand and brings it to his lips. A bump of pleasure lifts my heart as he kisses the skin, and then his grey eyes open to mine, lust and devotion swirling together.

We haven't really said much to each other since it all happened. It was hard getting a moment away from the people constantly visiting him, but now a heavy silence falls over us both.

"I need to change your bandage."

"So change it."

A wide smirk staggers over his face as I straddle his waist. I change his shoulder first, gently peeling the bandage coated with rusty blood. He doesn't make a sound, even though it must sting. His hands stroke my sides as his charcoal eyes never stray from my face.

All the unsaid things glow from Tony's eyes. I'm vividly aware that this is the first time we're actually alone together. No doctors to interrupt us, no mother to pop in unannounced, nothing. Heat builds up between us until I have to wipe my hands over my jeans.

Underneath my legs, I feel him hardening into a stiff rock. I meet his gaze warily and I inhale a sharp breath. Fuck, he just always looks so delectable. Even now with his five o' clock shadow, I just want to run my fingers along his jaw and stare into those deep eyes as he rams me hard.

"Tony, we can't. The doctor said—"

"The doctor said a lot of shit."

The heat in his voice makes me lick my lips. "Seriously, though. You could hurt yourself."

"I'll fuck you when I want to fuck you, stitches be damned."

He leans forward, kissing my neck. The feeling of his lips pressed against mine gently strokes the fire simmering inside me. It's been a couple weeks since I've felt him inside me. We've just had stolen kisses in the hospital bed, a hand job while the nurses were occupied, that's it. Tony's face blazes with need, his hair already tousled from the many times I've run my hands through it.

"Sweetie, let me do the work."

I lift myself and reach down, touching his iron-stiff cock.

"No, I'll never let you do that again."

I'm not sure what he's referring to, but then again, Tony's been odd lately. It must have been his close brush with death. He hasn't let me out of his sight.

He stands up and takes my hand, a devilish look on his face. Cock vivid against his jeans, he pulls them down, his biceps straining. I help him undress, kissing the hard bump straining against his briefs.

"This fucking wife of mine." He stares down at me, his eyes shining. "You saved my life, and I hate that. I hate that I put you in that position, but I love you for being so fucking brave."

My chest bursts with affection as I stand up in his arms, and he holds me as though he needs it, as though he's still beating himself up over it.

"I love you, Tony. I'd do anything for you. Always."

He takes me to the bedroom and pulls the t-shirt from my head. The bra unsnaps from my back with a twist of his hand, and that falls to the ground, too.

I love this, just being naked with him, our bodies exposed to one another. He touches me like I'm a piece of art, sadness still lingering in his eyes. I don't know why.

I take off my pants and he follows my every move. He watches as I struggle with the tightness of the fabric. It snags my panties and those drop down. He touches my belly again and I imagine what it'll be like when it starts kicking. My heart races whenever he puts his hands on me.

Then he lowers his head, lips brushing against my ear. "Having you there at the hospital was hell. They don't tell you about the raging hard-ons you get when you're naked under the sheets and your wife is right there, but you can't fuck her."

His hand covers my breast and I shudder at the contact. Hot lips sear against the side of my head as he pinches my hard nipple.

"You have me now."

He grabs the base of my neck gently and makes me sit down on the edge of the bed. I slide my hands up his muscular thighs and pull his black briefs down, so that his cock bounces free. I grab the veined, stiff cock and my lips roll over his head. Tony sighs and pulls away from me.

"I need your pussy right now."

Tony covers my body with his as he pushes me over the bed, spreading my thighs with his hand. The head of his burning cock pushes hard against the ache crying out for him, for his thickness. I love that sound he makes when he sheathes himself for the first time. My wetness gathers around him as he pulls out and shoves it back in, deep inside my pussy. He's never been this gentle with me. Never looked at me with so much love in his eyes. It's hard to describe, but they almost look fractured. In pain.

My body clenches around him as he pulses inside me, hammering my pussy as he breathes into my neck.

"I fuckin' need you."

He stops for a moment, grabbing my tits and then sinking his teeth into my neck.

I need him too—need this passion in my life. I need his cock inside me and his cum, too. The future unfolds for me. We'll have more kids, and we'll have a lot of fun making them. He makes me happier than I ever could have dreamed.

He kisses my damp neck as I dig my fingers into his back, screaming into the ceiling as he hits my g-spot with his cock. Then a groan shakes from his throat, and his cock stabs me hard. He empties his cock in my womb, and I feel the sticky warmth inside me.

We kiss like two teenagers who just discovered sex. He bites my bottom lip and butterflies flutter in my chest as he looks at me with that slightly drunken expression.

"I love you."

But a frown descends over his face.

"What's wrong?"

He rolls on his back and opens and closes his mouth a few times, staring at the ceiling. "You know what's wrong."

I rub my arm feverishly. Rafael. He's nowhere to be

found.

"It drives me insane knowing he's still out there."

"I don't think I'll be able to sleep. I just—I have no idea what his end game is."

Tony's eyes flick to me, and I almost flinch from the darkness. "You. You're his end game."

I don't like hearing that. Bitterness curls my lip. "I'm not a fucking trophy. I'm not a goddamn possession."

"I'm just as possessive as your ex. I just don't have to hurt anyone to keep what's mine." He takes my chin gently, and even though his words should make my blood run cold, they have the opposite effect. "There's no way in hell I'd let you go."

I don't want you to.

We lay there in bed for a while and gradually Tony closes his eyes. Sound asleep. I let him. The doctor said he needed rest, but I can't rest. My nerves are fucked from being back in this house, where Rafael knows exactly where to find us.

I get up from the bed and grab my phone off the nightstand, which lights up with a new text:

Need to see you. Tell no one, or I go to the police and tell them who really shot me.

The blood drains right out of me. I can almost feel it pooled at my feet.

He has my number from the phone he stole from Tony. He's still after me.

I look over at Tony's sleeping form, knowing how enraged he'd be if he knew that Rafael contacted me. He would want to find him, but what if he didn't? What if he went to the police?

The phone shakes in my hand. I don't know what to do.

What do you want?

Meet me here. Now.

The text has a map pointing to a motel outside of town. The hair rises on the back of my neck.

No fucking way I'm meeting you there.

Then enjoy prison, I guess.

A shock of cold horror runs through me, like a rippling wave. Prison. Either he could link the gun that shot him to me, or Tony.

I just want to talk.

I don't believe that for a second.

How stupid do you think I am? I'm not going anywhere near you.

I wonder if the guards will let me in the cell with you if I bribe them.

My lip curls as I stare at the screen. *Fuck you.* I am not going to jail, and neither is Tony. I won't be lured into a trap.

In the living room, I peel back the curtains and stare into the white streets, heart hammering. What should I do?

I could meet him.

I could kill him.

My heart seizes at the thought. I know I'm capable. I'll do anything to save Tony and my baby. And I owe him.

Just look at him. Look at what you cost him.

My heart breaks when I look at Tony's sleeping, exhausted body. He's been shot, and he's had one of his molars ripped out all because of me. Rafael's too smart to be tracked down, but maybe I can do the work for them. For fuck's sake, I don't want to rely on anyone anymore. I was Daddy's girl, but I'm not anymore. I'm not just Tony's wife, either.

I'm Elena, and I can handle this piece of shit.

I look at Tony, almost wishing he was awake so that he could stop me from leaving. My heart slams against my chest as I gather my purse and slip out the door, locking it behind me.

* * *

My footsteps echo hollowly through the mostly empty parking lot. A dirty, dingy motel lays in front of me.

It's dangerous. I know that, but I'm also familiar with Rafael's moods. Now that he actually thinks he's the father of my child, he won't hurt me.

Too bad I have no problem hurting him.

I knock on the door, legs shaking as the blinds ripple near the window. The door cracks open and I stare into the nozzle of a gun.

"You're alone?"

A sliver of a man shows through the door.

"Yeah."

"Good. Get in."

The door swings open and Rafael beckons me from the darkness. I hesitate, wavering on my feet, and he reaches forward and yanks me inside. The door slams shut and my back hits the solid wood as Rafael presses his angular body into mine, his hot, greedy lips at my neck. Hands touch my waist and a surge of vomit rises up my throat. I shove his chest hard and he stumbles backward.

"Don't *fucking* touch me."

Rafael doesn't look as coked out as he has the last few times I've seen him. He wears a white tank top and dark blue jeans, the bandage visible behind the shirt. A pained look crosses his face. For a moment I think it's remorse, then I notice the way his hand flies to his shoulder. I realize I shoved him where his wound was. Good.

"You wanted to talk. *So talk*."

That dangerous, calm look falls over his face as he corners me, close enough so that I can see every stubble on his cheek. His lips are inches from mine, and his eyes are clear. They're filled with deadly calm.

Oh God. I don't like this.

"Let me tell you what's going to happen if you don't do what I say. I'll tell the police who shot me, and after a short trial, you get a couple years in prison. Long enough for you to give birth there."

Where the fuck is this going?

Horror slowly fills my chest as a creeping smile spreads over his face. God, his smile used to make me glow. Now it just makes me sick. His fingers touch my frozen cheek, then my neck.

"They'll take the baby away from you soon as it's born. It'll be ripped from your arms."

It's like a grey cloud rolling over my head. I'm cast in a black shadow. Rafael seems to glorify my despair.

"Then I establish paternity for the kid, and I take it away from you."

"*No.*"

It's like a whisper. It barely passes from my lips, but Rafael hears it. His fingers brush over my bottom lip.

"Yes."

He can't do this to me. An image of my swollen self, pacing the small cell of a prison cell haunts my mind. Giving birth in prison, and almost immediately having a nurse rip the child away from my arms.

He can't do this.

"It's not even your baby!"

He raises his eyebrow, smile trembling. "Are you sure about that?"

No, I'm not. As much as I want the baby to be Tony's, as much as I hope that it's his, I'm not completely sure.

It's a horrifying image. As far-fetched I think his plan is—it still stabs my chest like a knife. I force myself to keep calm, to make myself seem like I really believe this shit. He'll drop his guard, and I'll get him. Somehow.

The room echoes with my shuddering gasps. I slump against the door, pretending to lose all strength in my limbs. Rafael wraps an arm around my waist, and I'm terrified by his warmth.

"I don't want to do this to us, Elena, but I will get what I want."

"You can't do this to me." I beg him with my eyes. "Please."

I'll kill you.

"You'll leave Tony, or you'll never see your kid again."

"Leave Tony?"

Leave the man I love? He must be insane if he thinks I'm going to actually go through with this, but inwardly I rejoice. He might as well have handed his head on a silver platter.

I'll go to Tony, sure. I'll tell him exactly where you are.

Rafael has the balls to grin at me. It's a wide, self-assured grin, not unlike the one Tony gives me, but so undeserving. He's such a piece of shit. A worm. A parasite unworthy to stand on the same ground as my beautiful, brave husband.

Rafael's sinewy arms wrap around me, pulling me against his chest. I ball my hands at my sides, holding them rigid as he wraps me inside his poisonous embrace.

"We belong together."

"We really fucking don't."

"I understand why you left, but it's different now. I'm off the coke." His lips hover right over my ear, just close enough to make me shiver violently. "I'll be a good father to our kid, and I sure as shit won't let another man come between us."

I let tears slip down my cheeks, and Rafael wipes them away greedily.

"No—I don't want—no!"

He grabs my jaw firmly as he plants his lips against my jaw. "I won, Elena. Just accept it."

I won't accept it.

The police in Montreal are not going to give a shit about a suspect for attempted murder if I'm in New York.

They'd have to extradite me, which could take weeks. He's out of his mind.

"You need to break up with him, and you need to make it convincing."

I screw up my face, pretending to be devastated. "I won't!"

He forces my jaw forward, so that I'm facing him. "Then I call the police right fucking now and they haul your ass to jail."

"This whole plan of yours makes no sense. Once they find out that you—you've coerced a member's wife, they'll kill you. Vincent will kill you."

"Not while this baby is mine." He growls in my face, reflexively grabbing my belly.

I slap his hand away, and he gives me an extremely offended look.

"I'm not yours to touch anymore. Keep your fucking hands to yourself."

Within seconds, his hand curls in my hair and he wrenches my neck hard, twisting my arm behind my back, making my cry out in pain. Deep loathing burns through my eyes as I look at Rafael's twisting grin. I hate how easy it is for him to make me cry out in pain. I struggle in his grasp, but it's useless. I'm no match for years and years of hardened brutality.

"These fucking tits."

He lets out a growl like a rabid animal and gropes my breast, his hand twisting my hair. The ugly violation boils my blood, but I'm powerless to stop him. He slides under my shirt and slips underneath my bra, mauling my sensitive flesh.

"Stop—please, stop!"

He lets me go so suddenly that I stumble to the floor. Immediately, I wrap my jacket around myself. Rafael's cruel laughter rings in the small room.

My fear makes him laugh.

"What's the matter, hon? You used to like it rough, remember? You used to *beg* for this." He grabs his cock and gives it a squeeze, and I turn away with a look of revulsion.

"Touch me again, and I'll scream."

His eyes narrow again and he digs a finger into the center of my chest. "You know what'll happen if you make one fucking sound."

Make him think you've lost. You've done it before.

My eyes lower from his and Rafael lets out a grunt, satisfied with my submission. This sudden surge of self-conscious introspection won't last, that I'm sure of. He'll go back to snorting lines and smacking me around.

Only this time, I'll be ready.

Because the first chance I get, I'm killing him.

The chair drags over the shitty carpet as Rafael pulls it out and sits down, stripping his white tank top from his shoulders. The bandage on his shoulder is soaked through, and he massages it with a tired look on his face. He beckons me with his finger.

"What?"

"Change my bandage."

I'll change your fucking bandage.

I step forward and rip the bandage from his shoulder, smirking as he lets out a sharp hiss.

"What the fuck is your problem?"

Are you seriously that stupid?

The genuine surprise on his face makes me livid. "You're insane, that's my problem. This fucking plan of yours isn't going to work. Tony is not going to let me go anywhere with you."

The slick grin on his face twitches as I slap the fresh bandage over his skin. He cocks his head, studying me. Then his hand shoots out, grabbing my wrist. I yank hard, and then I twist my arm. He bends my wrist in a painful position and tears spring to my eyes. He yanks my body so that I fall over his lap. I cringe from the warmth of his chest and his hand snaking around my waist.

"Then you better find a good reason to tell him to back

371

off."

I try to get up, my abdominal muscles tensing against his powerful arm, but I fall back onto his lap. "Let me go!"

"What the fuck is your problem? Why are you giving me such a hard time?"

I want to scream.

I dig my elbow in his wounded shoulder and he screams in pain, releasing me immediately. He stands up from the chair, a murderous look snarling his features. My heart stammers and I wonder what the hell I'm doing. Why am I provoking him? I forget all about my plan as rage bursts from my mouth.

"I don't want you! I can't fucking *stand* you. For months, I was biding my time until I had a chance to leave. I took it and never looked back. You were the one who couldn't fucking let go!"

His muscles tense as he screams. "Because you don't get to fucking decide when we're over, especially when you are carrying my fucking kid."

"It's not your kid!"

He grabs my arms, his thumbs digging in hard enough to make me moan. He looks as though he wants to throw me against the wall, and I wait for it. His lips tremble as he bares his teeth like an animal, but he slowly releases me, breathing in deeply.

"I won't hit you because you're pregnant."

"You're a scumbag and you don't deser—"

My face whips to the side as a stinging slap burns my cheek.

I fucking hate him.

"I have no problem with slapping you around when you give me a smart mouth. That won't hurt the baby."

"I'm glad you're so confident."

This time I catch a blur of his hand as it hits me again, my eyes stinging.

"Want another one, you stupid bitch?"

His hand hovers above my face and I watch it, hating the weak part of me that makes me shake my head.

* * *

Crowds of people jostle me as I make my way through throngs of people shopping, eagerly jabbering in French. My eyes sift through the crowd to find my husband's face.

So that I can tell him what I did.

He'll be furious with me. I spent the night under Rafael's watchful gaze as I sat in the chair, refusing to occupy the same space as him.

But now it's over. I know exactly where he is, and I'll point Tony in the direction. I stand there, brain abuzz with what I'm supposed to say to him.

I watch him check his phone anxiously. He runs a hand

over his face, looking stressed, and I feel a pang for the pain I've caused him. He looks over his hand and recognizes me. Relief floods his face and he gets up from the table. The relief melts away from the heat baking his skin. His jaw sets and he—there's no other word for it— he looks *pissed*. My heart squeezes at the sight of him looking so upset.

Tony's sculpted arms grab me, and for a moment I think he's going to throttle my neck, but he pulls me into his chest. He holds me so tightly that my lungs wheeze, and his fingers curl into my hair as a sound I've never heard from Tony shakes from his chest.

"I was so fucking worried, Elena. I had half my guys out looking for you."

The worry in his voice throttles my chest. It's torture. I bury my face in his chest without saying a word, inhaling the sharp spice of his deodorant. This is where I belong. It takes every effort inside me not to break down.

"I'm *fine*."

He pulls away from me, his hands still holding my shoulders as sharp eyes scan my face. Can he see the tracks on my face?

"You know you're a shit liar, right?"

"Tony—"

"*You left me in the middle of the night.*"

"I had to go."

Thick eyebrows narrow dangerously. "Lie again, and I'll bend you over my knee right here."

An involuntary shiver runs through my body at the image of that. Tony seems to sense how it makes me feel and a heart-stopping smile tiptoes across his face.

"Fuck."

His thumb sweeps across my bottom lip right before he crushes his mouth against mine.

He's watching you right now.

But right now I don't care. I'm in Tony's arms, and when I look at him I can't help but feel that everything's going to be all right.

"I think you better tell me where the fuck you were."

He drags me to the table and we sit down together, his eyes never leaving my face. Fuck, I can't breathe when he looks at me like that.

Tony makes an impatient growl at the back of his throat. "You better start talking, or I just might make good on my fucking promise."

"Just hear me out. Okay?"

Tears well up in my eyes, consumed with the vision of me behind bars. I swallow them down, trying to free that knot in my throat. Gentle fingers touch my cheek.

"It's him, isn't it?"

375

Tony's eyes widen as it dawns over him. Fists clenched, he stands up from the seat and stares into the crowds of people. "Where is that piece of shit? I'll kill him right now." He looks around the mall. "Is he here, watching us?" His fist slams into the table separating us. "Talk to me, Goddamnit!"

"He's here. I lured him here for you."

I don't expect him to be happy, but I expect him to be pleased, at least. His eyes are red-hot as they scorch through my skin. "What the hell were you thinking?"

"Tony, you don't understand. I can't—we can't—"

He yanks me back down on my seat, his snarling face right up against mine. People around us are starting to stare, and a man behind Tony gives me a concerned look. He digs his fingers into my hair.

"Tell me what happened."

"I met him at a motel. He said I'd go to jail if I didn't. I just wanted him to believe he had me under his control, so we could finally get rid of him." My voice cracks as I finally break in half, folding in on myself.

Tony's eyes smolder as his lips tremble, white with rage. "You went to a motel with him. Alone."

I know what he's thinking.

"I don't know what the fuck you were thinking—"

"He says I'm going to jail, Tony. I shot him. I needed

to do *something*."

I stand up again, hating how furious he is with me. He grabs my waist again and a flash of anger sears up my throat, which dissolves when he gives me that look.

"Then why not fucking tell me about it? Why the hell would you go off on your own?"

"I've already done enough to you."

It hurts me that he can't see that I was only trying to save him from whatever hell Rafael has planned for him.

"I can take care of myself, Elena." His eyes smolder. "How dare you make this decision without me? We're married, and that means you involve me in every fucking decision."

Tony's face looks somehow shadowed, even in the bright lights inside the mall. His black, flyaway hair hangs over his face, the stubble on his cheeks overgrown, but his eyes are cold. A chill emanates from them, and I wonder if I've crossed some boundary with him—if I've gone past the point of no forgiveness. He takes my face in his hands as my breaths quicken to short gasps that hardly give me any air.

"I don't know for sure if it's yours. And if it isn't, and if I'm in jail, then he gets custody—then *he* raises my kid."

Tony watches my face, speechless as tears slide down my face.

377

"Elena, that's a lot of 'ifs.' And it's not going to happen."

"You c—can't be sure."

"That baby inside you is mine and when I find him, I'll make the bastard pay for everything he's done to us."

"But Tony—"

"I don't give a fuck what he told you. You should never have left the apartment. It was *stupid* to put yourself in so much danger."

It stings to hear the truth lash across my face like that, even worse to see the pain fracturing his eyes.

"Don't you trust me to keep you safe?"

Of course I do.

"I just wanted to take care of him myself."

How can I tell him that I'm trying to be a better person? I don't want to have to rely on anyone. That's what I did before, with Dad. That's all.

"No. Your job is to stay home and keep your legs open for your husband, to take his cock whenever he needs you to. Protecting you is my job."

His hand suddenly grabs my ass as he leans in, crushing his lips to mine as his fingers burrow in my hair. My heart pounds as his tongue shoves inside my mouth, tasting me. Heat burns my face as I imagine the people in the mall, staring at the spectacle we're making. Nothing compares to the horror I feel—Rafael is watching. He's going to know something is up.

He ends the kiss, breathing hard as he rests his forehead against mine. "I can't fucking stand it—can't take it that he fucking had you in a motel room."

Bile rises up my throat. "Tony, nothing happened."

His hands shake at his sides as he looks away from me, overcome with emotion. He can't look at me.

It's as though he can't stand the sight of me.

My voice is small. "I'm sorry."

He explodes. "That fucker is the only one who's going to be sorry. He fucked my wife!"

The bottom drops out of my stomach. That's what he thinks? "I didn't let him. Tony, I swear!"

"FUCK!"

My heart hammers against my chest as he stands up, yanking me with him. I've never seen him so upset. The grip on my hand is almost painful as he marches me through the crowd, his chest pulsing like a bull's. His arms flush with blood. "I'm going to inflict as much pain on that bastard as possible."

I dig in my heels, stopping him. The face that looks at me isn't one I recognize. It's ugly, full of hate and a twisted malice.

"*Nothing happened.* I didn't let him touch me."

"It doesn't matter to them!"

His nostrils flare as he looks at me with a tortured look. *Them?*

"My boss—all my fucking colleagues are going to think that I'm some fucking joke."

"You know what really happened. Who gives a fuck what anyone thinks?"

He stares at me for a moment, his face blank. "My reputation matters, sweetheart. If people think I'm a chump, why the fuck should they pay up on time?" His seething heat surrounds me as he grabs my upper arm. "*You* matter to me. I care what people think of my wife. A man who can't keep his wife in line isn't a fucking man."

"I'm not your goddamn *property.*"

Then he draws me closer, until my fists are against his chest and a warm smile spreads across his face. "Yeah? That's not what you said last night."

I'm amazed at how hot my face gets when he gives me that searing, confident look and the smile that always makes my butterflies out of control.

Tension balls in my stomach as he leads us outside.

It feels like a fist inside me, squeezing my organs until stars burst in my vision. Oblivious to my anxiety, Tony pulls my hand and leads me into the crisp outdoors.

"Where is he?"

I expect Rafael to jump from around the corner, gun blazing.

"He's probably gone by now. He must know I didn't do what he wanted."

Anxiety trembles through my voice. My plan fell apart like a house of cards. I expect to see a shadow of him lurking somewhere, but there's no sign of him. It makes me uneasy. Tony yanks me across the parking lot and into his car.

Tony makes a few calls while he drives us away. I keep silent as he talks on the phone, trying to suppress the desire to lower my head from the window. Tony looks on edge, too.

Then he stops in front of *Le Zinc*, and a man comes outside to greet us.

"Go with him inside. I'm going to find parking."

He says it in a voice that bids no argument, and I reluctantly open the door to walk the short distance from the curb to the restaurant, the man following behind me.

It reminds me when my dad was still alive. Dad sent his guys to chaperone me to places, usually when he was in hot water. The familiarity calms me down somewhat. The restaurant is closed, but all of Johnny's people are there, standing in the middle of the dining area. At the sight of the Montreal boss, my insides tighten. He's never liked me.

Tommy stands apart from the guys, his arms crossed. I can feel the judgment rolling from his gaze heating my face.

He still thinks we're running a scam.

A wide, toothy smile spreads on Johnny's handsome face. He beckons me closer and I slide into a chair.

"You want anything to drink?"

I still haven't forgiven him for refusing to help me track down Tony. "No."

No, thanks, you mean.

The rudeness doesn't slide past Johnny, who frowns at me, saying nothing. I hate sitting here, being surrounded by all these men I don't trust. They look down at me, occasionally I catch a glimpse of a sneer and I wonder if they made their own minds about where I was last night.

Fuck.

French words and laughter surround me, and I wonder if they're talking about me. It seems like it from the way they glance away from me when I meet their eyes, and the way they laugh with their backs to me. An unpleasant, sick feeling festers in my stomach and I remember what Tony told me.

They want a fucking spectacle? I'll give them that.

I lift the napkin sitting on the table to my eyes and I screw up my face.

Cry. Cry, damn it.

Sobs break from my throat just as the door from the front of the yesterday swings open. The French chatter drops as my voice echoes through the restaurant, and suddenly Johnny's hand is on my back.

"What's the matter?"

"He took me," I wail. "He took me from the apartment. I stepped outside f—for some fresh air and he grabbed me. Then he took me t—to his motel—"

"All right," Johnny says in a leaden voice.

"He had a gun to my head. I thought I was going to die."

I lift my head from the tissue as the men glance at each other, looking more sympathetic.

"He wouldn't let me leave—"

"That's enough," Johnny says quellingly.

"It's not nearly enough."

Tony's gravelly voice rumbles behind me, and my sobs subside as he takes both shoulders in his hands.

"Johnny, I got to talk to you."

"All right. Let's go to my office."

He stands up, and to my surprise Tony tugs my shoulders. "C'mon."

Making a show of wiping my face, I follow Johnny into the back, passing Tommy's stony face. We file into Johnny's office, taking seats behind his desk as he takes his.

"Johnny, we need to—"

"Shut the fuck up."

My heart jumps at the sudden heat blazing from his voice. His hands grip the edge of the desk, his knuckles white.

"Tommy told me everything."

Fuck.

"Told you what?"

I stare at Tony, surprised by the hostility in his tone. *He's the boss! You can't talk like that to him!*

"I know the wedding and pregnancy were part of a giant scam. I know about the money, and I've already taken my cut." Johnny fumes at me across the table. "That's thirty-thousand dollars you'll never see again."

Behind my simmering fear, I feel a ripple of anger. He has no right to that money.

"I never took a dime from her, John. It is real, she showed me the tests."

"I don't give a fuck. You disrespected me by lying to my face. I should fucking kill you."

Tony clenches the arms of his chair, staring at Johnny. "What are you going to do about Rafael?"

"Why the fuck is that my problem? As far as I'm concerned, he's Vincent's problem."

"He tried to kill me. Did you forget about that?"

Johnny takes a pen from his desk and bends it in his hands, finally hurling it back down.

"That was before I knew you lied to me and brought all this bullshit on this family."

The breath catches in my throat as the last words fall from Johnny's lips like a battle-axe. Without their support, we really are fucked.

"I won't deny that she came to me and asked me to do this for her."

Johnny smiles bitterly.

"But I never took a dime from her, and she is carrying my kid. That's a fact. You want to believe a fucking Yankee over me, that's your fucking problem."

The boss' eyes flash dangerously. "I'm not convinced. Your wife gave quite a performance outside, when I know for a fact she left your apartment willingly because I had Tommy watch the place."

A knock at the door disturbs us, but I'm almost grateful for the intrusion. The tension between the two men is red hot, and deadly. The veins in Tony's neck stick out as if he was screaming. He turns around and snarls at the door.

"What?"

"Police, open the door!"

"Who the fuck let them in the restaurant?" Johnny snarls.

There's a brief moment of silence before the officer knocks on the door again. Having no choice, Tony stands up and opens the door. Men in blue stand at the threshold, Johnny's men not far behind them.

"Tony Vidal?"

My husband crosses his arms. "That's me."

"You're under arrest."

TONY

Elena's face pales as they slap handcuffs around my wrists.

I grimace as the prick cop yanks on them. "What the fuck for?"

"Attempted murder."

"Attempted murder? On who?"

He ignores my question and reads me my rights as drags me from the office, Johnny's malevolent face fixed on Elena. No, I can't leave her right now. I can't fucking go to jail right now.

This couldn't come at a worse fucking time. Johnny's eyes narrow dangerously at me. He's thinking that I fucked up and didn't get rid of one of the bodies correctly, but there's no fucking way.

She charges to the officer and steps in front of us, blocking the way. "Who filed the charges?"

"Ma'am, you're blocking the way."

She screams at the officer, mak laugh. "WHO IS IT? It's R

The officer's blank f?

sinks as I hear the trem.

That fucking cock-sucking

me right where he wants. She thought he was going to put her in jail, but it was really me he was planning to fuck over. Just so that he could have a clear shot at my wife.

"No, it's me—I'm—"

"Shut the hell up!" I turn to Johnny, who stands next to her. "Johnny, take her away from here."

That's all I fucking need. My wife to confess to shooting Rafael's worthless body.

I catch Tommy's eye desperately as I turn around. "Tommy, please. Keep my wife safe until I'm out."

He opens his mouth but I don't hear his reply when I'm hauled out of the restaurant. The cold bites my cheeks and my eyes burn instantly, and I think of her, surrounded by wolves.

* * *

I'm going to kill that prick.

When I find you, you rat fuck—

I can't even finish the sentence, because every method of torture I can think of is too good for that asshole. The dank cell echoes with my footsteps as I pace along its length. I'm stuck in here while Rafael is free to do God knows what to my wife, and who knows if Johnny will intervene to help her.

throat closes at the thought, and I grasp the bars. ings to my hands like dirt, and I think about

Elena's broken face as I was led out of that restaurant in cuffs. I hate this. Why the fuck did they have to cuff me in front of her?

The door to the prison cell cracks open. "Tony Vidal, lawyer!"

Fuck, the last person I give a shit about seeing. He's a sharply dressed Jew, a guy the mob keeps on retainer.

"When the fuck can I get out?"

"Unfortunately, the judge won't grant you a bail given your—eh, history."

Fucking hell. I knew it.

It's not a huge problem. I'll have to grease the judge.

"Who's the judge?"

He glances at some sheets of paper. "Judge Giuliani."

Inwardly, I smirk to myself. He's known to us because he nearly always accepts a well-paid bribe. It's tricky, though. I can't just fucking hand it to him, and there's no fucking way Johnny will front the cash for me, especially after what happened.

Elena, hang in there. Please.

My lawyer leaves, and I make a phone call to one of my associates, who agrees to send the bribe for me. Then it's back to pacing in this fucking cell, and going out of my mind with worry. I smash my fist into the bars, rattling this fucking cage. My wife—Jesus—what's going to happen to her?

"Tony Vidal, visitor!"

The guard yells into the room as the door unlocks, admitting a man. Please fucking tell me it's John. He steps into the light, a predatory smile spreading over his thin face.

"You fucking crazy moron."

Rafael came to visit me in jail. I cannot fucking believe this.

I clench the bars and boil with rage. He's so close—so fucking close. Rafael approaches the bars, almost close enough for me to reach his fucking neck.

"Before you spend the next decade rotting in jail, I just wanted to let you know I'll be getting my dick wet with your wife."

"FUCK YOU! I'LL FUCKING KILL YOU!" I slam my body against the bars, determined to force them apart.

His laughter reverberates throughout the room, echoing horribly in my ears. "She's in my car. The little bitch came running for me the moment you were arrested. Turns out, she'll suck anyone's cock for a favor."

The banging of my fists against the bars clashes with his horrible laughter. I don't believe it. I can't believe it. Still a nasty feeling rises up my throat.

"She wants me to drop the charges." He sucks on his

bottom lip and rolls his eyes as if in ecstasy. "But why should I let go of a pussy that sweet? She fits around my cock like a damn glove."

I stand there, shaking with all the energy coursing through my veins.

"When I get out of here, the first thing I'm going to rip off your balls and boil them in motor oil."

He smirks at me and takes a step backward. "Careful. You don't want them to hear you saying that."

My fingers curl around the bars. "Touch my wife again—"

"And you'll what? Hit the bars?" He gets close enough so that his breath billows across my face. "Face it, fuckwad. She belongs to me. There's no coincidence that she left me right around the time she got pregnant."

I laugh at the logic spinning this brain. This guy is as crazy as he is dangerous. "*She chose me.*"

"Maybe, but I'm taking her back."

He turns away from me, giving me a final grin over his shoulder as he walks to the door and pounds it. The bars vibrate, rattling like gongs as I tear into them, screaming until my voice is hoarse, until I can't even make out what the fuck I'm screaming.

* * *

My fist smashes against the door and it flies open,

banging against the opposite wall. Wiseguys look over their shoulders at the intrusion, scowling at me for letting the cold air inside. I power through the bar, only having eyes for the man behind the bar, who looks up at me with a smile.

"Hey, Tony. You got out fast."

I push the waitress who offers me a drink aside and grab his collar as his face barely registers surprise, slamming him against the wall.

"Where the fuck is she?"

The bottles rattle behind him as he looks at my hand grabbing his collar with a venomous look. "How the fuck should I know?"

"WHERE THE FUCK IS SHE?"

I shove his chest hard, and his arm knocks over a bottle of Windsor Canadian whiskey. It falls like a rock and shatters, spraying cheap whiskey all over the floor. I seize the broken neck of the bottle and lunge at Tommy's neck. His eyes widen as I grab the hair on his head and dig the broken, jagged edges of glass against his neck. Pinpricks of blood well up around the sharp pieces and he winces.

"What the fuck are you doing?"

"I asked you to watch over my wife."

"I think you can cut the act now. Johnny knows everything."

"THIS IS NOT A FUCKING ACT!"

Every rough syllable digs the glass deeper into Tommy's skin, and I hear a female scream behind me—one of the waitresses. Male voices urge me to calm down, or they otherwise laugh at the spectacle I'm giving them.

"Calm down, Tony—"

My voice dials down to a gritty whisper, and Tommy's anxious hazel eyes find mine. I don't give a fuck about slitting his throat, right here, right now, and he knows it.

"I will kill you right fucking here if you don't tell me where my wife is."

Tommy's throat bulges and he swallows hard. "She left with him, all right?"

With him.

They let her leave with that scumbag.

"Can I ask you something? Why the fuck do you care about her?"

The edge of the broken half of the bottle smashes over Tommy's head as I lunge at his face. I let him drop to the ground as he cradles his head.

He looks up at me through a haze of broken bits of glass and blood. "I'm going to kill you."

He lunges at my middle and I fall backward, my back hitting the hard ground. Pierre and Francois suddenly materialize out of thin air, grabbing Tommy's arms before he can swing a fist. An animalistic look snarls Tommy's face, and it takes four guys to hold him back.

The energy and the fight flows out of me when I realize Elena probably left with him because he promised to drop charges against me. He coerced her, but no one would have known or cared to stop her.

"She's pregnant, and you let her leave with that psycho."

Tommy's chest pulses as he struggles against the guys holding him. "It's a fucking scam!"

"No, it's not—that's what I've been trying to tell you, you stupid fuck!"

They finally let him go as I slump against the bar. It's as though he slid a knife between my ribs. Then I think of the girl I loved when I was seventeen, and how she turned up dead in the streets. I felt like the pain would kill me, but it's nothing compared to losing Elena.

I bury my face in my hands and my face screws up. The bar goes quiet—really quiet. No one's ever seen me like this and I'm aware that I must look like a pussy, but I don't care. She's everything to me, and I can't find her.

My shoulders shake and my eyes burn as if they're on the verge of tears. I feel out of control—completely fucking lost. Mad rage twists my guts, and I'm half tempted to walk to *Le Zinc* right now and put a bullet in

Johnny's fucking head for allowing her to leave.

A gruff voice whispers in my ear as someone pats my shoulder. "I'm sorry, Tony. I didn't know. I honestly didn't."

I lift my head miserably and see Tommy's battered face filled with remorse.

It doesn't do fuck all for me.

"I'll never forget this. You might as well leave town tonight, because I'm coming back for you."

He lets out air through his nose. "What if I help you find her?"

"They could be anywhere by now."

"Or he went back to New York." A nervous edge trembles in Tommy's voice. I know that he's not supposed to place a foot anywhere near the city. "I'll call Vince."

"If you really want to help, you'll come with me. I'm going now."

He runs a hand through his hair. "Fuck—fine. Let's go." Tommy addresses a waitress. "Clean up this shit and then put Jamie in charge."

* * *

The drive toward New York is spent in silence, with only the sound of Tommy drumming his fingers restlessly against the car door handle.

"Can you give it a rest with that shit?"

He lets out a long sigh. "Sorry. I'm not exactly welcome in New York anymore."

I look at him, watching the way his jaw tenses. "What did you do?"

And how are you still alive?

He gives me a dark look. "I helped whack the old New York boss."

Elena's father.

"So? You weren't the only one part of that fucking disaster."

"There were other things I did," he says unhelpfully. "Things I don't fucking regret, but still."

"Call him again."

He gives me a look before opening his phone and dialing the New York boss, putting the phone on speaker.

"*Vince.*"

"Hey, Vince, it's Tommy again."

"*I haven't found the little shit stain yet. He's not at his apartment.*"

"Listen, Tony and I are driving to New York right now." He winces as he finishes the sentence.

The phone crackles with silence for a moment before Vincent's indignant voice speaks again. "*You what? No— turn back around.*"

"Too late for that. We're already halfway."

"*You lost your New York privileges, remember?*"

"I'm just trying to help Tony."

"*What the fuck am I supposed to tell Paulie's cousins when they find out your ass is in town?*"

I don't really care about Vincent giving Tommy shit about returning to New York.

"Vince, what the fuck are you doing to find my wife?"

"*I don't like your fucking tone, asshole. Maybe you should've kept better track of your wife—*"

"Maybe you should have let me kill him when we had the chance. Then he wouldn't have ratted me out to the cops, or hired bikers to try to kill me, you arrogant prick!"

Tommy's face pales as the speaker screams in outrage.

"*Do you know who you're talking to?*"

"She's my wife, Vincent. She's pregnant. What if it was yours?"

The phone goes silent for a moment and then it crackles with a sigh. "*I'm doing what I can. I don't know if he's in New York, but I've been trying to find him for weeks.*"

Slippery fuck.

"All right. We'll call you when we're close."

The phone goes dead without a reply and Tommy gives me an angry voice. "Nice work. Calling the boss an arrogant prick was a really good idea."

"That's what he is."

He grins at me. "Yeah, and I think you're a hotheaded moron but you don't see me calling you that. Oh, wait."

Fuck, I can't stand the guys in the life. I want to reach over and smack the stupid smile off his face, but my phone buzzes with a text.

"Read it."

"It's from Elena: Don't come after me. Everything's under control."

He raises an eyebrow at me. "What should I say back?"

My heart clenches. I doubt the text is coming from her. "Ask her where she is."

I watch his fingers fly over the phone. "New York."

"He's leaving us a trail of breadcrumbs, or he's trying to throw us off."

"I'm going to bet that it's an ambush. Have Vince trace the call."

Fucking finally. We're one step closer.

ELENA

Duct tape is a lot stronger than it looks. It's amazing, really. A couple strips over my mouth, and I can't make a sound. My hands, feet, arms, everything. I'm like an insect struggling in flypaper.

Thinking about that is much more pleasant than thinking about the man I loathe, who sits on the bed with a gun trained at the door. I've already tried wrestling the gun from him, and he knocked me out. Couldn't believe that I'd actually want to kill "the father of his child."

Maniac.

He keeps glancing at his phone, waiting for some bit of horrible news about the ambush he has set up for Tony. First, he made me get my father's money from Tommy. Then he hired those fucking animals to kill my husband.

With my money.

He grabbed me the moment I left the restaurant. It was right out in the open and if any of Johnny's people saw, they didn't give a fuck. He forced me to go to Tommy to collect my money.

"Those fucks better take care of him. I swear to God. I've never paid so much for a fucking hit."

My murmured, unintelligible response doesn't go unnoticed by him. He cups his hand around his ear, looking at me.

"What was that? Couldn't quite make that out." He grins at the fury on my face.

I'm glad you're able to keep a sense of humor during this.

"Fuck it."

He bounces from the bed and grabs the corner of tape, ripping it off my face. Spittle drools down my cheek, and he wipes it off with his thumb.

"Rafael, let me go. *This is insane.*"

"Let you go so you can crack me over the head with that lamp?" He nods toward the heavy looking lamp on the nightstand that I've been eyeing. "I don't think so."

Rage boils in my chest as I struggle fruitlessly against my bounds.

"When he's dead, we'll go upstate. Hide out in some fucking farm. That money will last us a while."

He talks about it on the bed as though he's got everything figured out.

"Or maybe I can give it to Vince—get him to call off this shit."

"Yeah, do that so that I can watch him blow off your head."

It bursts out of me before I can swallow back the

words, and Rafael whirls around.

Oh fuck.

He gets up from the bed, gun dangling from his grip as he walks in front of me, his pelvis facing me. "You're a sick cunt," he says as he threads his hand through my hair, yanking viciously. "The moment this kid is born, I'm beating some fucking manners back into you."

The deepest loathing riles inside me as he gently cups my face, running his thumb over his bottom lip. Disgust swirls in my stomach as I see the bulge in his pants, growing larger by the second.

"Fuck, maybe I should just shove my cock down your throat to shut you up."

"I'll bite it off," I growl.

"You'll lose more than a couple teeth if you do that to me."

"No!" I squirm in my seat, terrified when he actually undoes his belt with a groan. He pulls his pants down and I scream.

He swears and smothers my mouth with his hand, and the door suddenly rattles as though a battering ram smashed into it.

"OPEN THE FUCK UP!"

"Tony!"

I manage to scream his name as his hand goes slack

around my mouth.

"Fuck," Rafael swears before he aims the gun at the door.

"NO DON'T!"

Too late.

The sounds of gunshots explode in my ears as he aims at the door and shoots. Black holes rip through the door and shatter through the window, which is covered with drapes. He clenches his face as he fires indiscriminately.

They're going to fire back. Fuck.

Using my weight, I swing so that my chair topples to the floor. Returning fire blasts the plaster above me, and a voice screams for them to stop.

BAM!

I see an image of Rafael frantically reloading his gun before he's blasted off his feet, back smashed against the floor. Blood streaks the wall as he slumps down.

Yes. *Finally.*

It all happened in an instant, and suddenly men pool in the room. They kick away Rafael's gun. I can only make out slacks and leather shoes before a familiar face drops down to my level and hauls me upright.

Tony gives me a sad smile as his hands briefly grasp mine.

"Hey there, troublemaker."

I'm so stunned to see him here that I'm convinced it's a figment of my imagination. "Tony? How—what about the ambush?"

"They were just low level street thugs. They backed off once they knew who they were dealing with and told us where to find you."

I can't believe it. My heart swells inside my chest as I realize that Tony is really here.

"Vincent, she's mine! Her baby is mine! Don't do this!"

"Shut him up."

Tommy sinks his fist between Rafael's ribs and he sputters with blood. Tony quickly cuts the duct tape from my hands and feet. A vicious surge of vengeance courses through my limbs.

"Let me do it. I want to."

Tony's face darkens. "No wife of mine is going to be an accomplice to murder."

"Vince, you still got my room at the deli?" Tommy's voice trembles with excitement.

The New York boss crosses his arms, looking angrier than I've ever seen him. "Yeah," he responds. "Tony, is that okay with you?"

"Let me take care of him, Tony."

I glance at Tommy, whose excited face shines with blood lust.

Tony doesn't seem to be listening to them. He wraps his arms around me and lifts me out of the chair, wrapping around me so tightly that I think he'll never be able to let go.

"We'll wait outside," Tommy says in a different voice.

Once the door shuts, he lets out a strangled gasp. "What the fuck did you do to me, Elena?"

He pulls my face toward his roughly and kisses me, tongue spearing through my mouth in a dance that makes my chest heat.

When he finally breaks away, I see tears swimming in his eyes.

* * *

Nothing feels the same anymore.

I think that to myself as I pace around Tony's apartment, waiting for him to come home. The charges against him were mysteriously dropped following the disappearance of Rafael. He left the motel with Tommy and the others, probably to torture the bastard before he killed him.

I find that I don't really mind much.

It's just hard for me to accept that things are finally getting back to normal.

The door opens.

The sound used to terrify me.

His deep footsteps creak over the floorboards, and I get up from the armchair in the living room, twisting my ring around my finger.

Tony gives me a heart-stopping smile the moment he sees me tiptoeing into the foyer. His smell wraps around me as he wraps an arm around my waist, hand curving protectively over my small baby bump. His coarse cheek scratches mine as he turns his face to tease me with his lips. Sparks travel down to my thighs.

He grasps me in his arms, pulling back to look at me with a smile I've never seen on his face.

"Baby, I'm out."

Out? Out of patience? Out of what?

A tentative smile creeps over my face when he laughs. Geez, I've never seen him like this.

"Johnny let me go. *He let me go, Elena!*"

He's out of the Mafia.

"Oh my God." Joy soars through my chest and tears spring to my eyes. "Really?"

"It's just me, you, and the baby now. I'm done with the life."

I bite my lip anxiously. Back home, I knew the rules. You don't leave the Mafia after signing up. It's a life of service or death.

"How?"

"Johnny wasn't happy with everything that went down. He didn't take the threat to my life seriously, and word is getting out about it. No one respects a boss like that, you know? He wanted to get rid of me—to transfer me to another family, but I told him I just wanted out. So I got out."

I can't believe it. We're so lucky. "So—so what are you going to do now?"

A hand slips down my jeans, pushing aside the fabric of my panties as he slowly strokes me. I gasp into his chest as a smirk widens his face.

"Right now, I'm going to fuck the shit out of you."

His face is filled with joyous energy as he suddenly lifts me into his arms. "Before I do though, I wanted to ask you something."

I cling to his shoulders smiling. "What?"

"Will you spend the rest of your life with me?"

He sets me down over the bed, and I try to suppress a smile. "We're married, Tony."

"Yeah, but it wasn't real." He bends over, planting his arms on either side of me as heat curls over my breasts from his fuck-me gaze.

"When you say 'yes,' I want you to mean it."

"I meant it then and I mean it now. I love you and I want you to fuck me. Is that good enough for you?"

Heat blazes through his eyes and the smirk tugs at his full lips.

It strikes me how things come full circle. My infatuation with bad boys could've landed me with another bad egg, but I got lucky. I got him.

He seals his lips against me and heat blazes through my chest. For the first time in a long time, I'm optimistic about the future. If he's in it, I know I'll be all right.

# # #

ABOUT THE AUTHOR

Vanessa Waltz loves to write romantic suspense novels. She lives in the Bay Area with two crazy cats and she loves mail from her fans: **waltzbooks@gmail.com.**

19794702R00249

Made in the USA
Middletown, DE
05 May 2015